County

KT-231-492

DISCARDED

014266012 1

The Bleak Midwinter

Also by L. C. Tyler

A Cruel Necessity
A Masterpiece of Corruption
The Plague Road
Fire

The Bleak Midwinter

L. C. Tyler

CONSTABLE

CONSTABLE

First published in Great Britain in 2018 by Constable

Copyright © L. C. Tyler, 2018

The moral right of the author has been asserted.

*All characters and events in this publication, other than
those clearly in the public domain, are fictitious
and any resemblance to real persons,
living or dead, is purely coincidental.*

All rights reserved.
No part of this publication may be reproduced, stored in a retrieval system,
or transmitted, in any form, or by any means, without the prior permission in writing
of the publisher, nor be otherwise circulated in any form of binding or cover other
than that in which it is published and without a similar condition including this
condition being imposed on the subsequent purchaser.

A CIP catalogue record for this book
is available from the British Library.

ISBN: 978-1-47212-855-3

Typeset in Adobe Caslon by SX Composing DTP, Rayleigh, Essex
Printed and bound in Great Britain by CPI Group (UK) Ltd, Croydon CR0 4YY

Papers used by Constable are from well-managed forests and
other responsible sources.

Constable
An imprint of
Little, Brown Book Group
Carmelite House
50 Victoria Embankment
London EC4Y 0DZ

An Hachette UK Company
www.hachette.co.uk

www.littlebrown.co.uk

To Catrin and Henry

Some persons in this book

John Grey – myself. Originally of Clavershall West in the low and misty county of Essex, more recently a lawyer at Lincoln's Inn and the occasional aider and abetter of the schemes of the King's spymaster, **Lord Arlington**. Now Lord of the Manor in the place of my birth following the sad death of

Mistress Payne – my mother, who, by means of a nicely judged second marriage to my stepfather, **Colonel Payne**, acquired the Big House and all pertaining to it, thus regaining what her ancestors had so carelessly lost, many years ago, to the family of

Sir Felix Clifford – debauched former cavalier, whose closeness to my mother has been a cause of concern to me in so many ways for so many years, and the father (according to the parish baptismal records at least) of my wife

Aminta Grey, née Clifford – noted London playwright, formerly married, due to an unfortunate oversight on my part, to

Roger Viscount Pole – who happily will feature in this story in no way whatsoever, being dead, as is

George Barwell – a carpenter with no discernible morals, the discovery of whose bloody remains one snowy afternoon proves inconvenient for

William Taylor – his father-in-law, who had felt obliged to remind Barwell, quite forcefully, of his obligation to marry his pregnant daughter, that is to say

Amy Taylor – now the briefly but respectably married Mistress Amy Barwell, whose grief at her husband's death is palpable, though her good friend

Margaret Platt – does not appear entirely displeased, perhaps in view of the fact that George Barwell had also undertaken to marry her along with

most of the girls in the village – who, though sharing Margaret's pain, are nevertheless happy to testify that she has been seen consorting with

Alice Mardike – believed to be a witch by anyone who believes in witches, maker of herbal remedies and possessor of a cat and a toad, these things being held sufficient proof in this part of Essex that it stands to reason she had something to do with Barwell's death, a view shared (enthusiastically) by

Dr Marcellus Bray – a papist in everything except his member-ship of the Church of England, recently installed Rector of Clavershall West, and (grudgingly) by

Jacob Platt – Margaret's father and (completely inexplicably) by

Nell Bowman – the surprisingly beautiful wife of

Ben Bowman – the fat (let's be honest) innkeeper and very reluctant village constable, who will soon be called away from his comfortable parlour to inspect a faceless corpse on a low Essex hill.

As indeed will you.

Prologue

December 1668

'You ever witched anyone to death, then?'

Alice Mardike considered this question carefully. There were two possible answers: one was a lie, the other unlikely to impress. It wasn't difficult to choose.

'Of course,' she said. 'Lots.'

Her much younger visitor nodded as if she would have expected nothing less from the owner of the most feared cat in North Essex. 'Anyone round here, was it?'

'Don't get to go anywhere else, do I, girl?'

'I thought witches could fly on a broomstick.'

'Well, maybe I can. When I wants to. But I don't poke my nose into other villages' business. One witch in a village is all you need.'

She looked her visitor in the eye as she said these words. The point needed to be made that there were no vacancies in Clavershall West. One village, one witch, one source of reasonably priced potions and charms. That's all you required.

In a village with two witches, nobody made a decent living. Her visitor sniffed but said nothing.

Alice continued to stir the small cauldron in front of her. The pleasant scent of rosemary, bay and juniper wafted through the cramped, smoky room that served as kitchen, parlour and bedchamber. The beams and plasterwork were a uniform shade of grey in this poor winter light. Bunches of dried but still green herbs, tied with dirty twine, hung from the low ceiling. In a glass jar on a shelf were the scaly remains of something that might once have been a snake. In another was a live toad. It looked as if it would have preferred to be somewhere else.

'What's that for?' asked her visitor, pointing to the pot.

'That, Margaret Platt, is for everything,' said Alice. 'It's called a universal elixir. That will cure every disease known to man. Doctors at the Royal College of Physicians of London would give anything for it. But to you, one Shilling a bottle.'

'What's in it exactly?'

Alice's darkest suspicions were again aroused. 'I don't give away my secrets to anyone – not even to you, Margaret Platt. I don't want to find every idiot in the village trying to brew up universal elixir. It's not as easy as you'd think, and if you don't do it right, then it could kill as easily as it could cure. One's every bit as likely as the other, now I come to think about it.'

Margaret did not dispute this, which was good, but something else was still troubling the younger woman, which wasn't.

'So, *who* did you kill then?' Margaret asked.

'None of your business, girl.'

'Just one. You could tell me one of them.'

'Can't. Wouldn't be proper to reveal the secrets of the coven.'

'Didn't think you had,' said Margaret Platt. She pursed her

thin lips in a way that had, from time to time, got up the noses of almost everyone in the village. It was the smirk of a younger sister who had just put one over on you. It could not be tolerated under any circumstance whatsoever.

'Didn't think I had what?' demanded Alice.

'Didn't think you'd really witched somebody to death.'

'Farmer Kerridge.' Alice spat the words rather than said them. She removed surplus spittle from her lips with the back of a wrinkled hand then helpfully clarified: 'Cursed him proper and he died. That good enough for you?'

Margaret, who was noted in the village for being just a little too clever, could see a flaw in that straight away. 'How come I saw him alive and walking through the village yesterday? If he's proper cursed and dead, like you say, he's no business doing that. None at all.'

'Not young Farmer Kerridge – not Giles. I mean old Farmer Kerridge. You won't remember him. Before your time, girl. Robert Kerridge. Giles's father.'

'What did he do to you?'

Alice sighed. What hadn't they all done to her? And to her mother before that. Nobody could blame her if she'd simply poisoned the entire population of Clavershall West. The jury would have understood what drove her to it. They'd have still hanged her of course. Just like they'd hanged her mother. Once your mother had been hanged for witchcraft there weren't many things you could do, except become a witch yourself and hope things might work out a bit better next time round. The boys hadn't exactly been queuing up to marry her. Not the daughter of a hanged witch. She'd liked the look of Robert Kerridge though, when he was younger. He'd kissed her once and she'd never forgotten it, though he clearly had, because he never kissed her a second time. And, now he'd been in his grave for twenty years, that was probably that.

'Old Farmer Kerridge?' Alice said, as if the memory of the kiss meant nothing to her. 'He showed me disrespect, so I gave him the evil eye.'

'And he dropped dead on the spot?'

'Not on the spot exactly. But he died all right.'

'He certainly did,' said Margaret. 'Seen his tombstone many a time. He learned his lesson.'

'There you are then. I gave him the evil eye, his horse kicked his skull in and now he's dead. What more do you want?'

'Nothing,' said Margaret, respectfully. 'You've got the true witch's powers, Alice Mardike. Everyone round here knows that.'

'Good,' said Alice. And it was just as well they did. She wasn't tormented by the local boys, unlike other more respectable old ladies in the village who were reputed to practise few or none of the Black Arts. People might not choose to pass the time of day with her, but they left her alone and gave her the correct change when she bought their butter. Steal a witch's money and you were in her power for ever. Nobody wanted to find themselves vomiting pins for the sake of a couple of worn halfpennies. Nobody wanted their cream to turn sour, even if it had been left out in the sun longer than it should be. Nobody wanted their best cow to sicken and die. Nobody wanted the Magistrate to discover that the weights they used on market day were a bit lighter than recommended. Life was already too full of uncertainty. There was no need to go upsetting witches.

'It's just . . .' Margaret began. She bit her lip.

'Just what?' asked Alice.

From the moment that Margaret had started to flatter her, Alice had known that a request of some sort would not be far behind.

'Since you're so good at it, could you learn me how to give somebody the evil eye?'

'No, I could not,' said Alice firmly. 'You can't just teach something like that. It's handed down, mother to daughter – like syphilis or being a member of the gentry. Anyway, you wouldn't want the power even if I could teach it to you. It's a terrible responsibility. And murder's against the Law, however you do it.'

'I know that,' said Margaret meekly. 'But—'

'Well, then,' said Alice firmly, before the rest of the sentence could be allowed to develop into something that might lead to the County Court.

Margaret gave a sob that was slightly too short to inspire pity, slightly too long to be involuntary. 'I don't know who else to turn to,' she said.

Alice sighed. 'Who do you want dead anyway?'

'George Barwell.'

'Any reason?'

'He married Amy Taylor and not me.'

'Did he say he would marry you?'

'Every single time.'

'More fool you, girl. Why did he marry Amy Taylor instead?'

'Her father made him. Wanted his daughter wed before the baby was born.'

'And you . . .'

'Fortunately not. Under the circumstances.'

Alice breathed a sigh of relief. At least she wasn't being asked to perform an abortion. She didn't do abortions. Sometimes, when she was watching the village children play, she'd think of all the babies she'd never have, not now at her age, and she'd have to stifle a sharp sob of pain.

'I thought George Barwell wasn't looking too happy at the wedding,' Alice said, poking the fire beneath the cauldron.

'He wasn't happy. And he won't ever be happy. Not with her. Stuck up little good-for-nothing. Killing him would be a mercy. If you won't learn me how, you could do it for me. You could do it easy. Like you did old Farmer Kerridge. The Taylors have got horses. Plenty of them. I bet one of them would kick him.'

Alice looked up at her mantelpiece. The toad was trying to hop his way through the glass, as he sometimes did. His previous failures had taught him nothing. Nothing at all. After a while he stopped and just sat there, staring out into the world he was not allowed to join.

'So, will you?' asked Margaret, with a child's insistence.

Alice tried to count the reasons why this would not be a good idea. There were at least seven or eight. She chose one that was irrefutable. 'You couldn't afford it,' she said. 'Not a bewitching to death. Much too expensive.'

Margaret knew when she was being spoken down to. It was something that happened far too often, in her humble opinion. Well, she didn't have to put up with it this time. She straightened her back and looked Alice in the eye. 'I can pay,' she said.

The younger woman took an old leather purse out of her pocket and opened it. In the dim light, Alice could see the silver glinting. It was the most beautiful thing she'd seen in many a year. It offered a new shawl and decently salted red meat for weeks to come.

'One Pound, ten and sixpence,' said Margaret. 'I've been saving. For something just like this. I'll give it all to you if you kill him for me.'

Alice shook her head.

'And these,' said Margaret, indicating her small gold earrings.

During a long lifetime, Alice had rarely been shown kindness, but she knew what it was and that it was a good thing. And taking the silver Shillings in front of her – let alone the silly child's earrings – would not be kind. She dismissed the Devil's temptation with a sigh, knowing that it might be some while before he could be bothered to tempt her again. 'Look, Margaret Platt, I won't kill him, and that's all there is to it.'

'You have to help me.' Margaret took out a dirty handkerchief and examined it, as if trying to decide whether she could produce a tear or two. But nothing in Alice Mardike's expression encouraged this. 'You have to help me,' Margaret repeated. 'The other men in the village all know I've been with George Barwell, because he's boasted to them that he did it with me. And the men have all told their wives I'm a trollop. They look at me as if I'm a bit of shit on their doormat. What else am I supposed to do with my savings? I certainly won't need them for a dowry.'

Alice sighed again. She'd have happily exchanged places with Margaret. Margaret's family was well off and nobody hanged you for being a trollop. 'See here,' she said, 'why don't you buy a couple of bottles of my universal elixir. Normally a Shilling each, but let's say one and six for the pair of them. And, absolutely free of charge, I'll throw in a general sort of curse for George Barwell. It may work or it may not – I can't say, and that's the honest truth. There's no refund if it doesn't work, mind; but if he does sicken and die, then you'll know you helped him on his way. That's rare value for eighteen pence, that is.'

'Thank you, Alice Mardike,' said Margaret. 'I'd like that very much. But sixpence a bottle seems fairer to me.' She took a Shilling out of her purse, folded the worn and cracked leather more firmly than might have been advisable and handed the coin to Alice. The older woman pocketed the money without comment.

'Take whichever bottles you want from the shelf over there,' she said. 'They're all much of a muchness, except the belladonna, which isn't. So keep your hands off that one. Now, run along, girl. I've got more potions to make.'

'With that old toad?' asked Margaret. 'Are you going to boil him up?'

Alice looked at the miserable prisoner. He'd be happier out in the fields, hopping around in the mud. Or maybe in her woodshed until it got warmer. She could still label the potion she made next spring as 'toad and nettle'. People would think it tasted better than usual but that would be all. 'Tomorrow that toad will no longer be here,' she said. 'I promise you that.'

Margaret stuffed the purse back in her pocket, through the placket in her fine woollen skirt.

'Is it true you have to sell your soul to the Devil?' she asked. 'To be a proper witch? And he rides you through the night to the witches' Sabbath? And you get to drink ale and fornicate with imps and goblins?'

'Haven't you done enough fornicating with imps for the time being? Whoever told you that nonsense anyway?'

'Martha Williams over at Saffron Walden. She said the Devil came to her cottage door in the form of an ordinary man dressed in black and he promised her anything she wanted if she sold her soul to him.'

'And did she let him have her soul?'

'Yes.'

'Good for her,' said Alice without enthusiasm.

'She said he never gave her anything in return, though.'

'So,' said Alice, in summary, 'he appeared to her as an ordinary man?'

'Yes.'

'And promised her the world?'

'Yes.'

'Then he didn't deliver in any way whatsoever?'

'Not a thing.'

'You'd have thought she would have seen that one coming,' said Alice.

Chapter One

Mr Morrell has news

I do not know how long I have been here. The winter sun is now low in the sky and the iron clouds presage another storm. The blank snow stretches before me without end. I should be somewhere else entirely but I am chained to this place by my own grief. In front of me is a slender sapling that may not survive the blasts of a winter that already has these low, white Essex hills in its grip. I am urging it to live; but have its roots, encased in the iron-hard soil, already given up hope? In a world in which everything seems dead, who can tell?

I feel her hand on my shoulder before I hear her footsteps. This snow deadens everything, within me and without. The soft fur lining of a warm cloak rubs gently against my face. In the midst of winter there is the pale summer scent of lavender.

'I thought this was where I'd find you,' says Aminta.

'It seemed a good place to come,' I say, placing my cold hand on Aminta's much warmer one. To her credit, she makes no complaint. 'That's the tree my mother planted before she passed away. It replaced a giant blown down in a storm a few months before – an oak that had been put there by her great-great-grandfather. She said she was planning to live until the new tree was as tall as the old one.'

'How old would she have been for that to happen?'

'About a hundred and fifty or a hundred and sixty, I think. She often spoke to me of the Old Countess of Desmond, who lived to be a hundred and forty and died after a fall from one of her own cherry trees. My mother would have contemplated nothing less for herself. It was one of many things that she considered she was entitled to.'

'If you want to live even to see the New Year, you should come indoors now, John. If the bitter wind doesn't persuade you of the truth of that, this spot will be a foot deep in snow by the morning. You can't stay here. The tree will have to look after itself.'

'My mother planted it. My mother watered it and mulched it. She would have expected it to look after itself thereafter and not complain. She didn't tolerate weakness – especially in other people. If the tree has inherited any of her single-mindedness, it will do well enough, snow or no snow.'

I rise slowly. I am still stiff with the cold – or am I just getting older? I feel a sharp stab of pain and rub my thigh, but not so much that Aminta will feel obliged to comment on it.

'How is little Charles's cough?' I ask, pre-empting any discussion of my leg.

'No better,' says Aminta. 'But our young son is strong. As your mother was. I don't think that the cough troubles him too much. I'm more worried, my dear husband, about your aged bones. And the wound that you received last spring.'

So, she has decided to remind me of my foolishness. It is

a wife's duty – or so she always tells me. But her warning is unnecessary. I'd already told Lord Arlington, even before I inherited my mother's estate, that I would undertake no further missions for him.

'The leg wound is healed and paid for,' I say. 'And I am unlikely to run the risk of another injury of that sort.'

'Are you?' asks Aminta. This is not as much of a question as it appears to be. She means that I ignored her warnings last time. She thinks that, one way or another, Arlington will persuade me to work for him again. I have already been stabbed (or shot) in the leg, shoulder and face. The next wound may be somewhere less convenient.

'Arlington has other agents. Men without the responsibilities I now have. They can take care of Dutch spies and Popish conspirators and anyone else who wants to plot against His Gracious Majesty King Charles the Second. I'll stick to my duties here. I'll plant trees, drain fields, be polite to the Rector and do as little as I need to do as Magistrate. I've seen enough blood to last me a lifetime – my own especially.'

Then we both notice a figure approaching, still small in the distance and very black against the untroubled white of the snow. He is not travelling fast except by his own standards. His body wobbles to and fro and his arms are flailing in an attempt to assist his progress. It is my mother's steward – now my steward – Morrell. Something must be amiss for him to abandon his usual ponderous dignity in this way. Something must be amiss for him not to send one of the lesser servants out into the cold. He does not like the cold any more than he likes the heat. He does not like running. He does not like the lesser servants.

'Can it concern Charles?' says my wife uncertainly.

'Surely not?' I reply. 'You left him only a few minutes ago. It must be some other urgent matter.'

But it is with trepidation that we walk, with Aminta clutching my arm, to meet the steward who is so newly my own.

'Slow down, Mr Morrell,' I call. 'This snow is treacherous.'

But he does not slacken his pace until he reaches us, far too out of breath to speak. For a moment he is bent double, his hands on his plump knees, puffing and coughing. Then he straightens up. His look is one of considerable concern.

'Nothing ails Charles, I hope?' asks Aminta. 'When I left him . . .'

Morrell holds up a hand, coughs again, then says: 'No, my Lady. Young Master Charles is wrapped up warm as you instructed and is refusing to eat his nutritious gruel in a most encouraging way.'

'Sir Felix?' I say.

'No, sir. Lady Grey's father is also well and was drinking your best wine by the fire when I left him. You need not be concerned about him either.'

'Then whatever has made you run here cannot be a matter of life or death,' I say.

Morrell smiles triumphantly. 'On the contrary, Master John . . . I mean Sir John . . . it is most certainly that. There has been a murder in the village. A horrible murder. Up on the hill, sir. One of the shepherds found him, just inside the wood.'

'Then I must go there without delay,' I say.

'There's no need to do that, John,' says Aminta. 'They can bring the body down to the village and place it in the church. If, as Magistrate, you really feel you have to view every dead body in the village, then you can view it there tomorrow. You're still limping with that wound of yours, which is far from healed and paid for by Arlington most inadequately. I don't want you going up to the wood in this snow. In fact, I forbid you to stir beyond the house tonight.'

'I wouldn't view it tomorrow either, sir, if I were you,' says Morrell. 'Leave it to the coroner. It's a horrible sight, sir. The shepherds say that he has no face left at all. It's been clawed away, as if by some great beast. Flesh ripped from the bone. Lidless eyes staring out from the skull.'

I nod. I had not realised that our Essex shepherds could be thus eloquent. The lidlessness of the eyes is a well-observed detail.

'Could the shepherds identify the body?' I ask.

'Only by his clothes,' says Morrell.

'And who is it?'

'George Barwell,' says Morrell. 'But this is no ordinary death, sir. No Christian man would do that to another. Only the Devil would rip the flesh so and leave a poor soul there unburied under the wide December sky. It's witchcraft, Sir John. George Barwell has been killed by witchcraft. You really don't need to see it. The constable just requires your permission to move the body to the church.'

My wife, standing beside me, sighs. 'Oh, he'll want to see it,' she says. 'You won't be able to keep him away from something as good as that.'

Chapter Two

I am introduced to George Barwell

By the time we reach the woods, the sky is blood red – not the scarlet of fresh blood, but the dark crimson of blood when it is old and dried. I've seen every shade of it and have no preference for one rather than another, but the sky is telling me that I have very little time to do my work.

Two shepherds are waiting there, both wrapped in old but very serviceable cloaks, doubtless to recount how the body was found and perhaps solicit a few pence for their trouble. Their stained leather hats are clamped firmly on their heads, the low crowns and broad brims dusted lightly with snow. They lean easily on their crooks, as if enjoying this rare moment of leisure. Ben Bowman is also standing under the trees, an odd place for an innkeeper to be at his busiest time of day, but Ben is village constable this year. He does not wish to be constable, but nor does anyone else and he had avoided taking his turn for as long as he decently could. It has the advantage that, for a year, he has the responsibility for the regulation of alehouses and the suppression of drunkenness. Other people having these duties has sometimes proved inconvenient for him. But, at this moment, he would rather be behind his counter, with the fire blazing in the hearth, serving mulled ale, while his wife Nell goes round trimming the smoky tallow candles. He has thoughtfully brought a lantern with him. We'll probably need it before we're done. The daylight fades last up on this modest Essex hill, but the fields below are already more than halfway on their journey into night.

'This is the body?' I ask, though it's unlikely that it's anything else.

'Indeed, Master John,' says Ben solemnly. He pauses and adds: 'Sir John, that is.'

I wonder how long it will take for people to address me as 'Sir John' without any hesitation. A year? Two years? Twenty years? I was, after all, 'young Master John' for a very long time and this isn't the sort of village where you are allowed to forget who you once were. Nor do I greatly value the knighthood that Arlington obtained for me. I would have preferred prompt payment of the fee originally agreed for the job.

'The King finds it cheaper to hand out titles than to pay his bills,' I say. 'I'm lucky he didn't owe me enough to make me an earl.'

Ben laughs uncertainly. One of the shepherds looks from me to Ben and back again, then he feels that it is safe to smile briefly and obsequiously. The other decides not to risk it. I can't see Morrell behind me, but I have no doubt that he disapproves of my levity. Titles are not to be mocked, especially one's own. Even Oliver Cromwell could not abolish titles of rank. Only a madman would even wish to do so.

'You're certain who it is?' I ask. 'I suppose most people round here are customers of yours.'

'It's Barwell – at least as far as anyone could tell with his face like that. But, as for his custom, he hasn't been to the inn lately. He's not much of a loss in that respect.'

'No money?' I ask.

'That or being under the thumb of his new wife. He enjoyed my ale well enough until recently,' says Ben.

There's a note of disdain in Ben's voice that goes well beyond Barwell's newly acquired vow of abstinence. He clearly didn't like Barwell that much, even when he was a dependable drunkard.

'When did you find the body?' I ask the shepherds.

'About two hours ago, sir,' says one of them. 'Tom went straight down to the village to report it to the constable. Mr Bowman came up to inspect it and said to send for you, in case you wanted to see it here. He said you knew more about dead men than he did.'

'You stayed close by in the meantime?' I ask.

'I carried on looking for our sheep,' he says. 'That's what we were here for. Mr Taylor doesn't pay us to be idle – so he always tells us. He'd regard our watching over a dead body for a couple of hours as a sorry waste of his money.'

'You didn't see the man who killed him then?'

The shepherd quickly looks around him, as if worried that the killer might still be in the undergrowth, listening to our conversation. Then he shakes his head. 'The killer? No, sir. Didn't see another living soul, sir. Not here or anywhere in the woods.'

The light remains good enough for me to inspect the murdered man without the lantern. The shepherds (or Morrell) exaggerated. There is still some flesh on the skull – more than half, I'd say. Most of the cheeks have gone, admittedly, but the scalp is intact. So is the nose. I kneel so that I can feel the neck and shoulders and note their stiffness, then my hands work their way down the body; the legs are less stiff, though they will soon be as rigid as the shoulders. There are no bullet holes in his coat, no stab wounds, no sign of a blow to the back of the head that might have killed him. Witchcraft it is then. Or it would be if there was any such thing.

I look at the ground that he is lying on. It has not been much disturbed – there is no sign of a struggle. I am struck more than anything by his insignificance. Barwell is quite a small man, and death diminishes everyone. Wrapped in his cloak, he rests lightly on a bed of brittle, frost-hardened leaves, the bare branches above protecting him from the worst of the snow. Only his lack of a face draws your gaze inexorably back to him.

There are many footprints leading to and away from the body, but at least four people have been here recently in addition to the killer. If our man was murdered two or three hours ago, as I think he was, then the prints of his attacker coming and going to the woods will have long since been covered by new snow and disturbed by far too many shepherds and innkeepers.

I have to shift my weight – kneeling like this is not comfortable, but the wound in my own leg is small compared to those I see before me. This was a savage attack.

I return to a close examination of what is left of the head. In one or two places even the bone has been shaved away. Then I look at the neck and frown. I check the face again. No, I wasn't mistaken. How odd. The face tells me one story and the neck another entirely.

'Is there a problem, Sir John?' asks Ben. 'Other than him being dead, of course. I can see that's not so good.' He blows on his fingers. He wants me to instruct the shepherds to carry the body down to the village, so that he can return to the warmth of his own house, his duties as unpaid constable fulfilled for the day. I think he's beginning to regret sending for me. If so, that was entirely his mistake.

'Look at this, Ben,' I say. 'See the redness of the eyes and the small pink spots on the skin that remains? This man was strangled. See too how little blood there is on the ground. He was dead before somebody decided to remove most of his face, so he has bled very little. If it was done while he was living, he would have lost a lot of blood along with his cheeks. And nothing around him seems to be disturbed, except by your own clumsy feet. He died without much of a fight – none at all, I'd have said.'

I stand, straightening my leg with difficulty. I rub it, but the pain is much the same as before. Aminta's right. Arlington didn't pay me anything like enough.

'If you say so, Sir John,' says Ben. 'Well, it must all be the same to him now.' He blows on his fingers again, mainly for my information, I think. 'So the man was ambushed by somebody and they strangled him quickly and without a fight. That's not unheard of, is it?'

'No, but what's odd is this. If he was strangled you'd expect fingermarks on his neck – or, more likely, raw, red rope marks if a ligature was used. There's almost nothing. Or nothing I can see at the moment.'

Ben helpfully lights the lantern and holds it over the body, but I am none the wiser for the pale glow it provides on a darkening evening.

'The Devil has his own ways of killing, sir,' says one of the shepherds.

'Can't expect it to appear natural when it's not,' says the other. 'Can we take him down now, Sir John? I don't want to be up here once the sun sets. Not with the Devil out on the prowl.'

'He wasn't killed by the Devil,' I say.

'We don't want to be here if his ghost comes back either,' says the first shepherd. 'Don't want to see that sort of thing again.'

I had forgotten the general prejudice here in favour of the existence of ghouls and goblins of all sorts. Everyone has a story of seeing at least one dead person strolling through the village at midnight. Usually shortly after the inn closed.

'His ghost isn't returning here any more than the Devil,' I say. 'You have my solemn word as His Majesty's representative that you will see neither this evening.'

The two shepherds look at each other. I have a certain authority in the village but it will take more than my saying so to convince them. Their views are already formed: anyone can see this is an unnatural killing. After all, what fellow human being would have done that to his face? And if you don't get to see a ghost after a murder like this one, when would you?

'Could a wild beast have gnawed at him?' asks Ben. 'I mean after he was strangled and left lying here?'

Well, perhaps. It's more likely to be a fox than it is to be Satan. I look to see signs of claw or teeth marks. The flesh, and in places the bone, has been hacked away in broad strips. Whatever animal did this must have had one enormous claw to rake the victim's face in this way. Very wide and very sharp. Just for a moment I too wonder if something strange and unnatural has been at work here. It wouldn't have occurred to me during the bright day; now, with the sun almost below the horizon, anything seems possible. But the thought is there only for a moment, then it is gone. There ought to be lumps of flesh on the ground, but they will have been snapped up by various small hungry creatures. He's lucky he's still got his eyes. It's a cold winter for everyone, the birds included.

'No,' I say. 'No wild animal could have done it. There's nothing large enough round here. It's three hundred years since wolves were last seen in Essex.'

'What about wild boar?' asks Ben.

Ben doesn't want to think it was a man, and certainly not a man from this village, which is charitable of him, but plain wrong.

'There were wild boar in Hampshire twenty or thirty years ago,' I say, 'but it would be a very long way for them to come on the off chance of a meal.'

Ben shakes his head. 'Sounds like Dick and Tom are right then,' he says, indicating the shepherds. 'It's the Devil's work. You've as much experience of dead bodies and their secrets as anyone round here. If you can't tell how this fellow was killed, Sir John, then it's a very strange business indeed.'

'I didn't say that I couldn't tell how he died, Ben. He's clearly been strangled, then attacked with a very sharp blade – wielded by a man, not the Devil. It's just that I don't understand why there are no marks around the neck or why somebody would wish to disfigure him like that. That's all very odd, but it isn't witchcraft.'

It wasn't my intention, but the word 'witchcraft' now hangs ominously in the misty December air. We all glance at each other, except Morrell who is looking nervously back down the hill. At first I am almost inclined to laugh at my steward's caution, then I realise that he has just heard something that the rest of us have missed. It is the rhythmic crunch of boots on crisp snow in the red stillness of a winter evening.

'There's somebody coming up the track,' he says in a hoarse whisper.

We all turn and see a dark figure marching determinedly towards us through the skeletal trees. He's a large man – almost unnaturally so against a landscape in which the usual benchmarks for size now lie beneath the snow. He carries in his hands a heavy wooden staff – good for balance on an icy surface or for close fighting. His features emerge slowly from the gloom. Fortunately he has neither horns nor tail. He has dark, flowing hair and a full beard. He is reassuringly well dressed too – a heavy woollen cloak, deep green and quite new, good-quality leather boots, and a tall, feathered beaver hat that warms you just looking at it. It's William Taylor. Of course, he'd come as soon as the news reached him. His daughter Amy is married – was married – to the man on the ground in front of us. The two shepherds immediately doff their own hats in a way that they didn't when I arrived. They do after all work for Taylor, whose farm is near here. The large man looks for a moment in our direction. Standing, as we are, beneath the trees, we see him better than he sees us. He squints for a moment into Ben's lantern light, then strides over to the dark huddle on the ground that was once his son-in-law.

'So, it's true then?' he says in a deep voice. 'Barwell's dead?'

'I'm afraid so,' I say.

'Who's that?' He quickly turns in my direction. 'Sorry, Sir John, I didn't see you standing there in the shadows. I apologise for not greeting you properly.' Taylor sweeps off his fur hat and gives me a business-like nod by way of greeting. He turns on his shepherds. 'And what do you think you were doing, standing there like fools with your heads covered in Sir John's presence?'

'It's cold, sir,' says Dick.

'Well, don't let me see you showing disrespect to the Lord of the Manor like that again. Not if you want to work for me. When you address gentry, your hat should be in your hand. Just as you do for me. Have I taught you nothing, the pair of you?'

'I'm sure they meant no harm by it,' I say.

'No? Well, they'll do as I tell them anyway, if they want to avoid a thrashing. So, how did my son-in-law die then, Sir John?'

I describe as best I can how I think he died – strangled in a way that I can't determine then disfigured for reasons I cannot explain, probably by somebody he knew or somebody who took him by surprise. I'm not sure I've told him much he can't see for himself.

'I'm sorry for your loss, Mr Taylor,' I add. 'And I'm sorry for your daughter's greater loss. They'd been married only a short time, I think?'

Taylor nods, as if more than satisfied with my account. 'Yes, a mercifully short time,' he says. 'I'm not surprised it's ended this way. The man was a knave and fool.'

He shows no more emotion than if he'd found one of his sheep dead of the cold. Rather less than if he'd found the tup dead. Barwell wasn't his most valuable asset by a long way.

'Well, he could have chosen a better time to get killed,' I say. 'So close to Christmas. And I understand your daughter is expecting their first child.'

'That's why she married him,' says Taylor. 'I can promise you she wouldn't have stooped so low otherwise. A poor husband, even judged by the very lowest standards, sir. Can't think why anyone would have taken him except to save their honour. He had good looks, but looks do not last.'

We all turn to the corpse before us. Barwell might reasonably have expected to retain his looks a little longer.

'He's from Suffolk,' says Ben, as if that explained everything. 'Came here a year or so ago, when you were living in London, Master John. A handsome enough man, as Mr Taylor says, when he still had a face. The maids all seemed to like him anyway. And some of the married ones, who should have known better. Supposedly a carpenter, though I never saw him doing much work with wood or anything else.'

'Nor me,' Taylor snaps. 'I'd hoped he'd help me run the farm, and to be fair he learned how to slaughter a sheep, but he wasn't of much use otherwise. Not yet, anyway. I might have made a good upstanding Essex yeoman of him, given time, even if he was born on the wrong side of the River Stour. You'll take him down to the church now? I'll pay whatever needs to be paid for his burial. He was part of my family, if a reluctant one.'

'The coroner will have to be informed before there can be any burial,' I say. 'He'll confirm how Barwell died, not that he's likely to rule it's anything other than murder. With his face like that, it's certainly not plague or suicide. There's no chance of a coroner getting here until the snow clears, but there will have to be an inquest, however tiresome that may be for you and your daughter. We have to know the truth. The killer is almost certainly still with us. The roads out of the village are all blocked with snow, so there's nowhere much he could have gone.'

'I'm sorry, Sir John, but I already know exactly how he died and who was responsible,' says Taylor.

'Who?' I ask.

'You know Alice Mardike?'

'Yes, of course. As Ben says, I've been away, but don't forget I grew up here. Alice Mardike is the old woman who brews potions and herbal remedies. I've known her since I was a child.'

'She's the witch who brews potions and herbal remedies,' says Taylor. 'And a lot more besides. You know she claims to be able to find any lost article, using magic?'

'She does indeed,' I say. 'My mother once consulted her. So have most people in the village. She doesn't always find the missing items but she's cheap. And Mistress Mardike did find my mother's gold pin. She was pleased to get it back. Alice Mardike is harmless.'

'You think so? Then listen to what I have to tell you, Sir John. Two days ago Barwell was out and about in the village. At the well, he met Alice Mardike and he suddenly realised that she was looking at him funny. Very funny. "What do you want, you foul old crone?" he asked. "Is that supposed to be the evil eye? If so, I don't think much of it." And he laughed. She didn't like that at all. "And *I* don't think much of your gallivanting with the maids in this village," she said to him. "It's not proper to promise them things so they'll let you do your dirty business with them. Especially not now you've got a wife and a baby on the way. You'll get your comeuppance, George Barwell, you see if you don't."

'Well, there were a lot of people listening by that time because you don't see a witch put the evil eye on somebody every day of the week, not even in Essex. "You don't frighten me," he said. "And I'll whip you round the village if you try anything." Alice Mardike looked one way, then the other, as if she didn't like the way things were going. "It will happen," she said. "Mark my words, George Barwell. Mark my words, all of you." And she flounced off, as well as she could with two wooden buckets full of water in her hands. Now, two days later, he's dead.

'I'm not saying I care much one way or the other, but I don't think you need to look very far for the culprit, do you? You just need to arrest Alice Mardike and give her a fair trial. Then you need to string her up by her neck. It can't be anyone else. This is no natural death, and there's only one witch in the village.'

Chapter Three

The Compleat Justice

The fire is blazing in the hearth, huge logs from the Park in the great stone fireplace. Sir Felix sits in a well-cushioned chair with a bottle of wine on the table beside him. The bottle is scarcely touched, which is commendable, but I think it may not be the first he has opened this evening. Candles have been lit and the oak-panelled walls flutter gently in their yellow light.

'A bad business, John,' he says. 'Barwell wasn't liked, but nobody wants to see somebody killed in that way.'

'They're saying it's witchcraft,' I say.

'Of course they are,' he says.

Sir Felix strokes his carefully trimmed beard. He has lately adopted the new fashion and purchased a periwig. The flowing jet-black curls suit him well. The dark-blue velvet of his coat glows in the candlelight. His lace cravat is immaculate. There is, in his own opinion and in the opinion of one or two widows in the village, still something about him of the dashing cavalier who once charged with Prince Rupert at Marston Moor. Like me, he's seen men die in a number of ways, and he has since had some leisure to consider which way is best. Barwell's death, neither glorious nor in a comfortable feather bed, is not one he would have chosen for himself.

'His father-in-law didn't seem too upset,' I say. 'He did little more than glance at the body.'

'Barwell seduced William Taylor's daughter and agreed to marry her only under extreme duress. There were one or two other ladies in the village to whom Barwell was also attached, and whom he thought he might prefer, if he were still free to choose. That Amy is now a respectable widow rather than the wife of a wastrel will not displease Taylor too much, I think.'

'I'll wager there are a lot of people in the village who won't mourn his passing,' I say. 'There will be a number of women, and their fathers and their brothers and their husbands. But not all of them will have been abroad at about one o'clock today, armed with a sharp blade.'

'You think that's when he was killed?'

'The cold will have slowed down the stiffening of the body but, when I inspected it, it was well advanced though not yet complete. Normally it would take three hours or so. With snow falling, maybe as much as four or five. That means he died late this morning, at the earliest, but more likely some time this afternoon. And he was strangled – the mutilation occurred later. It was no beast that clawed him though, for all that Ben wishes it was – the flesh had been hacked off in two-inch strips. That would be a mighty claw indeed, and a sharp one.'

'That's why you think it was some sort of blade?'

'Yes. Solid enough to chip bone away and as keen as a razor.'

'And you are ruling out witchcraft, in spite of the general prejudice of the village in that direction?' asks Sir Felix.

'I've seen men stabbed and choked and bludgeoned to death. I've never seen one killed by witchcraft and never expect to. You can't dispose of somebody that way. If it could be done, then my Lord Arlington would have long since adopted witchcraft as a cheaper way of dealing with the King's enemies. I've no plans to issue a warrant for the arrest of the Devil as principal or accessory. The only thing I do not understand is the lack of rope or fingermarks round the neck. I must look at him again when the light is better.'

Sir Felix shakes his head and pours himself some more wine. My wine, as Morrell has pointed out to me. 'You don't believe in witches because, like Lord Arlington, you are a modern man. I conversely am a child of King James's time. Everyone was allowed to believe in witches then. You may struggle to persuade some people round here that the Devil was not abroad this afternoon.'

'The older villagers, you mean?'

'And some of the younger ones. We still cherish the ancient customs here, as you know.'

'Well, Taylor has no doubt that Alice Mardike is a witch.'

'Of course she is,' says Sir Felix, wiping his lips with the back of his hand. 'So was her mother. Everyone in the village knows that. Alice keeps herself to herself and brews fairly harmless potions. She's also very good at discovering lost property. That's illegal of course, if magic is employed, but I wouldn't go to anyone else if I lost my horse – I certainly wouldn't waste my time going to the constable.'

'You'd trust her magic?'

'No, I'd trust to her knowing who'd suddenly acquired a new horse.'

'You never prosecuted her for witchcraft – I mean, when you were Magistrate here?'

'Why would I want to do that?'

'Because, as you say, it's illegal. Even finding lost property.'

Sir Felix sips his wine thoughtfully. 'A lot of things are illegal,' he says.

'I know,' I say. 'Don't forget I'm a lawyer, when I'm not working for Arlington.'

'But you've probably spent the last ten years drafting contracts and wills, when you weren't engaged in espionage. None of that will help you much in your new role as a Magistrate and Lord of the Manor. I doubt if you've had to deal with a single case of witchcraft in your entire time at Lincoln's Inn.'

'Of course not,' I say. 'Londoners – old or young – have little belief in the power of anything except hard cash.'

'Well, I can promise you that they don't mock witchcraft here,' says Sir Felix. 'And that's not just the common folk. You'll find a number of your fellow justices are equally superstitious. If you issue a warrant accusing Alice Mardike of witchcraft, you'll get a County Court judge prepared to try her – and a jury prepared to find her guilty, with or without the customary intimidation from the bench.

'Back in the forties they were hanging witches all over the county, with witch-hunters touring every town and hamlet. Not in this village of course. That Hopkins man showed his face at my door and offered to discover whether I had any witches in Clavershall West. Wanted a fee of five Pounds for each witch he detected. "I imagine you always find a few, Mr Hopkins?" I said. He grinned at me. "Never fail to find twenty Pounds-worth, my Lord," he said. "More if you wish. Just say how many you'd like." So I kicked him down the steps and he never came back. He didn't care. He and his gang just went on to Saffron Walden and earned a hundred Pounds in a couple of weeks. He'd ask around and see who had a reputation for being a witch, or was just bad-tempered and owned a cat. There were always plenty of neighbours who bore a grudge and were happy to put the recent death of one of their cows to good use. Hopkins would keep the poor woman awake all day and all night, and walk her up and down the room until she was exhausted. Or he'd throw her in the pond and swim her. They'd always confess to something eventually – usually consorting with the Devil. After they'd admitted that, they got to sleep in a warm, dry bed for the night. Then it was off to the county gaol. The trial a month or two later was a formality. Nothing the Judge could do if the witch had foolishly already admitted her guilt. She wouldn't be allowed to retract the confession and the Judge couldn't pardon her. Not a witch. After the hanging, Hopkins would collect his fee. One good thing about that man Cromwell – he at least put a stop to witch-hunting.'

'Then it doesn't sound as if you believe in witches any more than I do,' I say.

'There's a difference between believing in witches and paying charlatans by the hour to fabricate cases for me to try. I had better things to do. But the Bible says there are witches and the Law says there are witches. I never arrested any witches when I was Magistrate because nobody ever made a good enough case. But my father committed Alice Mardike's mother to the County Court and they found her guilty.'

'What's the relevant statute?' I ask.

'The Act of 1604,' says Sir Felix. 'In the first year of the reign of King James. You'll find a couple of helpful books on your shelves over there. Most were there in my time as owner of this house, but either your mother or your late stepfather seems to have added to them.'

I take down a small leather-bound book entitled *The Compleat Justice*, 'now amplified and purged from sundry errors which were in former impressions thereof'. I work my way through the table at the front of the book: 'Abduration, Absolve *vide* Treason, Accessory and Principal, Acquittal *vide* Enditements, Additions, Affray and Affrayers, Agnus Dei, Alehouses . . .' A Magistrate clearly has many interests, though I am not sure what crime is signified by Agnus Dei. My finger runs rapidly down the page to Watermen, Wax, Weirs and finally Witchcraft. I note the page number and locate the relevant section.

'Well, it seems clear enough,' I say. 'The invocation, conjuration, consultation, entertainment, employment, feeding or rewarding any evil spirit, taking up of dead bodies, or any part thereof to be employed in Witchcraft or Charms or using any manner of Witchcraft whereby any person shall be killed or any part of them wasted or lamed and also the accessaries is a felony without the benefit of clergy.'

'Quite. A most serious offence, so no benefit of clergy allowed. You may hang even our new Rector if he is found to be indulging in the black arts,' says Sir Felix.

'Only if there is proof that he fed or rewarded an evil spirit,' I say. 'I'm not sure that he has. Or more to the point that he or anyone else has ever used witchcraft to kill somebody.'

'Your London scepticism does you much credit,' says Sir Felix, 'but what I mean is that, as you have already confirmed, the Law exists. You can't say that there's no such thing as witchcraft if Parliament has kindly gone to the trouble to approve a statute against it. The only position you can take, as the King's representative here, is that there are witches and that they do sometimes dig up dead bodies and feed evil spirits. Otherwise our Monarch and his Parliament are a pack of fools.'

'God forbid that I should ever suggest such a thing. But, equally, there's no dispute that highway robbery exists. Proof is nevertheless required in order to convict an individual highwayman.'

'You will find that the best authorities regard witchcraft as a crime apart, in which the normal rules can be ignored. How can you produce two witnesses when the whole thing is done secretly? You can't, so they're not required. For most crimes, an alibi is a more or less complete defence. But a witch can work her spells from anywhere, so evidence that she was in another place when the crime was committed counts for little. If she was somewhere else when the victim died, it just shows how devious she is. Proof in a witchcraft trial is not the same as proof in the sort of cases you've dealt with before. That's the first thing you are going to have to remember, Mr City Lawyer.'

'So, if Taylor drags Alice Mardike in front of me, I must commit her to the County Gaol unless she can establish she didn't do it? Even if he has no good evidence that she did? I simply have to believe him?'

'Well, not if somebody else clearly murdered Barwell without supernatural help. I think Mistress Mardike would then be off the hook until the next time a sheep dies in suspicious circumstances.'

'It sounds as if Barwell was generally unloved,' I say. 'I don't think Ben liked him much and his father-in-law liked him even less. What do you know about him, other than his extensive love life?'

'Very little. Don't forget I moved back here only last summer,' says Sir Felix. 'I was elsewhere when Barwell first arrived. And my years in Paris and Brussels and London have made me almost as much a foreigner in my own village as you are. There are two types of people, in the eyes of Clavershall West. On the one hand, there are those who properly stay where they belong and don't question the views of their forefathers. On the other, there are those who discover a broader allegiance to the wide world. In London there are plenty of people like us – here, not so many. That's why, these days, people don't necessarily tell me everything they know; and they definitely won't tell you more than they have to. But a few questions asked in the inn might establish for you exactly how many tearful young ladies Barwell had promised to marry. And how many vengeful fathers and brothers were prepared to teach him a lesson. A journey across the border into his native Suffolk might also yield results.'

I look out of the window. The night is deep black, but enough candlelight escapes the room to reveal the snow falling heavily in the Park, flake upon flake. I won't be going to Suffolk tomorrow. Or anywhere beyond the village. Clavershall West has been cut off from the rest of the world since yesterday, which is how Clavershall West likes it.

'I'll speak to Amy Barwell,' I say. 'When an unfaithful husband dies, the wife is often a good starting place. Even if she didn't kill him, I'm fairly sure she'll have some idea which other women he was friendly with. Wives tend to notice.'

'You might also ask her where her father was early this afternoon,' says Sir Felix.

'Yes,' I say. 'I'll do that too.'

Chapter Four

I discuss Leviticus with the Rector

It still seems strange to have a man bring my horse round to the front door for me. But I am, after all, Sir John Grey, and cannot be expected to fetch it from the stables myself as rascally lawyer John Grey once did. And the lord of the manor cannot be expected to walk into the village on a day like this.

The snow was already impossibly deep in places, but, during the night, somebody has draped a thick white sheet over the Park that surrounds the manor house. The long, straight gravel path has now completely vanished. We have not seen grass for some days, but even the hedges have become low, snaking ridges of snow. The trees bear white robes, streaked with black where the bare branches show a little. Only the sky retains the colour it remembers from last summer.

My brown Welsh cob trudges through it all, unimpressed by this English weather, kicking the snow away as if it were thistledown. Steam rises from his nostrils as he jogs along at his own slow pace. I am cold even before I reach the inn, but I do not stop there. I press on to the church and to the Rector's house, that lies just beyond it.

The Rector is no more pleased to see me than he was to receive George Barwell yesterday. Barwell is there by my command and the ground will soon be too cold to bury him. The Rector feels I might have been more considerate.

I do not know this new incumbent well. Dr Marcellus Bray's arrival was also while I was away. I met him first at my mother's funeral. He is slightly built, but wiry and, I suspect, with some strength in his arms and legs: a grey-muzzled terrier of a man, always ready to growl at anything he disapproves of. His nose is red with the cold or drinking too much Canary. He is completely bald under his broad-brimmed hat. Like me, he dresses severely in black, but two starched white linen bands descend from his throat to his breast. I do not know precisely what his views are on many things, but I think he is a High Church man, of whom the King would approve. Almost, but not quite, a Catholic. It is what you need to be nowadays if you want preferment. Almost that, but not quite. Just like the King.

And I detect a strange ambivalence in Marcellus Bray's attitude to me, which I also noticed at my mother's funeral. It is as if he wishes to be my friend but thinks it beneath him to ask. Why? He has nothing to fear from me. He does not need my approval. Now he has been appointed, only the Bishop can unseat him. His income from tithes and the church lands is secure and rumoured to be good. And yet I can tell he would like me to offer some word of reassurance to him. And, until I offer it, he has decided to treat me with caution.

'You plan to remain in the village, Sir John?' he asks.

'With the snow, I have little choice.'

'As do we all. I meant that you do not plan to return to your Law practice in the City?'

I pause, without knowing why. My mind is, after all, made up on this. 'No,' I say. 'I've no plans to return to London. Now that my mother is dead, the running of the estate falls to me.'

He nods. 'Your mother will be greatly missed,' he says. 'I hope that she gave you a good report of me?'

'Of course,' I say. 'She was most complimentary in all respects.'

My mother in fact said little to me about Dr Bray; but I have, in Arlington's service, become nothing if not a practised liar. And yet I think Dr Bray can detect my insincerity. He looks me up and down again, taking in my full blackness, then sighs and wraps a grey woollen shawl round his shoulders. With slow steps, he ushers me to the unheated vestry, where his guest has been laid out for further inspection by me or the coroner or anyone else who might be interested.

Barwell looks in no better health today than he did yesterday. The blood has congealed and darkened. The remaining flesh on his face seems to have dried and shrunk, like well-hung meat. The body is stiff, as if with the cold, though this change happens too on the warmest day, and happens faster. The deep pink spots that I observed on the face are still clear, but the neck is strangely untroubled. Then I see some small red creases.

'Mr Taylor says this was the work of the Devil,' says the Rector, behind me. 'He says that his men and the village constable are convinced of that too. But you seemed unwilling to credit that the Devil could walk amongst us.'

I straighten my back and turn to him. 'I make no claims to

be a theologian, of course, but I can assure you no witchcraft was involved in this killing. Barwell was strangled. But not with an ordinary rope or by somebody's hands. I'd recognise the marks. This was different, and now, in better light, I think I understand that too. I've heard of a silken rope being used in the East. Something of the sort was employed here.'

'Why?' asks the Rector.

Well, that's a very relevant question. Hempen rope is good enough for most people. Why buy in silk for Barwell?

'I've no idea,' I say.

'And where would you get a silken rope in Essex? What use does it have, other than a murder of this sort?'

'That too is something I cannot tell you,' I say.

He looks down his nose at me and sniffs. Lord Arlington, at his most haughty, could not have conveyed his contempt for my lack of progress more succinctly.

'If he was simply strangled, as you say, why should anyone claw away at his face like that?' he says. 'What was the need for it?'

'Because his killer disliked him very much,' I say. 'Perhaps they wanted him to be thus for all eternity.'

I smile, but I think I have somehow offended the Rector.

'That is poor theology, Sir John,' he says. 'Pagan savages may believe that to be possible, but Scripture teaches otherwise. We shall not take our mortal bodies with us to Heaven. St Paul says, in his First Epistle to the Corinthians, that we shall be raised incorruptible and that we shall all be changed. George Barwell will, once in the presence of the Almighty, have a perfectly good face again. Perhaps not his original one – St Paul is unclear on that point – but an adequate replacement for a person of his standing in society.'

'The murderer may not be familiar with St Paul,' I say. 'He may not have realised that this disfigurement was an unfortunate waste of his time.'

The Rector sniffs again. He had hoped for better from me. Or perhaps he just has a cold.

'The Devil can read the Bible as well as anyone else,' he says. 'And the Devil can cite Scripture for his purpose.'

'A man killed him and a man did this,' I say. 'A belief in witchcraft is heathen superstition – and a dangerous one if people can hang because of it. Surely, as a learned man and a doctor of divinity, you don't believe in witches yourself?'

'On the contrary,' he says. 'I have preached a number of sermons on the subject. The village is aware that I abhor witchcraft as much as they do.'

Well, that may explain how I have upset him. If he's gone to the trouble to write sermons warning the Parish against the ever-present danger of witches, he won't be happy with a Lord of the Manor who doesn't think they even exist.

'I do of course respect your views,' I say.

'Respect *my* views? We are talking about God's views, Sir John. Deuteronomy teaches us that wizardry and necromancy are an abomination unto the Lord. Leviticus urges that we should stone witches to death with stones – though I am uncertain what else would be used for stoning other than stones. Still, the general intention is perfectly clear. It adds quite reasonably that their blood shall be upon them. Those who stone a witch bear no blame. Exodus Chapter 18, verse 22 states: "thou shalt not suffer a witch to live". Exodus, Leviticus *and* Deuteronomy, Sir John. You are not, I hope, claiming that Moses was a heathen? He was of course a Jew, and therefore most regrettably burns in Hell, but he is not to be accounted a heathen for all that. His opinion is good enough for most practical purposes.'

I wonder whether to tell the Rector that I don't think Moses is actually in Hell, but the idea clearly pleases him and Moses isn't a client of mine. Perhaps it would be better not to annoy him further. 'I bow to your greater learning,' I say.

Dr Bray sniffs. Yes, I think he does have a cold. It is icy in this vestry and it would be unkind to keep him long. Hopefully I'll decide not to.

'What do you know of George Barwell?' I ask.

'A liar and fornicator,' he says, wrapping the shawl more closely round himself for protection. 'A man of loose morals, inclined to uttering foul oaths. An ungodly person, even by the standards of this village.'

He'll be down there chatting with Moses, then.

'A carpenter by trade?' I ask.

'He claimed to be. I rarely saw him work at it. I offered him a little employment here, as you may have heard – repairing some of the panelling in the church – very much out of Christian charity. In truth, the work did not need doing. But ...'

He looks at me. He wants me to know this, but perhaps not much more. Again I think he has considered to what extent I am to be trusted and come to no firm conclusion.

'And yet he had money?' I say. 'Ben says he spent freely, at least when he first arrived.'

'Is that what they say in the village? It may be true. I saw no evidence of it myself, and it did him very little good if he had it. St Matthew of course reminds us that we should not lay up for ourselves treasures upon earth, but rather we should lay up for ourselves treasures in heaven, where neither moth nor rust doth corrupt, and where thieves do not break through nor steal.'

'When I practised Law,' I say, 'my fees were always quoted in corruptible currency. My clerk was instructed never to take the other sort.'

The Rector is unimpressed by my bookkeeping.

'I had not expected a Puritan to mock the scriptures in the Lord's own house,' he says.

'I mock nothing,' I say. 'Nor do I know who might have informed you that I was a Puritan.'

Perhaps he is judging me again by my attire. He clearly thinks the Lord of the Manor should be arrayed in brighter colours than a Rector. Nobody in the village has forgotten that I was at the University of Cambridge at its most puritanical. I could disown the entire Bible, from Genesis to The Revelation of St John the Divine, and the accusation of undue sanctity would still hang over me like the hot steam from a dunghill.

'I hope that Barwell had indeed laid up some treasure in heaven,' I add. 'Just as I hope that I have and you have. We'll all need it one day, and perhaps sooner than many of us expect. But, as St Matthew points out, it wouldn't have tempted thieves to commit murder. Any gold he was carrying may have done.'

'Whatever he may have possessed, he had very little money with him when he was killed – only a few pence in his pockets,' says the Rector. 'I counted it. Just that and a small door key. The money and key are in the Rectory, in the chest with my maniple and cope, if you wish to examine them.'

Maniple *and* cope. I try to remember what they are. Popish vestments of some sort. It wouldn't surprise me if he went over to Rome this afternoon.

'Then thieves may have taken the rest of his cash,' I say. 'Unless Barwell gave it to the poor.'

For the first time, the Rector allows himself a smile. 'That is improbable,' he says. 'He had little interest in the poor, unless they happily chanced to be young and female. What am I to do with the body?'

'You'll need to keep it here until the coroner can be summoned.'

'I would prefer to bury him as soon as the weather permits.'

We both look out of the window. Snow has started to fall again. Clergymen have to be as aware as farmers of the state of the ground and what can and can't be done with it.

'I cannot say whether the coroner or a thaw will come first.'

'Then I must be host to Mr Barwell for a few more days,' says the Rector. 'Until a convenient and lawful time presents itself for his interment. I really must find something to cover what is left of his face. It is most unpleasant.'

Taylor's farm is on the edge of the village, on slightly higher ground. I am glad that it has a large stable, with room for my cob. Even he struggled the last few yards. He'll be pleased to be rubbed down by one of Taylor's men and given some water and good clean hay.

I offer Amy Barwell my condolences. She nods without saying anything and wipes away a tear. She does not seem to share her father's view that she's much better off without a husband. She looks up at me with red eyes. 'They won't let me see his body,' she says.

She's young – sixteen or seventeen. Her skin is pale, her hair is red and there are many small brown freckles on her face. There is a fragility to her body and to her beauty. Either could be blown away in an instant. A father would want to protect a girl like that from a man like Barwell. In her current state, she must be a constant reminder to Taylor that he didn't. In just a few months Taylor will have a grandchild.

'I think it's as well that you don't,' I say. 'Whoever killed him . . .' I pause, wondering how this sentence might end. Is there any pleasant way to describe his disfigurement?

'I know what happened. I'd rather see him, whatever they did to his face,' she says. She's fragile, but I don't doubt her bravery. Even so . . .

'Better perhaps to remember him as he was,' I say. 'Your father identified his body. That is sufficient. There is no need for you to do so.'

'I *will* see him,' she says. 'I won't let him go to his grave without a final farewell. It is my right. Neither you nor my father will stop me.'

'I agree that you don't need my permission,' I say. 'Nor your father's. Your late husband lies in the vestry, and the Rector will scarcely deny a wife's request to see him.'

'I'm a widow,' she says. 'I was a wife until yesterday afternoon. Now I'm a widow. I may as well get used to calling myself one.'

'Of course,' I say. My mother never hesitated to describe herself as a widow, if it suited her to do so, even when her first husband was alive. It created the legal fiction that was so necessary for her second marriage to take place.

'As George's widow, I shall go there today,' Amy says.

I admire her determination and her spirit. I really think she deserved better than Barwell.

'Your late husband was a carpenter?' I ask.

'There was little work for him here.'

'Do people no longer need items made of wood?'

'He was skilled in fine carving, not making common stools and buckets.'

'The Rector says that he gave him some work.'

Amy looks surprised. Had her husband not told her that? 'Of course,' she says. 'So he did.'

'He came from Suffolk?' I ask.

'Sudbury.'

'Why did he settle here if there was no suitable employment for him?'

She smiles. 'He had been working in Cambridge, making panels for the chapel of one of the Colleges. He stopped here for the night, at the inn, on his way to London. We met on the road the next morning, before he left. He asked Ben who I was. He didn't go to London after all.'

'Because of you?'

'Because of me. He spoke a few words to me on my way to market and he never looked at another woman afterwards.'

I consider this idea carefully.

'You were not aware that he might have had an interest . . . that there might have been other ladies in the village to whom he was in some way . . . attached?'

'If anyone has told you that, it is a lie,' says Amy. 'He was completely faithful to me. Don't you think I would know?'

For a moment, I am almost convinced myself. Could the Rector – indeed could the entire population of Clavershall West – be mistaken as to Barwell's character? I am in no doubt that she's heard the same rumours as I have. But she didn't believe them. And still doesn't. Perhaps some wives do operate on that basis. I'll have to ask Aminta.

'Did he just live off your father?' I ask. 'If he didn't find much work here?'

The answer shoots back. 'He had money. He was paid well for the job in Cambridge – and other places. He could carve scrolls and musical instruments and birds and fruit and flowers. He showed me one of the birds. You would have expected it to hop onto your finger and sing.'

'Ben thought that he had run out of money lately – he was seen rarely at the inn.'

She laughs. 'He had no need to go to the inn. Not once we were married.'

Well, even if she didn't credit the rumours about other women, she believed in keeping him well away from temptation.

'Do you know why he went up to the woods? The day was bleak and he had no cause to go there.'

'He would sometimes take walks. He said that he needed to study nature. As models for his work.'

'Of course,' I say, but I must have raised an eyebrow slightly further than I intended. Amy rounds on me.

'It wasn't to meet some slutty village girl if that's what you're thinking. Why would he want one of them if he had me?'

Because that's what men like Barwell do, whoever they are married to. You might as well ask why a fox visits the hen house again when he's taken a chicken the night before.

'Did he tell you where he was going yesterday?' I ask.

'No. He didn't tell me anything.'

'So he just went for a walk in the snow?'

'I thought I had already told you that.'

Amy stares at me as if I were an imbecile. I wonder how long she can maintain that look of disdain. A minute? Two minutes? Surely she must be aware what her husband was like? But, no, apparently not. Perhaps I'm forgetting how young she is. Things are much clearer at that age. Right and wrong haven't started to overlap. The man you love is perfect in all respects.

'Do you know what time he left home?'

She shakes her head. 'I didn't notice him go,' she says. 'I don't . . . didn't . . . watch him the whole time. I trusted him. Anyway, I had work to do on the farm.'

'Do you know if he took much money with him?' I ask. 'He had only a few pence in his purse when he was found.'

'Then perhaps that's all he took. He had plenty back at the house, I can assure you. He didn't need my father's charity.'

We look at each other. If she knows more, she's not planning to tell me what it is. Certainly not if it does no credit to her late husband's memory. He may be a dead blasphemer and fornicator, but she wants me to think well of him nevertheless.

'I must talk to your father,' I say.

'He's out, up on the hill, gathering in the last of the sheep. Says the snow's as bad as he's known, but it's only going to get worse.'

'Was he doing the same yesterday? Up on the hill, over by the woods, I mean.'

'Two of his shepherds were.'

'I know. I met them. They found your husband's body. He wasn't with them then? Perhaps he prefers just to send his men out on a day like that?'

She shakes her head. We both know that isn't what Taylor would do. He'd have been out there somewhere, guiding, directing, chastising. He knows his duty to his men as well as he knows his men's duty to him.

'You'll have to ask him,' says Amy. 'When he's back.'

I nod. 'Do you know who might have wanted to kill your husband, Amy?'

'Of course. It was Alice Mardike.'

'I'm aware that she and your late husband had words,' I say. 'And I shall of course question her. But was there nobody else in the village with a grudge? Had anyone else ever threatened him?'

She shakes her head, making the fiery locks swing across her face. Her fists are clenched in her apron pockets.

'Everyone liked George,' she says. 'Everyone except that old witch. She slandered him, then said she'd kill him. And that's exactly what she's done. How much more proof do you want? Your duty, Sir John, is to arrest her, try her and burn her. And, if that takes more of a man than you are, I'm sure my father will happily do your job for you.'

Chapter Five

The examination of witches – theory

I need to return to the centre of the village then ride out on the way to Royston to reach the next house that I have to visit. It is a little off the main road, down a track that is normally muddy and rutted, but which today is smooth and white, like everything else. Footprints on the main road are few, but nobody at all has ventured down this track today. The snow is virgin pure.

The house itself is small and composed of black timber, newly whitewashed clay and dirty, much-repaired thatch. Its windows are small squares of leaded glass, smeared with grime inside and out. Nobody knows how old the house is, but Sir Felix once told me that it was mentioned in the very earliest of the surviving records of the manor. Many have lived and died here. If there are ghosts anywhere, this is where they'd be. Not up on the hill. The cottage is surrounded by a small, neat garden and overshadowed by a great, leafless oak, perhaps even older than the building itself. There is no chimney, but a thin, parsimonious trickle of white smoke rises from a hole in the roof. I knock on the low door. Were people once smaller? Or was it just the people who lived here?

'Piss off, there's nobody home,' calls a voice from inside.

'And a very good morning to you, Mistress Mardike,' I say, as I duck and enter.

Alice Mardike looks up from adding a small log to her fire. She scowls but doesn't throw it at me. By her standards this is a warm welcome. I'm honoured.

'Good morning, boy,' she says. 'My condolences on the sad loss of your mother. I'd have come to pay my respects, but folk don't always like to see witches at their mother's funeral. Lowers the tone.'

'You found her gold pin for her,' I say. 'The one that was her grandmother's. She was always grateful for that.'

She winks at me across the smoky room. We both know that good deed was technically illegal. My eyes are getting used to the perpetual twilight of a witch's parlour, and I can finally study her. She has scarcely changed at all since I lived here ten years ago. Her dress, a castoff from a previous decade, is an indeterminate grey-green colour, though it might once have been something else entirely. She has an even older shawl round her shoulders. Her untidy white hair is stuffed into an off-white linen cap, tied loosely under her chin. Her mouth is set in a thin firm line, but she can't stop the twinkle in her eye, try as she does.

'I knew I'd see you today, Master John,' she says.

'Your magical powers, no doubt,' I say.

'Didn't need them. Not this time. I'd just heard that no-good George Barwell was dead. When somebody dies, it never takes long for the village to accuse me of cursing him, and in this case that's exactly what I did. So I was expecting you or Ben Bowman – Magistrate or Constable – one or the other. Bit too cold today for Ben, I suppose?'

'He has an inn to run,' I say. 'It seemed unkind to insist that he brought you to me, when he'd already had to waste an afternoon up at the woods. In any case, I can come to you more easily than you can come to the Big House. Unless you've bought a horse recently?'

'Ain't you forgetting a witch's broomstick, boy?'

'Very useful for sweeping the floor,' I say. 'A horse is better in the snow.'

She thinks about smiling, then doesn't. A smiling witch would be like a smiling grave digger. She has a professional reputation to consider. 'You never were afraid of me, were you, Master John?'

'I'm afraid of a man with a sword, when all I've got is a single pistol and my powder is wet,' I say. 'And I'm afraid when I have a sick child and no idea how to make him better. Most other things I can take as they come.'

'I wouldn't know about gunpowder, but I do know you always were a handful when you were a child yourself.'

I wonder if she still sees me now as a ten-year-old. Should I tell her about my knighthood? Maybe she's already heard. I doubt it would have interested her very much if she has.

'I thought I was obedient and studious as a boy,' I say. 'That's how I remember things.'

'Which afternoon was that, then? Forever up to mischief, you and your friend Dickon. Dickon was always the stronger of the two of you, but you were more devious.'

'Dickon's dead now,' I say, staring into the fire.

'I know,' she says.

'Yes, of course you do. I've seen a lot of other men die since then.'

'As a lawyer?'

'Working for Lord Arlington.'

She nods as if she is well acquainted with His Majesty's spymaster and Secretary of State for the Southern Department. It's possible she is. After all, Arlington has agents everywhere. He'll employ anyone if they're cheap enough and don't complain.

'You're limping,' she says.

'A sword wound,' I say.

'How's that then, boy?'

'It's because the last man I saw die was trying to kill me at the time.'

She considers this. 'What about that scar on your face? Did the man who gave you that happen to die too?'

'Yes,' I say. 'Shortly after he did it.'

She nods. 'I'll try not to get on the wrong side of you then. Do they know who killed George Barwell?'

'You did, apparently.'

'Who says?'

'William Taylor.'

'Did he see me do it, then? I must be getting careless in my old age.'

'I'd have said that was unlikely – unless you know different.'

'He's a cruel man,' says Alice. 'Beats those who work for him. Beat his wife, when she was alive. Beats his poor little daughter, I don't doubt.'

'His poor little daughter also says you're a murderer.'

'Does she? In that case, she's a pert little ginger-haired madam. Too good for any of the village boys, now the Taylors have money. She and Barwell deserved each other. Always said so.' She gives the fire a cruel and unnecessary poke. The small flame goes out, but a tenacious trickle of smoke continues to rise from the glowing ashes.

'I think she genuinely loved him,' I say. 'In another couple of years she might have seen him for what he was, but not yet.'

Alice Mardike nods, as if acknowledging the sublime power of love to mess things up for everyone. But in the end she just mutters: 'Young maids be fools. All of them. Well, almost all. You married the best one in the village.'

'So she tells me,' I say.

'Took your time doing it though.'

'I was lucky,' I say. 'I had more time than I thought. A second chance. Sometimes you get them.'

I look round the room as much as the light from one small window will allow. The rough sheets and blankets may be threadbare, but the bed is neatly made. The rushes on the floor are fresh. Everything that can be made clean cheaply is clean. If the windows are filthy, it is because the dirt offers privacy at a lower cost than curtains. Dirt doesn't need washing or mending. On the mantelpiece is a jar with the remains of a snake in it. There is another empty jar beside it. There are bundles of dried leaves everywhere and some bottles of herbal remedies on a long wooden shelf. There is no fireplace. The logs burn on an iron grate in the centre of the room, and the smoke rises in a leisurely way through the hole in the roof.

'Where were you yesterday, around noon?' I ask.

'Was that when young Barwell died, or just your own curiosity, boy?'

'Both.'

'Went to the well just before noon. Like always. It's warmer then if you've got to wait while others go first. Witches always go last at the well. That way we can't poison the water. I usually spits in it though, when I remembers. A good gob of phlegm, when I've got it in me to do it.'

'Really?'

'I will one day. You just watch out.'

'We've got our own well at the Big House. You can spit in the other one whenever you want. Did anyone see you there?'

'Lots around. Can't say if any of them saw me. Sometimes witches are invisible to normal folk. You say hello and they look straight through you. I'd call that magic, wouldn't you?'

'So, you didn't speak to any of them?'

She considers. 'Harry Hardy,' she says after a while. 'He gave me good morning.'

I nod. Harry Hardy must be eighty by now. I wonder whether he'll survive another winter.

'And later?'

'How much later would that be, boy?'

'Did you see anyone during the afternoon?'

'Curiosity again?'

'I don't know exactly when Barwell died. Could be as late as two o'clock.'

'Makes no difference to me when it was. I was still doing the same things. After dinner, I gathered vegetables in the garden. Digging them before the snow got worse. Davies, the smith, came by. The Quaker. He spoke to me. Always does.'

'What time?'

'Time? Do you think I have a silver pocket watch, boy?'

'You could hear the church clock.'

'True. The clock was striking as we spoke, now I think about it. Maybe that would be one o'clock, then.'

'Did you leave your cottage after that?'

'Course not. Snow was falling hard by that time. Stayed in by the fire, same as normal folk what can't fly on broomsticks.'

'You say you cursed Barwell?'

'In a manner of speaking.'

'What did you say exactly?'

'I told him to stay away from silly young village wenches, now he was married and had a baby on the way. It wasn't right.'

'That merely sounds like good advice,' I say.

'I may have added that I hoped he'd drop dead of the Plague.'

'Those words exactly?'

'How should I know? I hadn't expected to be answering questions about it, or I might have written it down in my memorandum book.'

'And people heard you?'

'If I say good morning to folk, everyone seems deaf. If I tell somebody to drop dead, they can hear me on the other side of the village.'

She pulls her shawl more closely round her. She needs a thicker one.

'Are you still brewing your cough recipes?' I ask.

'Of course. Your mother used to make that too.'

'Yes, she did.'

'Better if she hadn't given it away free to anyone who asked. How did she expect me to make a living if folk could get it for nothing from her?'

'It wouldn't have occurred to her. She came from a family that had scorned trade of any kind for over five hundred years. Only money gained through inheritance or marriage was in any way creditable.'

Alice sighs. 'A sad loss to the village, Master John. Always a friendly word when I saw her.'

'Perhaps I could buy some medicine from you now. Young Charles has a cough.'

Alice takes down a bottle of thick green syrup.

'How much?' I ask.

'To you? Same as your mother used to charge,' she says.

'I'd better pay something,' I say. 'You can't be seen bribing the judiciary.'

'Tuppence, then.'

'That wouldn't even pay for the honey in it,' I say.

I give her a Shilling. She takes it without comment and wraps herself tightly in her threadbare shawl again. She pokes the fire once more, then shivers. There's a limit to how much heat you can get out of a couple of smouldering logs, however much you threaten them with violence.

'I'll see if I can find you one of my mother's old cloaks,' I say. 'It's going to be a cold winter.'

She shakes her head. 'You can't afford to have your mother's cloak going round the village with a witch inside it,' she says. 'The taint would stick to your mother's memory and to you. Thank you kindly, but I'll have to be warm enough in this.'

'I'd like you to have it nevertheless.'

She shakes her head. 'Can't be done, boy. Trust me on that. You go straight home with that cordial and don't tell nobody where you've been. Don't worry about me and my aches and pains. Old age doesn't come alone, as you'll find out yourself one day. For the moment, you just look after Master Charles. That's your main concern.'

'The whole village is my concern now,' I say. 'Thank you for the cordial, Mistress Mardike. I'd stay indoors if I were you. I think things will get worse before they get better.'

Chapter Six

I am politely warned

The snow is falling hard again. Soft white flakes, drifting down from the heavens. It is like one of the autumn mists that floats in from the fields, obscuring anything more than a few yards ahead. I scarcely notice Harry Hardy's cottage until I am upon it. I dismount and wade through the snow up to his front door.

'Good morning, Sir John,' says Harry. 'You'd better come in.'

I look back at my cob, who is now much more white than brown, standing patiently by the road, staring straight ahead. This is nothing to him. They breed them tough in Wales.

'Just for a moment,' I say.

Harry's cottage is a slightly larger and brighter version of Alice's. More of the thin winter light enters through the snow-caked windows. The fire is larger. He has a chimney. His oak chair by the hearth has a padded seat and back, covered with an embroidered fabric. Pewter plates and tankards gleam on the oak dresser. A ham hangs from the ceiling close by. This is comfort that previous generations of villagers would have envied. Modernity is knocking at the door, even in Clavershall West.

Harry's clothes are not the latest London fashion, any more than Alice's are – the short, dark green jacket and the ample breeches probably came from Saffron Walden market and he may not have been to the first or even the second to wear them. Still, they are unpatched and keep him warm. His hat is a little battered and, like the shepherds, he has chosen to keep it on for warmth rather than remove it out of respect for my knighthood.

'How are you, Harry?' I ask. 'Do you have everything you need in this cold weather?'

'Well enough for my age, and thank you, sir, and I have firewood and food aplenty. Are you back for good then, after your travels?'

Once again, I pause. Yesterday I would just have said 'yes'. Why am I now uncertain? I have little desire to return to being a lawyer – less still to working for Arlington. Aminta seems content here, writing plays in the country for the London stage. I'd be a fool to set foot in the noisy, grimy City again.

'Probably,' I say.

'Lawyers still make good money down there, I hear.'

'Yes, nothing changes. But now I also have responsibilities here.'

'So you do,' he says. 'Well, if you choose to stay, I think folk will be very happy to hear it. They were very fond of your mother. Less so of your stepfather, if you don't mind my saying. But he wasn't from round here.'

'No,' I say. 'He wasn't. I don't think Colonel Payne was ever really at ease being Lord of the Manor. He was happier being a soldier. He saw the village as a company of infantry that he could never quite train as he wished.'

'We don't take kindly to being told what to do. Not in Essex, we don't. But you and your wife, sir – your two families have both been here for a long time. You know how things work. Folk trust you to run things as they were run in times past – I mean, before that man Oliver. The King back on the throne and your family back in the Big House. I'm glad I lived to see it, sir.'

'I'll do my best,' I say. 'One small matter, Harry – do you remember seeing Alice Mardike at the well yesterday?'

'Does she say I did?'

'Yes. She told me this morning.'

He nods. 'Maybe she was there, then. If that's what she says.'

'And you spoke to her?'

'Any reason why I shouldn't?'

'None at all, Harry. Don't worry. It was kind of you to do so, when so many don't. What time was that?'

'A bit before dinner. Maybe eleven or half past. Half past, I think, because it was a while since I'd heard the church clock strike.'

'Did you see her later?'

'Not me. Come home as fast as I could with my rheumatics. Snow was getting worse.'

'Did you see anyone else heading off towards the woods, then or later?'

'Can't say I did. Not sure it would amount to much if I had.'

'Why not?'

'Because everyone knows it was Alice Mardike, sir.'

'Everyone in the village?'

'Everyone I've spoken to.'

'But you don't believe them?'

'I'm not saying that. I've known her for years. Knew her mother, up to when they hanged her. Knew her well. All they ever wanted was to be left alone. When I first heard, I thought, What would Alice Mardike be doing killing George Barwell when she didn't need to?'

'My thoughts exactly. Thank you, Harry. I'll have to make enquiries elsewhere.'

Harry shakes his head, then says: 'I hope you won't mind me giving you advice, Sir John . . .'

'Of course not,' I say. 'We've known each other a long time.'

'So we have, sir. Thank you for saying so. It's like this, sir – you did well to question Alice Mardike straight away. Folk will appreciate that. They'll feel it's what you should do. But I wouldn't waste your time in looking for anyone else who might have done it. I mean, somebody in the village, sir. Questioning them all about where they were. People might feel it wasn't respectful if you were suggesting they were no more to be trusted than an old witch.'

I nod. I think I already knew that. Still, the reminder is timely.

'The scar on your face has healed well,' Harry adds.

'It's the wound in my leg that is troubled by the cold,' I say. 'I fear it may not be wholly mended until the spring. Though I might not admit that so freely to my wife.'

Harry nods. He was married once.

'Cold gets in everywhere,' says Harry. 'And at any season. At least it does at my age. But you've got another fifty years before you'll have to worry about being my age.'

He gives me a look that says: 'if you live that long'. It's the same look that Alice Mardike gave me. It's the same look Aminta gives me from time to time.

'Let me know if there's anything you need,' I say.

'Thank you, Sir John, but you don't want to trouble yourself about me,' says Harry.

'My mother would have done,' I say.

'That's true,' says Harry. 'She would. She understood us well and was as generous with your stepfather's money as she could get away with. I hope you do too, sir. Understand us, I mean. For everyone's sake.'

My cob is pleased to see his stable again. He's tough, but he knows he deserves some respite. I would be happy to rub him down and feed him myself, but the bridle is taken from me and I am ordered indoors to warm myself by the fire.

The parlour is, however, empty when I reach it.

'Where is Lady Grey?' I ask.

'Gone into the village, sir,' says Morrell. 'She wished to take food to one or two of the poorer inhabitants.' His tone implies that it would be better if the poor starved quietly and did not put the gentry to needless trouble.

'Could you not have gone for her?' I ask.

'I suggested that, and she declined my offer. She said that your mother would not have allowed it. It was, and always has been, the custom for viands to be delivered by the lady of the house in person.'

'And Master Charles?'

'He is well. The housekeeper is looking after him.'

'Sir Felix?'

'Lady Grey's father has taken to his bed, sir. He has a chill.'

'Then please take him a bottle of Canary,' I say. 'With my compliments.'

'He commanded me to do so an hour ago,' says Morrell. 'I shall of course give him your compliments and enquire whether he requires a second bottle.'

Morrell approves of Sir Felix Clifford in a way that those who know him better do not. The Cliffords, as Morrell is aware, are an important family. One of the King's ministers, Sir Thomas Clifford, is a distant cousin. And Sir Felix is in a way a reformed character. Most of the things that he enjoys doing in London are simply not possible here in the country at any price. Drinking my wine in a soft feather bed is the closest he can get to debauchery.

I hear a door bang and a moment later Aminta is with us, still shaking the snow from her fur-lined cloak. Her cheeks are flushed but there is a triumphant gleam in her eye.

'I hope that the recipients of your bounty were grateful, my Lady,' says Morrell.

Aminta looks blank for a moment and then says: 'Of course, Mr Morrell. They were touchingly indebted. It brought a tear to my eye. Could I trouble you to fetch me a glass of Sack? I am stiff with cold and would like it at once. At once, if you please, Mr Morrell.'

He bows. After all, Aminta was a Clifford too before she took my less impressive surname. Her desires are, for him, the most absolute of commands. And her commands are his greatest, possibly his only, pleasures. 'I shall do so instantly, my Lady.'

She watches him leave, then says very quickly: 'I went to the inn to see Ben's wife, Nell.'

'Why?' I ask.

'Because you can pick up all sorts of gossip at the inn and, unlike Ben, Nell actually listens to people.'

'And did you discover anything?'

'I hope you realise that you said that with a sickeningly condescending tone. I'm almost inclined not to tell you what I found out.'

'But you are going to?'

'Yes, John, because you really need to know this. It is all so much worse than we thought.'

Chapter Seven

The Platts let me know they have money

'So what did Nell have to say?' I ask.

I've known and respected Nell for many years. Her father once ran a theatre company in London. Nell helped him manage it and, it was always rumoured, had even appeared on stage in the days when such things were strictly forbidden by the Law. She's younger than Ben – not so much older than I am. And very pretty. The only thing that convinces me that witchcraft might be possible is that Ben has managed to keep Nell to himself for so long. She must have had plenty of better offers.

'Nell confirmed that George Barwell had promised almost every girl over the age of fourteen in the village that he would wed her,' says Aminta. 'There was much maidenly consternation when he chose to marry Amy Taylor.'

'So half the village is with child?'

'Some fortunately recalled the advice of the Rector and their mothers just in time to avoid conception. None of them has been left in an awkward position, as far as Nell knows.'

'But we have many possible suspects for Barwell's murder?'

'No. At least not according to Nell. The scales fell from the eyes of the maidens of Clavershall West once it was clear that George had promised himself so generously. One by one, the women of the village began to doubt his good taste. He became an object of their scorn and pity rather than their hatred.'

'That was wise of them.'

'Except perhaps for one young woman.'

'Who?' I ask.

'Margaret Platt,' says Aminta.

I try to remember who she is. Since I was last resident here, families have expanded, and once familiar children grown into unrecognisable adults. The Platts have a farm of middling size on the London road. Jacob Platt comes from a long line of yeomen and he has managed his inheritance well. He's not yet as rich as Taylor but he's one of the better-off villagers these days.

'You'll know her,' says Aminta. 'The Platts' youngest child. Small, mousy girl – about the same age as Amy, I think. Not popular, apparently, amongst the other village girls, though she and Amy were good friends when they were younger. Thought to be rather clever, which isn't a compliment round here, as you know. Reads and writes very well. Margaret was expecting George Barwell to marry her, until she discovered one morning that he'd married her best friend. She's not the sort to shrug that off and wish them a long and happy life together.'

'The Platts' youngest? Yes, I remember her now,' I say. 'A sister married to a farmer in Royston and a brother living in Colchester, I think. She'd be the last of the Platt children still at home. I may need to go and speak to her.'

'Precisely, John. That's why I'm telling you. You need to speak to her. What Nell added was that Margaret had been seen visiting Alice Mardike, a few days before Barwell died. Tongues would doubtless have been wagging about that anyway. But then Margaret told more people than was advisable that she would soon have her revenge on George Barwell. Nobody took that too seriously at the time, because nobody takes anything she says too seriously; but now people are starting to wonder more than a little at the coincidence.'

'But she wasn't seen out and about when Barwell was killed?'

'Nobody Nell's spoken to says she was, and Nell seems to have spoken to a lot of people. But it was a cold day and no one was out who didn't need to be – especially after about eleven o'clock.'

'That's interesting,' I say. 'But I'm surprised that Nell is spreading gossip even to that extent.'

'It's called evidence, not gossip, though I don't think Nell likes Margaret that much. Margaret seems quite good at annoying people.'

'Very well, I commend Nell for providing this important and impartial evidence. But how does it make things so much worse? It sounds as if Margaret has acted unadvisedly, but if nobody saw her out that day, then it's unlikely she killed Barwell.'

'It was what Nell said afterwards. She and Ben have never had a child.'

'I know. I think it is a sadness to both of them that they do not.'

'Nell says it is because Alice Mardike cursed her.'

'She's never said that to me.'

'Nor to me. Nor has Ben ever said anything. But today Nell

told me that, shortly after she came to the village, she had an argument with Mistress Mardike. Mardike came to the inn and customers complained, so rather reluctantly Nell told her she'd best leave to avoid any trouble. There was some slight altercation, because Mistress Mardike thought her money as good as anyone else's. Mistress Mardike said something that Nell didn't quite hear but that, with hindsight, Nell believes to have been a witch's curse. Nell thinks that her failure to conceive is a result of that curse. Now she considers the matter properly, nothing else can explain it.'

'Why bring that up now?'

'Because, now, Alice Mardike stands accused of witchcraft.'

It is as if an icy wind has entered the room. Of course. Now the seed of witchcraft has been planted it will start to grow everywhere.

'In the eyes of the Law, Alice currently stands accused of nothing,' I say. 'I do not regard Taylor's outburst as a formal accusation.'

'The eyes of the Law are lagging behind those of the village,' says Aminta. 'I do not doubt that half the folk here are racking their brains to try to remember what injuries they have suffered over the past thirty years and whether Alice Mardike could have had a hand in them. Anyone who's ever offered Mistress Mardike an insult will be wondering which of their later misfortunes were caused by her sorcery.'

'Insulted her? That's more like the whole village than half of it,' I say. 'But surely Nell of all people knows that witchcraft is a mere phantasm?'

'I certainly thought that she did. And I don't believe she'll go so far as to give evidence against Alice in court. But she'd like it to be true. She'd like to believe that all that stands between her and a child is the lifting of a curse. Some small part of her is convinced that, if Alice Mardike is hanged, then all will be well.'

I shake my head. 'Nell's not the sort to believe in witches. Taylor's shepherds may fear ghosts up on the hill, but Nell doesn't believe in that type of thing any more than I do.'

'Do you not? You say that now, here in your own drawing room. But if I asked you in the churchyard on a misty November evening . . . Would your answer still be the same?'

I remember the brief moment in the woods, with the sun almost set and a cold wind blowing, when I almost believed Barwell had been killed supernaturally.

'The facts would be the same,' I say.

'I'm not talking about facts. Nell has been here a long time amongst these damp Essex fields and low Essex hills. She's in the churchyard – a metaphorical one admittedly – wondering if the approaching shape is a man or a ghoul. Set her down in Spring Gardens in London, in a dazzling blaze of candlelight, and you might get a different answer. I've talked to Nell about the theatre. I've discussed Shakespeare with her and Marlowe and Jonson. She's an intelligent woman, who has seen much of the world and knows there are better things in life than mud and sheep. But at the moment she truly believes that hanging Mistress Mardike will let her have a baby.'

'There may be another reason,' I say. 'By condemning Alice, Nell also puts herself safely on the side of the majority. I offered Alice Mardike one of my mother's old cloaks. She said it would endanger us if she accepted. You don't want to be seen too close to a witch. Sir Felix mentioned Matthew Hopkins. I don't remember his coming here, but I do know that he rarely found just one witch. When they find one, they look for others. They could accuse any woman in the village. Especially one who has brazenly appeared on the stage. But a victim of witchcraft would come under less suspicion. Nell may not be the last to feel the need to demonstrate her virtue.'

'Well, as a playwright, and above all as a writer of comedies, I am clearly already in league with the Devil and a lost cause. But I have no intention of condemning Alice Mardike simply to show the village how virtuous I am.'

'Of course not. Our safety lies in sticking firmly to the letter of the Law. Nobody can blame me if I do that. It's my job. I will question everyone who might know about the murder in the most impartial way. Then I shall decide whether Alice has any case to answer. Or indeed, more likely, whether Taylor has a case to answer.'

'You think he killed his son-in-law?'

'As I've said, he showed no emotion when he saw the body. He seemed to know exactly where it was. He went straight to it, even though it was already so dark that he couldn't see me under the trees. He confessed to me that he disliked him. Taylor is the one who is most insistent that we find Alice guilty and do so without further investigation. And there's one other thing. I'd been trying to think what you'd use to take a man's face off. According to Amy, George Barwell specialised in fine carvings. You'd need all manner of chisels and gouges for that work – and you'd need to keep them razor-sharp. Barwell had them when he came here, because he was on his way to London, where he had work. They'd have been at Taylor's house. Taylor would have known where they were.'

'Taylor's wife died a few years ago,' says Aminta.

'How?'

'A fall, they say. At least, nobody was willing to give evidence to the contrary.'

'Alice Mardike said Taylor used to beat her.'

'It's his right,' says Aminta. 'As a lawyer I thought you'd know that. He's allowed to chastise his wife. Doubtless he'd feel he had the right to beat his son-in-law too.'

'And strangle him?'

'Men like Taylor, who are used to violence, don't always know when to stop.'

'We'd need witnesses to convict him of Barwell's killing, but we might get them – an ill-treated farm worker, for example, or a daughter who realises that her father has just murdered her much-loved husband.'

'From what I've heard, it's unlikely that Amy Barwell will give evidence against her father,' says Aminta. 'She's too frightened of him.'

'I doubt that his shepherds will either,' I say. 'They seem thoroughly cowed. Well, I'll go and speak to Margaret Platt next anyway. She may have something useful to tell us. We need to find out who the real killer was before the whole village decides it was Alice Mardike.'

'I think you'll find they've already decided,' says Aminta.

The Platts have prospered. Their brick-built farmhouse is not the largest in the village, but it is new and has six chimneys rising above the tile roof. No smoke rising from a hole in the thatch for them. Above the front door is a lozenge bearing the inscription 'JP 1660 AP'. As long as the wall stands, it will proudly record that Jacob and Ann Platt built the house in the same year that His Majesty the King was restored to the thrones of England, Scotland, France and Ireland. One day the bricks will doubtless mellow, but for the moment the house is proudly red. It has modern sash windows, a novelty that is still remarked on in the village.

Jacob Platt looks at me in surprise when he opens the door. 'Sir John! What are you doing abroad in this weather? And with the Devil stalking the village . . .'

Well, I probably don't need to ask if he's heard that Barwell is dead.

'It's about that that I've come, Mr Platt,' I say.

'I know nothing about his death, other than what I've heard. He won't be missed. A man of ill repute and a seducer of young maids.'

It sounds as if I don't really need to ask if he knows what his daughter was up to either. Still, I might enquire later – after I've talked to Margaret.

'It was your daughter that I wished to speak to,' I say.

'Surely not? She is understandably upset about the death of the husband of one of her friends. Our son is away in Colchester at present – he knew Barwell better than I do – but in his absence I'm sure I can tell you whatever it is you need to know. You don't need to trouble my daughter.'

'I think Margaret probably knows him best of all,' I say.

Jacob Platt looks at me and swallows hard. He'd hoped the rumours were less well known than they clearly are.

'It's not true,' he says. 'It's not true, Sir John, what they're saying about Margaret. Any attachment to Barwell . . . it's just her fancy. But the silly village girls will gossip anyway.'

He doesn't regard Margaret as one of the silly village girls. That remains to be seen.

'I'm speaking to many people in the village,' I say, 'including the Rector. I don't listen to gossip, unless it is relevant to my investigation, and I am accusing your daughter of nothing. Indeed, for the moment I'm accusing nobody of anything.'

'The new Rector?' says Platt scathingly. 'You know he's a papist, I suppose? The vestry's full of robes and stoles of every colour under the sun.'

I think of the Rector's assurance that Barwell's pence are safely stored with his maniple. Is that a type of robe? Something suspiciously Roman, anyway. We certainly never had them at Cambridge in its Puritan days.

'Yes, I noticed,' I say.

'Well, that's the sort of man the King appoints now. Nobody asks us who we want. They just send us a papist.'

Much of this is true, though Dr Bray was presumably my mother's choice for the post. Perhaps it just amused her that everyone in a low church village would have to sit and listen to high church sermons for the next thirty years.

'I do need to talk to Margaret,' I say.

Platt nods. 'I'll get one of the men to take your horse to the stable, Sir John. It's a fine, clear day, but it's still cold, even for a tough little cob like that.'

Margaret looks nervous, as well she might. Her faithless former lover is dead and she's been seen consulting the village witch.

'Sit down, Margaret,' I say.

Though it had not been my intention, seating her has made her look even more insignificant than before. She is pale, with dark hair. Her nose is sharp and her tongue, though I cannot see it, is reputed to be sharper. She wears a simple but very warm grey woollen dress and a fine linen apron over it. Her hair is tied back tightly in a way that seems to stretch her skin to a perfect smoothness, revealing in the process two small gold earrings.

'Can my father overhear us?' she asks.

'I don't think so. I said I needed to speak to you alone. He said he was going to the barn.'

Margaret makes an almost audible gulp and looks round the newly panelled room. The oak is still pale gold, though Mistress Platt has already managed to give it a fine, hard polish. The stone fireplace is the warm yellow of newly quarried stone. There is some silver amongst the pewter on the dresser. The Platts are coming up in the world. Wooden platters to silver plate in a single generation. Have they risen far enough to save Margaret? If you have enough money, you can consult witches with impunity. But how much is enough? That is the question that is currently running through her mind, and she hasn't yet answered it.

'What do you want to know?' she asks. She strokes her skirt. It's good quality, plain broadcloth. It could act as a character witness in any court in the county.

'Is it true that you and George Barwell had some sort of understanding? You're not under oath here, but I may need to ask you the same question formally under oath, and it would be convenient for everyone if your answer remained much the same.'

'He promised to marry me,' she says in a whisper.

'They say you claimed you would get your revenge on him for deserting you.'

'I said he'd get what he deserved. I never said I'd do anything. I never said witchcraft. Never. I'll swear that on the Bible, Sir John, whenever you want. Bring me one now and I'll swear.' She gives me a crooked smile. I nod. She'll need to do much better than that if she has to testify under oath. Unless she really wants the jury to think she's a devious little minx as well as a murderess.

'Where were you yesterday?' I ask.

'Here all day. My mother will vouch for that. And my father.'

'I do not doubt that they will. You didn't go out at all?'

Again there is the look of cunning, without which she seems unable to lie. 'No,' she says. 'Not at all.'

'If you did go out,' I say, 'somebody will have seen you. That is how it works in this village. Don't imagine that, just because the shutters are closed, nobody is watching you. You can't walk down the street without two women asking their husbands where that girl can possibly be going at this time of day.'

She nods thoughtfully. Her mother probably does that too.

'Yes, I remember now,' she says quickly. 'I went out for about an hour.'

'When?'

There is a long pause for consideration, quite unjustified by the answer that follows.

'I don't know. Maybe a little before midday.'

'And where did you go?'

'To . . . to the well. The well in the village.'

'Do you not have your own well here at the farm?'

'Yes, but I went to meet my friends.'

'So, they'll have seen you there?'

'No . . . that is, they weren't there. I waited for them, but they did not come. Or perhaps they were there earlier and I missed of their coming. I don't know.'

I nod. Harry Hardy had been there then and reported that a number of villagers were drawing water at about half past eleven. But perhaps they had all wisely departed before midday.

'It must have been cold waiting there?' I say.

'Yes. It had started to snow hard. That's why I came back. That's all there was to it.'

From her smile, she clearly thinks I believe some part of her story.

'So nobody saw you there?' I ask.

Another long pause. 'No,' she says.

I take out a notebook and my pencil. She starts to look worried as I write this all down.

'What are you writing?'

'Just what you've told me. George Barwell promised to marry you, but you claim you made no threats against him when he did not. You say you went out for an hour yesterday to meet your friends, but they did not come. It was late morning, after most people had gone home because of the snow. Nobody saw you. Otherwise you were here at the house.'

She bites her lip. 'That's right,' she says. 'Is that all?'

'No,' I say. 'You were seen visiting Alice Mardike.'

'Which time?' she asks. Then she falls silent.

'I only know of one visit,' I say. 'I cannot say exactly when – but within the last few days. With hindsight, it was an unfortunate thing to have done, however few times you did it.'

'I needed some medicine,' she says.

'What for?'

'Women's troubles,' she says.

She knows from experience that, as a man, I'm unlikely to question that.

'You didn't discuss George Barwell in any way?'

'What do you think?' she says with contempt.

'I think you probably did discuss him. But all I need to know at the moment is what you will say under oath.'

Again, the look of surprise that I am not wholly convinced by her evasions and half-truths. If she was one of my witnesses, I'd think twice about putting her before a judge at all.

'We didn't discuss George Barwell.' Her hand grips a fold in her skirt tightly. Her knuckles are white.

'Good,' I say. 'That was very wise. If you had, then things would look pretty bad for you. It's fortunate that you didn't.'

She swallows hard again. I wait and see what she will say next. The Platts' new clock ticks in the background. It is a pleasant sound, but Margaret does not find it soothing.

'Do you need to know any more?' she asks eventually.

'Not for the moment.'

I close my notebook and stuff it into my pocket.

'Will you speak to my mother? She'll tell you I was in all day.'

'I'm sure she will tell me that. If I had a daughter I'd probably say much the same. Thank you, Margaret, but I don't need to speak to anyone else at present.'

'I didn't kill him, Sir John.'

'Well, that's clear enough.'

Margaret looks at my pocket to see if I'll take the book out again to note this. I pull my cloak around me and fasten it.

'I don't do witchcraft,' she says.

'I haven't said that you did.'

'I only went there for some medicine.'

'I hope you're feeling better,' I say.

'So, Margaret Platt wanted Alice Mardike to help her get George Barwell back?'

'Or kill him,' I say.

'I think she'd try to lure him back first,' says Aminta.

'He was married to Amy.'

'I don't think that would have stopped either of them. Anyway, only marriage to Barwell would have restored her reputation. His murder simply makes things worse. At least, before all this, she'd been seduced by a respectable married man – the village wouldn't have approved but it would have sympathised, knowing what married men are like. The notoriety of Barwell's death will now cling to her, one way or another.'

'Margaret and Amy – they're quite alike in many ways. I mean, Amy has red hair and Margaret has black, Amy has freckles and Margaret has none, but they are a similar build and similar temperament. Both quite well off. Both a bit too good for this village, if you see what I mean.'

'Barwell obviously liked them almost equally.'

'True. I wonder which he would have chosen if he'd been free to make his own selection. I had another thought as I rode back here, by the way. The silken rope that was used to strangle George Barwell . . .'

'Yes?'

'Could it perhaps have been a woman's stocking?'

'There would be few silk stockings in this village. Other than my own. Wool is good enough for most women here.'

'Both Amy's and Margaret's families are prosperous enough, though. The fields are full of Taylor's sheep. The Platts have spent a great deal of money rebuilding their house. These days, people have money for silk, even in this place.'

'I'll see if anyone knows who in the village wears silk under their skirts. It's better I ask. It would not seem decorous that you enquire after ladies' stockings, even dressed in a sober black coat.'

'Not Alice Mardike anyway,' I say. 'She says she was at home, and, anyway, she'd never have gone to the woods and lain in wait for Barwell in her threadbare shawl. She'd have been dead of cold in ten minutes. Nor is anyone really likely to believe she sent her cat to kill him. That cat has a mind of its own. As the evidence grows, I think people will soon have to admit that she had nothing to do with Barwell's death.'

The parlour door is flung open, allowing in a gust of cold air, which we can feel even by the fire. For the second time in two days, Morrell is gasping for breath.

'You must come quickly, Sir John,' he gasps. 'They've taken Mistress Mardike to the millpond. And they say they're going to drown her.'

Chapter Eight

The examination of witches – practical

I hear the group, through the low river mist, long before I see them. A happy babble of voices and an ominous, urgent splashing. They all have their backs to me. They are very intent on what is happening in the millpond. As Aminta and I approach, one turns, then a second, then a third. The cheerful noise becomes less cheerful. Then it stops.

'What's going on?' I demand as I approach them.

There are about twenty of them – equal parts men and women – all warmly dressed, but with cheeks made red by the cold air and their excitement.

'Nothing for you to worry about, Sir John,' says Taylor, finally turning to face me. He seems to be the spokesman for the group. He holds in his hands a rope, which dangles down into the millpond. Attached to the other end of it, and thrashing around in the freezing water, is Alice Mardike. They've broken a large hole in the ice to get her in. That's thoughtful of them.

'Pull her out of there at once,' I say.

'We're swimming her,' he says, without moving. 'Don't worry. It's all being done properly, according to ancient custom. I've got a rope here to save her if she goes under. Plenty of witnesses to give evidence if she floats. We'll make sure she's handed over to you alive, so that she can face justice.'

'Thank you, Mr Taylor. That's very reassuring,' I say. 'So what are your conclusions?'

'You can see for yourself, Sir John: the Devil's keeping his own afloat. She'll not drown. Not her. No witch drowns.'

'Then your test is complete. Pull her in now, Mr Taylor – and I do mean now – or I'll have you all arrested for assault.'

Taylor is genuinely puzzled. 'Assault? But she's a witch.'

'Do it now,' I say. 'I'll explain the Law later.'

Taylor passes the rope to one of his men. 'Pull her in,' he growls. 'Like the Magistrate says. He's seen she's a witch. She floats. No point in our standing around in the cold now the job's done.'

I watch as Alice is pulled up the bank, across the mixed ice and mud and snow. Green water streams from her hair and from her skirts. Her face is white. She lies there coughing and gulping air and shivering. Her eyes are wide open and staring up at the grey sky, but she doesn't seem to see me or anything else. All her strength is concentrated on just breathing in the freezing air, one gasp at a time.

'You're lucky she's still alive,' I say. 'You're lucky you haven't murdered her.'

'We're within our rights, Sir John,' says Taylor. 'We are entitled, by long-standing tradition, to discover whether there are witches amongst us. You've seen the proof. Your duty now is to arrest her. We look to you to ensure the safety of the village.'

There is a general murmur of approval. They've all seen the witch swim. Not as much as they'd have liked, but enough to be sure they've made no mistake. Now they want to see an arrest, before they go home to mulled ale and cakes in front of the fire.

Ignoring the stab of pain that I knew would be coming, I kneel down beside Alice in the snow. 'How are you faring, Mistress Mardike?' I ask.

'Cold,' is all she can say between her sobs.

'She says she's cold,' I say to Taylor. 'Give her your cloak.'

'Give my new cloak to a witch?' He laughs. Then he realises I'm not joking and have no plans to joke with him. 'I won't do it.'

'You got her cold and wet. You can get her warm again,' I say. 'So I'd be obliged if you'd lend her some dry clothes.'

He looks at me and in particular at the scar on my face. Something tells me that he may not be brave enough to refuse a polite request from a Justice of the Peace. Even with his men standing by his shoulder. His gaze shifts from my face to my belt to see if I am wearing a sword. I'm not. He decides on balance he still won't risk it. He unfastens the cloak at the neck.

'It's only a loan,' I say. 'You'll get it back.'

'As if I'd wear it again after a witch had touched it. Take the thing.'

He sweeps off the thick cape and flings it down next to Alice. Aminta picks it up, brushes the snow off and, half raising Alice, wraps it round the old woman's shoulders.

'I'll take her back to her house,' Aminta says. 'She'll certainly die if I don't get her in front of a fire quickly.'

'You'd no business doing that,' Taylor says to me. 'I was acting within my rights, Sir John, and you know it.'

Then, with immaculate timing, Ben comes puffing up out of the mist. Morrell must have alerted him too. Ben looks at Aminta helping Alice away, then at me without a sword, then at Taylor, standing defiantly with no cloak. In a moment he'll spot the rope lying by the bank. It won't take Ben long to catch up with events by the millpond.

'Well, if that's all, Sir John, I'm going home to get a new cloak,' says Taylor. 'We've done our work for today. I'll leave you and the constable to do yours.'

'Not so fast,' I say. 'You've accused Alice Mardike of witchcraft.'

'I've proved she's a witch and you've shown little enough gratitude for it.'

'And why do you think she's a witch?'

'Because she floated,' he says. 'Everyone knows that is proof positive.'

'So, anyone who floats is a witch?' I ask.

The crowd has been subdued since I arrived, but suddenly there is complete silence. They want to know where this is going. It may be good. Better even than half drowning an old woman.

'Yes,' he says. 'Of course.'

'And you, for example, Mr Taylor. Would you float?'

He shakes his head. 'That's of no account, Sir John. I'm clearly not a witch.'

'Really? Let's see how you fare once you are in the water, then,' I say. 'We live in an age of scientific enquiry. Let's find out if swimming really is a good test for sorcery. I can write to the President of the Royal Society and let him know the results of our experiment. Our hypothesis is that, as an innocent man, you'll sink like a stone. So do you want to jump in, Mr Taylor, or do you want me to order the constable here to tie you up first? Please don't hold it against him if he does. He is obliged to carry out any instruction I give him or risk a fine himself.'

He stares at me. There is frost on his beard and moustache from his breath. It's a cold day.

'Jump into that water? It would ruin my suit of clothes,' Taylor says.

'Take your coat off then,' I say.

'This is a jest . . .'

I shake my head. 'Not at all. You may as well take your breeches off too. You wouldn't want pond water all over them – you saw how Alice Mardike had her dress spoiled.'

There is a laugh from the crowd behind him. They are seeing better sport than they expected.

'You are not entitled under English Law to treat me with such contempt. I am a yeoman of this village. This is wrong and without precedent.'

'You've created a precedent yourself by swimming Mistress Mardike. But first, tell me because I am curious to know: when we throw you in – what's your money on? Do you think that you'll sink or float?'

'I swim well enough,' he says.

'You swim? So, do you confess now to being a sorcerer?'

'Of course not.'

'No, I don't think you are either. Nor does anyone here. So, perhaps we are wasting our time, because we will all now have deduced logically that some can swim who are not witches. In which case Alice Mardike's immersion proved very little. I hope everyone here has noted that that is the case.'

There is a ripple of laughter.

'Go home, Mr Taylor,' I say. 'Button your coat and go home.

I'll get one of my footmen to bring you your cloak when I've had it dried and brushed clean of witch. Go home all of you. Go back to your fires and warm yourselves. The entertainment is over for today.'

Ben and I watch as they troop off, a long line snaking across the meadow, vanishing into the mist. One or two glance back at us. At least nobody, other than Taylor, has sought to question my knowledge of the Law.

'I shall go to Mistress Mardike's house,' I say. 'And see that all is well. I don't think they'll try to swim her again.'

'No, Sir John,' says Ben. 'I don't think they'll try swimming anyone for a while.' He's respectful but a little sullen.

'Come now, Ben,' I say. 'What's amiss? We've seen them off.'

'You shouldn't have made a fool of Taylor, sir. He won't forget that.'

'That was my intention,' I say. 'I want them all to remember. I don't want to see an old woman thrown in the millpond ever again.'

'Fine,' says Ben. 'Then you've had a good afternoon, Sir John. So has the village. But they still think Alice Mardike is a witch for all that. They haven't finished with her. You should have let her drown. It would have been kinder than what's coming to her.'

By the time I reach Alice Mardike's cottage Aminta has already helped her change into her other dress and her wet clothes are dripping and steaming by the fire. She is wrapped in Taylor's cloak but her face is blue and she is shivering.

'Thank you, Sir John,' she says. 'But it will do no good. They mean to hang me, and that's what will happen, if I don't die of pneumonia first.'

'The Rule of Law applies here as much as anywhere,' I say.

'In which case they'd hang me anywhere,' she says. 'Nowhere's safe. Not for a witch. You don't remember Hopkins back in forty-five, do you, boy? You'd have been just a child then. He went all over Essex and Suffolk and Cambridge, and everywhere he claimed he'd detected a witch they hanged her. The woman might have been somebody they'd known for years – a neighbour, a cousin, a godmother, a grandmother. But once she was touched by the accusation of witchcraft that was the end of her. You can't disprove it. You can't say it's right. And nobody can stand beside a witch and comfort her in case they get accused too. Touch a witch and you've got witch on your own fingers too. There's always plenty of witch to go round. And it ain't like good Essex mud – it don't clean off easy.'

'Sir Felix remembers Hopkins' visitation well,' I say. 'But things are different now. Anyway, even some of the women Hopkins accused were found not guilty.'

'Not many.'

'No, not many,' I say. 'But some.'

I look at the cottage door, but it is closed firmly. The cold air I just felt must have come from somewhere else. Alice too draws the cloak more tightly to her.

'You've been very kind to me, Sir John,' she says, 'and so have you, Lady Grey. I'm very grateful to both of you. But I'll manage here on my own now. Not many of them dare to come to this house, and the snow won't make them any braver. I've got my cat. If I need anything I can always send him to fetch it from Old Nick, can't I? The Devil looks after his own, so I'm told.'

'As a Magistrate, I've sworn to uphold the King's Peace. I shall not let them harm you, Mistress Mardike.'

'Thank you, but it may not be within your power to decide whether I am to be harmed or not.'

'I'll visit you tomorrow,' I say. 'In the meantime, we'll send Morrell over with some firewood and food.'

'He won't like doing that,' she says. 'Mr Morrell likes things done proper. And it ain't proper keeping a witch warm with wood intended for the use of the gentry. Still less taking leftovers from your table that your cook might otherwise be able to sell.'

'The wood will burn just the same here as at the Big House,' I say. 'Morrell can get one of the boys to pull the sledge. It won't be much effort for him. And I'll look out one of my mother's old cloaks. It will be of more use here than in a chest at home.'

Alice shakes her head sadly. But this time she doesn't decline the offer.

My own fire is roaring and crackling. Morrell has heaped logs onto it. As he has observed, if I have good timber to waste on witches, then there is no point in husbanding our supplies. He did not like delivering wood to Mistress Mardike, still less presenting her with my mother's oldest cape – a faded but well-made garment that dates back to the gracious days before the war.

'Taylor will have to tolerate your treatment of him,' says Sir Felix, now happily recovered from the mild chill that threatened his life a few hours before. 'As a Justice of the Peace, you have too many ways of making life awkward for him. You *are* the Law here in this village. You can't do entirely as you like, but you can fine him next time he gets drunk and you can uphold any complaints his neighbours bring against him, justified or not. He may own his farm outright, but he can't afford to upset you. Anyway, you're gentry, he's not. You've met the King, he hasn't. That's all that matters. He can't win in a fight with the Lord of the Manor.'

A blast of wind rattles the windows, and we all turn towards the dark night that lies beyond this little pool of warmth. There's nothing to be seen outside, except the stars and the red glow of somebody's fire in the distance. I wonder briefly what anyone can be burning outdoors at this hour. Could it come from a brazier? Perhaps Ben has set a nightwatchman by the inn, though the chances of any traveller coming to the village in this weather and at this hour are remote. And the flames look somehow wrong – flickering erratically rather than the steady glow of charcoal.

'What's that light?' asks Aminta, getting up and going over to the window.

I walk across the room and put my arm round her. 'It's the wrong direction for Mistress Mardike's cottage,' I say. 'If it gets bigger, I'll go and investigate. It could be somebody's unswept chimney out of control. If so, there'll be plenty of people on hand already to help put out the flames, but I'd better be sure.'

'It looks as if it's getting closer,' says Aminta. 'That's no chimney fire.'

'How many guns do you have in the house?' asks Sir Felix.

'I have a pair of pistols,' I say. 'There is a musket in the cupboard over there.'

'How much shot?'

'A dozen rounds for the pistol. There is a small box of musket balls. The gunpowder is in the cellar.'

'I'll get Morrell to fetch the powder,' says Sir Felix. 'We may need it before the evening is out. I'll look out my sword.

That fire is definitely coming our way. The question is, John, who is bringing it to us and what do they plan to do with it when they get here? I'll collect your sword too. You never were a very good shot, but I seem to recall you are a competent and thoroughly unprincipled swordsman.'

Chapter Nine

The village expresses its opinion on witchcraft

We watch the flickering lights proceed up the drive from the village, orange flame licking the white snow, under a starry sky. Beneath and around the torches we can now make out a dark mass of people. They move slowly, almost reluctantly, and even that pace slackens as they approach the house. Sir Felix has already laid out on the oak table my two pistols, the musket and our swords. He has just finished loading the second pistol.

'How reliable are these little toys?' he asks.

'They were made by Harman Barne in London,' I say. 'The barrels are rifled, as you'll have already noticed. He told me that the ball would pierce a breastplate, though he didn't say from what distance.'

'You weren't interested enough to ask?'

'The chances of finding an enemy agent wearing a breastplate seemed sufficiently remote that I didn't enquire. Anyway, these are accurate enough that I could have simply aimed for the forehead. Prince Rupert apparently hit a weathercock on a church steeple with an identical one. Then he did it again, just to prove it wasn't luck. I've made sure all of the doors are locked. I've closed the shutters on the ground floor except those over there. Morrell is extinguishing any candles that we don't need. He's armed the footmen with some rusty pikes that I never knew we had and which they won't know how to use. Now we just wait.'

'They'll have seen us making preparations for them.'

'I doubt they were expecting to take us by surprise. Not with a dozen or so torches.'

Those leading the crowd are now almost below the parlour window. I can finally see their faces by the light of the flickering flames. They are upturned, open-mouthed, hesitant, like fish taking flies from the surface of a lake. Their cheeks glowing. A quantity of beer may have been consumed prior to this trespass across my land.

Taylor is at the front, carrying a well-polished musket. He can afford the best. Its barrel gleams red in the torchlight. He'll have plenty of powder and shot too, if he really means business. Platt has a pistol tucked into his belt; I hope it isn't loaded and cocked, because it's pointing at his left foot and he'll need both feet to get back home. Harry Hardy is further back, unarmed as far as I can tell. Two of the Grices, brothers of my old friend Dickon, carry scythes. Their ice-cold blades flash red, as if taken straight from the forge. It is mainly the men of the village here, though Margaret Platt's mother is present, as is Margaret herself, both wrapped in furs. They'll want to know what people are saying. I also think I can see Amy Barwell. There is no sign of the village constable, though they must have been drinking his ale. He'll be counting his takings very carefully before he ventures out in the cause of justice. First things first.

'Twenty of them?' says Sir Felix.

'Thirty at least,' I say. 'I'll go and speak to them. There's no point in sending Morrell to say that Sir John Grey regrets he is not at home to callers.'

'I'd take both pistols with you,' says Sir Felix.

'Killing two still leaves twenty-eight,' I say. 'And wounding two still leaves thirty. I'll speak to them unarmed. But stand behind me when I go out and, if any one of them shoots me out of hand, then you can aim for his head with complete confidence. Tell them it's with Prince Rupert's compliments.'

Sir Felix and I go into the hallway and I unbar the door. At first, the blaze of light makes it difficult for me to see what is happening, but Taylor steps forward out of the dark mass. He is dressed comfortably in a new cloak and his beaver hat. Their warmth on a cold night gives him assurance. That and whatever he's been drinking.

'Good evening, Sir John,' he says. His deep voice carries well to the whole crowd. The words are only slightly slurred. 'I'm pleased to find you still up and about. Keeping London hours, no doubt.'

I note that he's kept his hat on when addressing me. I may have to reprimand him for that.

'Good evening, Mr Taylor,' I say. 'I wasn't expecting a visit so late on such a cold evening. What can I do for you all? Are you mummers, come to perform a Christmas play? If so, you are most welcome.'

Taylor frowns. He thinks all of the irony round here belongs to him, like the sheep. Well, I own some sheep too and some deer, and the freehold of most of the houses in the village.

'What can you do? You can do your duty, Sir John. We've brought the witch to you. You wanted it done legal and above board. I respect that. That's your job, just as mine is herding. So, now you can try her. I've got all of the witnesses you could need, right here. Two is plenty according to the Law. I've brought you a half dozen at least. All good honest yeomen and their wives and daughters.'

'I've already spoken to some witnesses,' I say. 'I've not been idle, Mr Taylor. I shall speak to the others in my own time. It was kind but unnecessary to trouble these good people on such a night.'

'Maybe you will speak to them all, Sir John – in secret. But we want to hear the evidence ourselves. We want a proper hearing in public. Because that's what's right. Afterwards, we'll abide by your decision, sir. But if she's to hang, as she rightly should, then she hangs at first light.'

The crowd mutters its agreement. First light is best. You'd miss the look on her face if you strung her up in the dark.

'I've no powers to hang anyone,' I say. 'Only to investigate and commit a suspected felon to the Assizes in Braintree.'

'We'll do the hanging then,' says Taylor. 'We won't trouble you with that.'

Without warning, Alice Mardike emerges from the crowd as if thrust forward by unseen hands. Her wrists are bound and it may be she has already experienced some rough treatment. There is blood on her face. Some people here clearly subscribe to the theory that scratching a witch sometimes undoes a curse. There's also what appears to be a bruise on her cheek. They haven't beaten her enough to kill her, but bringing her out like this, after her immersion today, may have the same effect.

Taylor places a hand on her shoulder. At first it seems a friendly gesture, but it is only to force her down.

'On your knees, witch,' he says. 'This is the man who is going to judge you. Then you're ours.'

'That remains to be seen,' I say.

She looks up at me wearily. 'Think of yourself and your family, Sir John,' she says. 'You're a good man, and I'd be as happy to be tried by you as any other, but you can see they've made up their minds already. Nothing you can do about it. They're too many for me and too many for you.'

'If I have to, I'll shoot the first person who tries to tie a noose round this woman's neck,' I say. 'And the rest of you I'll have transported to grow sugar cane in the West Indies until you expire from the heat and exhaustion and the children you've left behind die of hunger.'

'Brave words, Sir John,' says Taylor very slowly. 'But they won't stop us.'

'Really? Then, having been duly warned to depart, you will have taken part in an insurrection against His Majesty,' I say. 'It will be an act of treason, and you know the penalty for that.'

'Treason? I don't think so. We know our rights under the ancient laws of England. If Magna Carta says anything, then it says you can burn witches.'

There is another general murmuring of agreement. They've clearly all read Magna Carta. And that's definitely what it says. If it says anything.

'I'll send to London for a troop of dragoons to teach you constitutional history,' I say.

'Not in this weather you won't,' says Taylor. He smiles and strokes his beard. We both know I'm outnumbered, with no prospect of reinforcements. I can't be certain even that my own servants will try to resist their brothers and cousins in the mob. The old manor house – the one my mother's family built in King Henry's time – was designed to withstand a siege, but this new one is all classical columns, high glass windows and fine oak panels. It will burn well, with everyone in it. By the time the authorities arrive to make enquiries, the blackened timbers will be cold and the village will have closed ranks. The tragic loss of the Big House with its family and its servants, in a fire of unknown origin, will be recounted over and over again without any variation of detail whatsoever. One or two villagers may actually be commended for trying unsuccessfully to rescue us from the flames. If that's part of the story they decide to tell. The death of the village witch will not even be mentioned.

'We don't want to hurt you or your family,' says Taylor in a conciliatory tone. 'And especially not young Master Charles. But I want justice for my son-in-law. My daughter wants justice for her husband.'

'I can't hang Mistress Mardike,' I say. 'I can't hang her however much that might please you all. A hanging goes well beyond the powers of a country Magistrate. I can try all manner of minor offences. And I am obliged to investigate any murder that takes place within my jurisdiction. That's what I'm doing.'

'Murder by witchcraft.'

'Barwell was strangled. No witchcraft was required. There'll be no hanging here tomorrow morning or any morning. Go home, all of you.'

There's a shuffling of feet in the snow. This isn't as easy as Taylor told them it would be. Most of them would like to go home, or at least back to the inn.

'Look,' says Taylor. 'These folk here are your friends and neighbours, Sir John. They only mean well. I've told them that you will hear their case fairly. That's right and proper, and I'm sure that's what you'll do. If I did wrong this afternoon, swimming the witch before you wanted us to, then I'm truly sorry. But you're one of us, Sir John – Essex born and bred. We expect you to give us justice, as your ancestors did before you.'

'That's right, Sir John,' says Harry Hardy. 'We only want what your forebears would have done. We're entitled to it.'

'Times have changed, Harry. The lord of the manor can't just hang whomever he thinks fit to hang.'

'They were better times then,' says Harry. 'England was a happier place. Before it changed.'

'Happier for some,' I say.

'Listen to what the witch tells you herself then,' says Taylor. 'You should think of your family. Do they deserve to die while you protect a murderer?'

'I thought you and your friends meant well?'

'We repay loyalty with loyalty,' he says. 'As we always have. I can't answer for what they'll think if you don't do right by them *as they see it*.'

I turn. Sir Felix and Aminta are now standing behind me, just inside the door. I'm not sure who is looking more defiant. Aminta probably. Yes, definitely Aminta. It's fortunate for Taylor that she doesn't have the musket in her hands or he'd be a bleeding mess on the ground, with less of a face than George Barwell still possesses. Sir Felix, though his hands clutch the pistols, is considering whether a compromise might be possible. Years of following Prince Rupert have convinced him that charging headlong into battle, with your spurs dug into your horse's sides, doesn't always produce the desired results.

'Stay where you are,' I say to Taylor. 'Take another step and I'll kill you with my bare hands if I have to. And don't even touch Mistress Mardike.'

Taylor says nothing. I think that the scar on my face, the one that reaches almost to my eye socket, looks particularly fine by torchlight. It's worth an extra brace of pistols on any dark night, though maybe not much more than that.

I turn my back on them and retrace my steps to where Sir Felix and Aminta are standing. I do not close the door, but I take them both to one side.

'My advice would be to say you will hear the case, as they wish,' says Sir Felix, 'and ignore any legal technicalities that they cannot be expected to like or understand. Convene a court or a committee of enquiry or whatever you want to call it. Listen to the witnesses, both those you have spoken to and those you have not. Then look very grave and say you will reserve your judgment until a later time. Send them all home. Their heads will be cooler for a day in court and by Christmas we may have a thaw and a clear road from London for your troop of constitutional historians.'

'It would be better if Aminta and Charles could get away first,' I say. 'I'm happy to convene the tribunal, but the only outcome that may be acceptable to the village is that we hang Mistress Mardike on the green before dinner tomorrow. When they don't get what they want, then I fear Taylor will try to force matters again.'

'I've no intention of leaving you,' says Aminta. 'In any case, I doubt that I would get more than a mile, even on your cob. The roads are blocked now and there may be more snow before morning.'

'I meant elsewhere in the village,' I say. 'The inn would be safer than here. Or . . .' But I struggle to think of anywhere. Who can I trust? Not Nell by the sound of it. Not the Rector. Perhaps Ifnot Davies, the blacksmith – but what could he do alone against the whole village? He has a certain amount of moral authority as a Quaker, but limited firepower.

'During the late wars, manor houses less well fortified than this held out against the armies of Parliament,' says Aminta. 'At least, when a woman had been left in charge, defending her home and family.'

'For a few days,' I say, 'if well garrisoned, well supplied and facing only a small force that wished to avoid casualties itself and was prepared to wait for the defenders to despair of rescue. Sir Felix is the only soldier amongst us.'

'And I would advise that you have powder and shot to last less than an hour,' he says. 'Not even Prince Rupert would have recommended sallying out against our besiegers with a handful of serving men wielding pikes. And how many people from your own village are you prepared to kill? No, I think we shall have to use honeyed words and legal trickery. Unless you would prefer to offer up Mistress Mardike to the mob? Most justices would consider it a small price to ensure that their glass windows remained intact, let alone to avoid harm to their families.'

'We've had one murder in this village,' I say. 'I've no intention of allowing Taylor to commit another.'

I take half a dozen strides and stand again at the top of my steps, looking out at the crowd. The icy air strikes my face. The starry night is sucking the warmth and all compassion from the land. Taylor's rabble are rubbing their arms and stamping their feet. The dark and the growing cold will not encourage them to stay here longer than they have to.

Before I can say anything, however, Ben emerges from the darkness, a lantern raised high. He looks at me and at Taylor uncertainly. Since the deputation probably set out from his inn, nothing he sees will be exactly unexpected. Ben has come to check, after a carefully judged interval, whether the manor house has been burned down or not. As constable, he might have to do something about it. It's best to know.

'I'd thought that I might be needed, Sir John,' he says. 'So I came to see what instructions you had for me.'

'You certainly are needed, Ben,' I say. 'Please help Mistress Mardike to her feet, then untie her hands and escort her safely to her cottage. Bring her back here at ten tomorrow morning, when I shall convene a hearing into the murder of George Barwell. I'll send you a list by eight o'clock of other witnesses who may need to be summoned. As for the rest of you, go home to bed. There's nothing more for you here. I would not wish to be responsible for the deaths of any of you by cold.'

Taylor nods. He thinks he's won. Let the witch live until tomorrow if that will make me happy. The village won't begrudge me that one small pleasure. My mother's family has owned the village, with one short interregnum, since the time of William the Conqueror. The crowd turns silently, relieved that things have gone so well, and the flickering of the torches begins its slow progress across the park. The lights get smaller and dimmer and eventually vanish, close to the inn. They'll all need a drink after this. Let's hope Ben's cellars are full.

'You're right,' says Sir Felix. 'Only a hanging will satisfy them. From the moment Taylor accused her, Alice Mardike knew she would hang, just as her mother did. Whatever any of the village might be willing to say to you in private, nobody will give evidence for her in public. It isn't safe to do so. Like Nell, they'll be queuing up to show that they are as opposed to witchcraft as the next man. Or woman. Nobody can say witchcraft is a good thing. Can't be done.'

'I intend to find out who killed George Barwell,' I say.

'And how do you know it wasn't Alice Mardike? She clearly didn't like him. Unlike you, I don't think the lack of a good cloak would have stopped her following him up the hill if she wanted to kill him enough. She's as tough as an old boot. She may well possess at least one silk stocking. She would have had the stomach to take a sharp blade to his face. You've asked why any Christian man would do that. Well, nobody's allowed Alice Mardike in the church for as long as I can recall. It might come easier to her than most. I can see why you may not share Taylor's conviction that her guilt is manifest, but I can't see why you are so certain of her innocence. Forget witchcraft. She may have just strangled him in the ordinary way of things.'

'She's a good person,' I say. 'She's suffered a lot at the hands of the village.'

'That doesn't mean she didn't do it. It just gives her a stronger motive to kill one of them. Any of them.'

'I know,' I say. 'As for the church, even the Rector wants to see her hang. Quoted to me from the Bible. He referred to Exodus Chapter 18 about not allowing a witch to live.'

'Chapter 22,' says Sir Felix. 'It's one that's stuck in my memory. It was one of my father's favourites when trying witches. It's Chapter 22, verse 18 – mark my words.'

'No, I'm sure he said Chapter 18, verse 22,' I say. 'A clergyman wouldn't get that wrong.'

'Well this one did,' says Sir Felix, refilling his glass.

'If you say so. It's a small error and I won't take him to task over that, but I shall do so in no uncertain terms if he tries to get Alice Mardike hanged,' I say.

Sir Felix shakes his head. 'You're going to be lord of the manor here for another thirty or forty years, God willing. Dr Bray could be here almost as long. You don't want him as an enemy. But that's not the only reason for proceeding cautiously. Do the wrong thing now, John, and nobody here will trust your judgment for the rest of your life.'

'Am I the only one who wants Alice Mardike to have a fair hearing?'

'No, Aminta does too. I hope it doesn't cost you both your lives. There's one small crumb of comfort, though: I think whatever they do, they won't kill the child – or not intentionally.'

'Thank you, Sir Felix,' I say. 'I'm grateful for that.'

'I try to do my best,' he says. 'Could you please ask Morrell to fetch up a couple more bottles of Sack? I feel that dangerous chill coming on again. Anyway, I'd rather not go to my maker entirely sober. He might not recognise me.'

Chapter Ten

I do as my ancestors did before me

My mother, who might possibly have been able to remember, once told me that, in the old house built by her family, there was a dais at one end of the great hall, where the family dined and from which the Lord of the Manor gave judgment when sitting at the manorial court. When the Wests were evicted, following their conviction for treason, and the Cliffords built this house on the foundations of the old one, Sir Felix's father constructed a perfectly adequate drawing room and dining room in place of the hall, and saw no need for a dais of any sort, which would have spoilt the strict classical proportions of the rooms. He preferred to try cases of drunkenness or petty theft at the village inn and save wear and tear on the carpets, which, contrary to all previous practice in the village, were placed on the floor, not over tables. Though the dining room looks well for today's hearing, I would have welcomed a raised platform to impress the majesty of the Law upon the crowds who are already starting to assemble. Many of those who have come early are sitting while examining the ceiling above them, which is twice the height of their parlours at home. The intricate plasterwork, with its many geometrical shapes and its strange allegorical figures, now looks old-fashioned to me, but is still a source of wonder to them. Men who have never seen the sea knowledgeably point out mermaids and tritons to each other.

The Platts are seated in the front row, on my mother's good padded dining chairs. The Grices are further back, on hard oak benches from the servants' hall. Taylor is standing in one corner of the room, in deep conversation with the Rector. They'll both need to take seats soon if they don't want to remain on their feet all morning.

Ben has been scurrying round the village since before sunrise, assembling the witnesses. He has just brought in Mistress Mardike. She is wearing the dress in which she was swum, now dried and brushed and looking slightly better than it did before her ducking, with my mother's old cloak over it. She seems to have suffered less from her immersion than I feared. After much consultation with Ben, we have seated her on a stool, far enough from the other witnesses not to give offence, but not so far as to imply that her status is different from anyone else's. This is an enquiry into a murder, not a trial for witchcraft, as I may need to keep reminding everyone. She sits patiently, avoiding everyone's eye, including my own.

Outside, the sky is a brilliant, cloudless blue, broken into small sapphire lozenges by the leaded windows. Where the sunlight strikes them, the floor of the dining room and the seated witnesses are also decorated with the same lattice, elongated by the lowness of the winter sun. There has been no snow overnight. Ben reports that tracks have been worn through the drifts in the village and that it is, for the first time in days, possible to move about with some ease. The roads leading out remain blocked, however, in all four directions. It will be a while until I can summon help.

An empty seat by the window, guarded constantly by Morrell, is for Aminta. Charles's cough is worse this morning and her concerns are spread between the courtroom and the nursery. Eventually she takes her place. Ben brings in Harry Hardy, who is clearly still resentful that he has had to extinguish his clay pipe. When hearings took place at the inn, everyone was allowed to smoke and drink as much as they wished; most change is for the worse.

Ben gives me a nod. We have all of the witnesses we need for the moment. I thump the table three times with my fist. Silence descends on the happy, chattering room. The court is in session.

I explain very carefully, and with much reference to the relevant Laws, what I intend to do. I distinguish between my role in trying minor crimes and my role in investigating felonies and binding the accused over to appear at the next assize. The immediate answering cries of 'burn the witch' suggest that I may have wasted my time, but no matter.

'I'll take the evidence of Amy Barwell first,' I say.

'We only need to hear the witch,' somebody yells out. 'We all know what she's accused of.'

Those who had previously held back now add their comments, while others repeat them for the benefit of those who didn't hear them the first time.

'No need even to hear her,' calls somebody else. 'She'll only lie.'

'You need to examine her for the Devil's marks. They're a sure sign.'

'We all saw she could swim. That's proof. Always was. No need for more than that.'

At this point Taylor, who has seated himself next to Platt, stands and turns to the crowd. 'Listen to me, all of you,' he says. 'We have to let Sir John do this his way. Do any of you know the Law?' He scans the now silent room. 'No? I didn't think so. Did any of you go to the famous University at Cambridge? No. So, be schooled by him. He'll do right by you. I promise you that. And you, Amy, go and stand over there and answer whatever questions Sir John asks you – answer them truthfully and you've nothing to fear from him or from me.'

Amy stands and takes a couple of steps forward. She doesn't like doing this, but she's more afraid of her father than she is of looking foolish. Anyway, she wants her husband's murderer caught and punished.

'Do you want me to swear a Bible oath, Sir John?' she asks.

'No, just to tell the truth as your father has requested,' I say. She nods. 'What do you want to know?'

Now she's here, she's actually quite confident and assured. I can see more than a little of her father in her.

'Were you able to see your husband's body?' I ask.

'Yes,' she says. 'Of course.'

'You were certain of his identity, disfigured as he was?'

She doesn't flinch. She's got courage. No doubt about that. 'None at all. You saw him yourself.'

'I'm sorry to say that I didn't know him well. It is helpful that you can confirm it is him.'

'My father saw him too. So did the Rector.'

'Indeed. So they have. You told me that you didn't know who he had gone to meet at the woods.'

'Yes.'

'You haven't thought of anyone since then?'

'I told you, he sometimes went for walks on his own.'

There is a murmur of disbelief amongst the crowd. They know something of George Barwell's walks. Perhaps holding this hearing in public will not prove unuseful after all. Amy turns on her neighbours and silences them with a look. It seems to be a skill that runs in the family.

'Do you know of anyone who might have wished to kill your husband?'

'Only that witch.'

The crowd turns to where Alice is sitting, very still, on her low seat. She doesn't look at Amy. She doesn't look at anyone. She knows how easily this assembly could turn into a public hanging. A friendly smile at the wrong person could do it.

'Why do you say that?' I ask.

'George told me.'

'And what did he tell you exactly?'

'Just that she cursed him.'

'He didn't say how?'

She pauses. I'm sure she knows the full story. 'No,' she says. 'He didn't.'

There is a great shuffling of feet. Everyone here is happily aware that Alice accused George of being less than faithful to Amy. News like that can't be kept in its box for long. But will anyone be prepared to say it? A lot of the people here work for the Taylors or owe them money. Most of the rest wouldn't want a confrontation with them.

'Did you and your husband agree well?' I ask. 'Or did you argue about anything?'

Amy flashes a look at her father, who is frowning. 'I loved him,' she says.

I don't doubt that. Almost alone in Clavershall West, she still holds George Barwell in high regard.

'Will you need to ask my daughter anything else, Sir John?' says Taylor. 'She's told you what she knows. I'd ask you to respect her grief at her husband's death.'

'No, Mr Taylor, I don't think I do need ask her more. You may go and sit down, Amy. I'd like to ask the Rector some questions next.'

'Really?' says the Rector. 'I don't think I can help you very much, Sir John. I told you the little I can.'

Once more I have the feeling that I have let him down – the Rector and the Lord of the Manor should be allies in this and everything else. I am causing him unnecessary inconvenience. He's quite comfortable just sitting and watching the proceedings.

'Of course you have,' I say. 'But there are still matters that I would like you to clarify. Could you please oblige me, Dr Bray, and come and stand over here.'

'You wish me to *stand*?' His dignity is greatly offended, but I am unaware of any law that says in terms that clergymen must give evidence sitting on one of my mother's dining chairs.

'Yes, please,' I say. 'If you don't mind, Rector. You can stand where Amy stood.'

'I suppose that you'll want me to swear on the Bible,' he says, getting out of his comfortable seat and advancing to the table.

'I place no value on a Bible oath from the clergy or laity,' I say. 'Not in a hearing of this sort. Men lie under oath every bit as much as they do on ordinary days.'

This too does not please him.

'You seem willing to disregard large parts of the Bible entirely, Sir John,' he says. 'That you place no value on oaths does not surprise me.'

There is a sharp intake of breath. The village has long regarded me as a Puritan and, as such, a man of strange and dangerous beliefs. But they had scarcely hoped to have this confirmed by the Rector in my own dining room.

'My respect for the scriptures is as great as your own,' I say.

'I would remind you that, only yesterday, you mocked St Paul,' says the Rector.

The crowd nods thoughtfully. Puritans mock St Paul, do they? That's no surprise to them.

'What I said was merely a jest,' I say.

'You jest about sacred scripture?'

'I jested about mankind's love of money – my own faults as much as anyone else's. The flesh is weak. We are all sinners. St Paul said that too.'

'You accuse me of being a sinner, Sir John?'

'You'll find it in the Bible,' I say.

This gets better and better. Those with Bibles will be checking, as soon as they get home, exactly what St Paul said about the Rector.

'How well did you know George Barwell?' I ask.

'Not well,' he says.

I wait for him to say more, but he doesn't.

'But he was one of your parishioners?' I say.

'Of course. You know that. He lived here. He was not a Catholic or a Hindu or a Mohammedan.'

'And so you would recognise him – the body you have at the church is George Barwell?'

'Yes. You've already heard his wife testify.'

'Did he attend church regularly – when he was alive?'

'Sometimes. When he had nothing more pressing to do.'

'What was your opinion of him?'

The Rector pauses. He had not held back on this when I last spoke to him. I recall that he described him as a man of loose morals, amongst other things. 'This is not the time or place to speak ill of the dead,' he says. 'Really, I think I have said all I can on the matter.'

'You had previously led me to believe that you did not think highly of him.'

'We are all sinners, as you have just reminded us, Sir John.' The Rector turns and smiles indulgently at his congregation. They nod thoughtfully. The new Rector's told them they can all sin a bit if they want to. He's better than the old one.

'You told me you gave him work – repairing some panelling in the church, even though it did not need doing.'

There are one or two puzzled looks in the crowd, but there's no reason why this should generally be known.

'I don't think I quite said that. The panelling was somewhat decayed. But I gave him the work out of charity.'

'How much did the church pay him?'

'I don't recall.'

'Would you like a moment or two to try to remember?'

The Rector seems very uncomfortable, but Taylor comes to his rescue. 'Is this relevant, Sir John? Nobody, least of all me, would suggest that my son-in-law was worthy of the Rector's generosity. I am grateful to him for his kindness. But the precise amount is surely not important, if the Rector can't remember it?'

I look at the Rector. I think the amount is important, but I don't know why.

'This is my court, Mr Taylor, and I'll ask the questions I have to ask,' I say. 'I'll need to see the church account book, Rector. I assume there is such a thing? Good. For the moment, that is all.'

Taylor stands. 'May I please ask the Rector a question, Sir John?'

'If you feel there is something I have missed,' I say. 'But please be brief.'

'Thank you, Sir John. I'm very grateful to you. Rector, do you believe in witches?'

'Of course, Mr Taylor. I have said so in my sermons, as everyone here is aware. The Bible is quite explicit. King Saul consulted the witch of Endor, leading to his own defeat and destruction. The witch was capable of raising the spirits of the dead. It is impossible for any Christian man to say that witches do not exist or that they exist but are powerless to harm us.'

'And what attitude should we take towards witches?'

'Exodus teaches us that we are not to suffer a witch to live. Moreover, the Law of this country states . . .'

Taylor holds up his hand. 'I'm happy that Sir John advises us on the Law of this country,' he says. 'Whenever he sees fit to do so. But I'm much obliged to you, Rector, for reminding us what the Book of Samuel has to say. Even Kings can't afford to associate with witches, it would seem. They always bring you down in the end. Whoever you are.'

I look at Taylor. He has the calm expression of somebody who knows he is right. If God saw fit to punish King Saul of Israel, He'll have no scruples in dealing with a Justice of the Peace from Essex.

'Thank you, Dr Bray,' I say. 'Very informative, I'm sure. We'll hear the evidence of Margaret Platt next.'

'I'll try to keep you for as short a time as I can,' I say. 'When we last spoke you said George Barwell promised to marry you. Is that true?'

Margaret glances at her father. 'Not a promise as such,' she says.

I look at her. Is nobody – nobody at all – intending to repeat in public what they told me in private?

'No?' I say. 'I thought you were very clear on that point.'

'Perhaps, now I think about it, sir, I was mistaken. That that was not the meaning of his words.'

'So, what did he say exactly?' I ask.

'I . . . I don't recall . . .'

'He merely spoke of his admiration and respect for her,' says Jacob Platt, as if repeating a much-rehearsed line. 'There was no question of any attachment.'

'I was asking your daughter, Mr Platt,' I say. 'I'd be grateful if you let her answer.'

'What my father says is true,' says Margaret. 'He merely expressed a . . . fondness. In the playful way that boys do. It meant nothing. Not to him or to me. We both knew that. I was pleased that he married Amy.'

I look at my notes. There is little point in asking whether she made threats against him. Why should she threaten a man who had simply paid her a few compliments? And if she's willing to say that she was happy for Amy then she'll be willing to say anything.

'And on the day George Barwell died, you were at home?' I say.

'Yes, sir.'

'Except for a short visit to the well?'

There is a low buzz of surprise in the room, which I halt with a glance. That's interesting, though.

'I told you, Sir John, I went to meet friends.'

'Which friends? Or don't you now recall?'

She shakes her head. Perhaps she hasn't had the foresight to get any of her friends to lie about it, and can't just make something up in a room packed with people who might know better.

'But you do admit to visiting Mistress Mardike?' I ask.

'Just to buy medicines, sir. As almost everyone here does.'

One or two of the crowd nod, though cautiously. Actually they will all have bought from her at some time. She's the only witch in the village.

'And you didn't fear to go there?'

'Fear, sir?'

'You do not fear her magic powers?'

'No, of course not.' She looks at her father. Was that the wrong answer? Is it safer to fear witches? Probably.

'I wouldn't go near her,' mutters Harry Hardy. 'Rather have rheumatics than her potions.'

I look at him. I don't remember him saying that when we were alone either.

'Me too,' says his neighbour. 'Bought some of her concoctions once. Almost killed me. Better die in a godly manner than submit to a witch's care.'

'Been buying them all my life,' says another. 'Never did me any good at all.'

Suddenly there is a loud and general agreement that none of them has ever bought her goods or, if they did, then they were lucky still to be alive. I bang my fist on the table again.

'Do you possess silk stockings, Mistress Platt?' I ask.

'Sir?'

'You heard the question.'

'No, sir. Just woollen ones.'

She looks genuinely puzzled. But Morrell is trying to get my attention. I suspend proceedings for a quarter of an hour and allow him to lead me into the next room.

Aminta is already there, looking concerned.

'Charles is worse,' she says. 'He is almost exhausted with coughing. And we have used all of the syrup that you bought from Mistress Mardike.'

'Is there anything else that will soothe him?'

'Nothing that we have found so far.'

'Well, whatever we do, I can't go back into the dining room and ask Alice Mardike to kindly bring us some more.'

'We could send a footman to her cottage – it won't be locked. He can take two bottles from the shelf and leave half a crown in payment. Alice will understand why we've done it that way.'

'He would do well to avoid being seen anywhere near the cottage,' says Sir Felix. 'Until a few minutes ago, it might not have mattered, but I think you have just made not buying from witches a touchstone of respectability. I don't know what Taylor is planning, but he's just a little too polite for my liking. You don't want him accusing you of bias, now or later.'

'Send Jack,' I say. 'He grew up here, so he'll know where the cottage is and how best to get to it without being noticed. I've no doubt he's been there before on errands for his mother. He'd better go on foot – less conspicuous. But he should wait until we reconvene and everyone is occupied here.'

'I think it will snow again soon,' says Sir Felix, indicating the darkening sky. It is the mottled grey of a fresh bruise. 'That's not what we wanted.'

'No,' I say. 'But it's what we have, for all that. There'll be no escape from this village before the New Year.'

'Don't worry,' says Aminta, touching my arm. 'You're doing well – except for that reference to silk stockings.'

'An indelicate question?'

'More that they now all know we're looking for somebody who possesses them.'

'True,' I say. 'Somebody will have picked that up. Maybe it will cause them to make a false move.'

'You'd better get the hearing started again,' says Aminta. 'If they're all still stranded here tonight, I've no idea how we'll feed them.'

Chapter Eleven

We have more witches than we thought possible

As I re-enter the dining room, Taylor stands and everyone else follows his lead. They remain on their feet until I sit, then there is much shuffling of feet and a harsh scraping of chairs on my polished floor. I can see why Sir Felix's father preferred to hold court at the inn.

And yet, for all this show of respect, the atmosphere in the room has changed. It's difficult to describe what it is, except that I've felt it many times before. You have infiltrated a group of Catholic plotters, say, to oblige Lord Arlington. You have got them to trust you, because for some reason they believe you to be a priest from Douai named Father Dominic – a mistake on their part that you have not been so rude as to correct. They were about to give you some information, for which it is already clear Arlington is paying you much too little. Then, you observe the way they are looking at each other. You notice they are avoiding your frank and open smile. You wonder if the false papers that Arlington gave you are quite as good as he told you they were. You check which wall you'd like your back against, if things get nasty, and you measure the distance to the nearest door with your eye. If you are lucky, then you've already loaded the pistol that is in your pocket. If you haven't, then you hope that none of the gentlemen you've deceived is a better swordsman than you are. And, still smiling in a friendly way, you take the first cautious, hopefully imperceptible, sideways step.

But until now I've never had to do it with my infant son next door.

I look round the room. Nobody's eye meets my gaze.

'Very well,' I say. 'We still have a number of witnesses to hear, but not too many—'

'With respect, Sir John,' says Taylor, 'several of your friends here have something to say. We've been talking amongst ourselves while you were out of the room, and there are facts we think you should hear.'

I nod. I could inform Taylor in the clearest possible terms that I have no intention of allowing him to give me instructions in my own court. I could tell him that he can produce as many witnesses as he wishes, but there will still be no such thing as a witch. Or I can pretend that I shall listen to the evidence as if it were sane and rational. It is, after all, a good principle never to admit to being a double agent until you have to. Let them tell me whatever they have to tell me. I'll pretend that I don't think that it's superstitious nonsense. As long as I don't believe it myself, it won't hurt me, and outside, drop by icy drop, the snow will eventually melt. Help will come. 'Who wishes to give evidence?' I ask.

'Eliza Grice,' says Taylor.

I turn to where the Grice brothers are sitting. Their youngest sister is with them. Like all the Grices, she's solidly built. You could throw a cannonball at her and it might not knock her over. Her fair hair is drawn back and hidden beneath a lace-fringed cap, tied neatly under her chin. Her dress is plain but quite new – a rich wine colour, enhanced with a little cream lace at the neck and cuffs. She has a single row of small fresh-water pearls round her chubby neck. Few of the villagers knew pearls existed, back in the days they now all so fondly remember.

'Very well, Eliza,' I say. 'Can you please come and stand in front of me over here?'

She walks forward confidently. 'Is this good enough?' she asks, stopping and throwing her head back. I don't think she lacks confidence either.

'That will do nicely, Eliza. Now, I'm not going to make you swear an oath, but you do need to tell me the truth and you may need to attend the assize next year if you have anything of importance to say. If you do, you'll be under oath there.'

'I don't mind,' she says. 'All the same to me. Wouldn't mind getting out of this village. Long time since I been to Braintree. I can buy me some ribbons while I'm there. Red would be nice.'

Most of those gathered in the room are watching with mild interest, but then I notice that little Margaret Platt is terrified. Her father turns to her, puzzled.

'So what have you to say to us?' I ask.

'It's about young Mistress Platt,' she says, pointing to Margaret. 'She told me she was a witch.'

'I never!' says Margaret.

'You did!'

'I didn't!' Margaret is on her feet now, tears streaming down her thin cheeks.

'Sit down, Margaret,' I say. 'You'll get a chance to answer these accusations, if they need answering, in a moment. What are you accusing Margaret of saying?' I ask Eliza.

'She swore me to secrecy and told me she was going to get Alice Mardike to learn her how to be a witch. She'd thirty Shillings to pay for it. Money from when her grandmother died. Showed it to me. Once she'd studied how to make curses and fly through the air on a broom, she would kill George Barwell because he married Amy Taylor and not her. And if she denies it, as I'm sure she's going to, then she's a horrid little liar.'

'I'm not!' exclaims Margaret Platt.

'She is!' says Eliza Grice.

'You're the liar!'

'Silence!' I say. 'I am taking Mistress Grice's evidence. I wish to hear from nobody else.'

Eliza Grice smiles triumphantly. She'd stick her tongue out if it wasn't beneath the owner of a fine pearl necklace.

'So,' I continue, 'you're saying Margaret Platt threatened to kill George Barwell?' My pen hovers above the sheet of paper on the table, but for the moment it declines to make a record of this.

'With witchcraft,' says Eliza.

'I see. That's what she told you. And *did* she in fact go to Alice Mardike?'

'So she said.'

'Very well, your evidence is that she stated a desire to learn witchcraft and later said that she'd visited Mistress Mardike, possibly to that end. And what do you say happened next?'

'Alice Mardike wouldn't let her in on her secrets. Margaret said she'd paid Alice a Shilling, though, to curse George

Barwell for her. And if that didn't work, she knew somebody in Saffron Walden who was a better witch than Alice ever was and would learn her everything she needed to know, including how to fly a broomstick and . . . do things with imps. And that's God's own truth, sir. Cross my heart and hope to die, if I ever tell a lie.'

I write all this down, forming each word carefully. I note that the cost of the curse was excellent value at one Shilling. I make sure I give God a large capital G. I record her unwisely qualified hopes for death. I leave out the bit about imps. 'And why are you telling me this now?'

'Because I can't stand hearing her deny what she did with George Barwell, little slut. Don't just take my word for it. Any of the women here will tell you the same. The men might too, if there's any here haven't done it with her, which I doubt.'

Amy is looking at Margaret as if she would like to kill her. Is this the moment when she finally realises what George Barwell was like? The men are looking at nobody in particular. Taylor is smiling to himself. Perhaps he has a score to settle with the Platts anyway. Most people have a score to settle with somebody in the village. If so, he's succeeded very well indeed.

'What do you have to say, Margaret?' I ask.

'It's all a lie,' she says. 'It's all a lie, sir. I'm no witch.' She tries to stand, but her legs decide otherwise.

'So, you didn't ask Alice Mardike to kill anyone for you?'

'Not exactly, sir.'

'Not exactly?'

'Not at all, sir.'

'Did you pay her a Shilling?' I ask.

'Only for medicine, Sir John. She didn't make me a witch. She wanted to, but I said I'd never do it. Let me swear an oath, sir. A proper Bible oath. Witches can't swear Bible oaths, sir. It chokes them up something horrid.'

'It's prayers witches can't say,' yells somebody from the back row. 'The Lord's Prayer is a sure test. Always was. Holiest prayer there is, that one. Get her to say it.'

'Yes, make her say the Lord's Prayer,' somebody else calls out. 'She won't get past "hallowed be Thy name".'

'I *can* do that,' says Margaret. She stands with great effort and begins. 'Our Father, which art in Heaven, hallowed be Thy name, Thy kingdom come, Thy will be done on earth as it is in heaven . . .' Then, fatally, she pauses. 'Forgive us this day . . . no, that's not it. *Give* us this day . . .' There is a roar of laughter that drowns out whatever she says next. 'For ever and ever, Amen,' I hear her conclude, though I doubt anyone else does.

Harry Hardy coughs and everyone turns respectfully towards him. He's got the longest memory of all and he's never, ever said anything in favour of witches. Not much against them, but nothing in their favour. They all want to hear what advice he has. 'When Matthew Hopkins came here in 1645,' he says, 'he told us that you never find just one witch. They always infect others with their poison. Young lasses very often. Most of the maids here are sensible, but that Margaret Platt was always scatty. Never had any respect for those of us who might have given a word or two of wisdom if she'd just stopped to listen. Cheeked me something terrible when I did try to learn her something. Well, now you see the result. I'm sorry for it, but there it is. The two of them can hang together, and the village will be a safer place for it.'

One of the men close to Harry pats him on the shoulder. He likes the old man's words very much. 'That needed saying, Harry,' he observes. 'You tell 'em, boy.'

'I'm not afraid to speak up against them,' Harry says. 'Unlike some here.'

Again, I'm surprised at Harry, but I remember what Aminta said. Soon we'll all have to be on one side or the other. The safe side or the dangerous one. Harry's gone firmly for the safe side. I can't say I blame him.

'Alice Mardike cursed my father,' says young Giles Kerridge. 'Bewitched his horse. That gelding was as placid as anything before my dad fell out with her. No village is safe with a witch in it.'

'True enough,' says Harry Hardy. 'Made one of her familiars get the horse to kick him. Crushed his skull right in.'

'For the last time,' I say, 'I am not taking evidence on witchcraft. Only on the death of George Barwell.'

'That's still what happened,' says Giles Kerridge. He seems to resent the fact that nobody was hanged for the actions of his father's gelding. Two or three people are now standing, ready to tell me of further misfortunes in the distant past.

'Sir John,' says Margaret desperately, 'I confess – I did go and see Alice Mardike. I was very foolish. I did ask her to curse George Barwell, because he had wronged me, as everyone here knows. But then ... I changed my mind. I told her I wouldn't listen to her blasphemies. Not me. I'm no witch. I've never seen the Devil, not once. Or his imps. And I don't want to neither. I don't even own a cat. George's death is nothing to do with me. I wanted him dead, but I didn't do it. It must be somebody who hated him even more than I did—'

'Enough, girl,' hisses her father. 'Don't make it worse. Hold your stupid girl's tongue before it hangs you.'

'Very well, Mr Platt,' I say. 'Did you know anything of this?'

'I knew Barwell had been sniffing around my door,' he

says. 'Before and after his marriage. But Margaret is just a silly maid. She doesn't know what she's saying. I apologise, sir, for what she's done, but it wasn't malicious. I am sorry and she is sorry and I hope you'll all forgive us. Please don't judge us too harshly. It was just . . . just a fancy, sir. She didn't mean anything by it.'

There are tears running down his cheeks, but he doesn't seem to have noticed.

'You should be ashamed of yourself, Jacob Platt,' says one of the Grice boys. 'Bringing up a witch.'

'I've always warned her to stay away from witchcraft,' Platt says. 'I brought her up to fear the Good Lord and to reject the works of the Devil. She knows the harm that one can do.' He looks around, hoping for encouragement, but there is none. He's one of the richest men in the village and it's done him no good. He's got a witch in the family.

'Slut!' yells Eliza Grice.

'Whore!' yells another girl.

'Jade!'

'Sorceress!'

'Jezebel!'

I turn. This last was from the good, kind, sensible Nell. She's staring at Margaret with fury.

Margaret herself is sitting open-mouthed. All her life, she thought she had had friends. Now she knows she didn't. Not one. She looks round the room at her neighbours and sees only their scorn and hate. She's going to die at the end of a rope. She is aware that, if she was on the ground now, they'd kick her to death. She's made of sterner stuff than her father, though. At least she has no plans to beg for forgiveness for things she hasn't done. She stands again and turns on them.

'Every one of you has visited Alice Mardike for some reason,' she says. 'I've been there no more than the rest of you.'

'That may be true,' says Taylor, 'but it depends why they went. Sir John here visited her very recently.' He looks at me and smiles. I smile back. It's a skill I've learned. 'But that was just so Sir John could question her about her crimes. The crimes that will shortly be punished. Nobody here would criticise Sir John for that, would they?'

The profundity of Taylor's voice has calmed things. For the moment the name-calling has ceased.

'Sir John knows what's right,' says Harry Hardy. 'His mother was a West and he's married to a Clifford. Both fine local families. That's good enough for me.'

'Of course he knows what's right,' says Taylor. 'And so do all of you. If any of you have ever been to her cottage – and I won't enquire who has and who hasn't – then it wasn't to ask her to kill somebody for you. Was it?'

They all nod. It might have been to get a cow cursed or somebody's leg broken, but not to expedite the painful death of a neighbour. Or not that they can now recall, anyway.

'Has anyone else told you they wish to speak?' I ask Taylor. 'Because nobody has informed me. If this were a court—'

'But it isn't,' says Taylor, 'as you have so helpfully schooled us, Sir John. This is an enquiry into a murder. And you have to speak to anyone with evidence, do you not? It might go hard with you, sir, at the assize if it were found you had concealed any material fact. I should be sorry if that happened, since you have listened to us so patiently. We only want things to go well for you.'

I would be within my rights to throw Taylor out of my dining room, but I know this is not the course of action that Sir Felix would recommend. I smile again, just to show that I haven't forgotten how to do it. Always keep smiling, until slightly after the moment when you have to draw your sword.

'Who wishes to speak next, Mr Taylor?' I ask pleasantly.

'Nell Bowman,' he says.

I look at Nell sitting in the second row. Actually, I don't think she wants to speak at all, but she's going to. Taylor's just told her she has no choice.

'I don't have to take the oath either, Master John?' she asks. 'I mean, Sir John . . .'

Nell is another who still sees me as the twenty-year-old I once was. That is perfectly fair. I can't deny that I used to be twenty. It is one of my many faults.

'Only if you wish to take it, Nell,' I say.

She pauses, in a way in which she would not ten years ago, to see if I am jesting. Ten years ago she would have known. Ten years ago she had a ready retort for anything Dickon or I might say. Not now.

'I don't mind,' she says uncertainly.

'Then just tell me what you'd like us to know.'

While she is making up her mind what it is that she wants to reveal to us, I write on the paper in front of me: 'EVIDENCE OF MISTRESS NELL BOWMAN'. I underline it, for want of anything better to do, then look up.

'Ben and I have been married fifteen years,' she says. 'As you know.'

I nod.

'In the normal course of things, we'd have been blessed with half a dozen children by now. But soon after I came here,

I had to ask Mistress Mardike to leave the inn, on account of complaints from other customers.'

'What was she doing?' I ask.

'Doing?'

'Why did people ask you to make her leave?'

Again she looks perplexed. Isn't the answer obvious? 'She's a witch.'

'Very well. Your other customers believed her to be a witch and requested she should leave. What happened next?'

'Well, she cursed me on the spot. And now we're childless.'

'I'm sorry for that,' I say, 'but I can't see that it is in any way relevant,' I say.

'It's true,' says Nell. 'Ask her if it isn't true.'

'I mean that it has no bearing on the murder of George Barwell.'

'But it's true. I'm a victim of witchcraft. You have to believe me.'

Slowly and reluctantly I turn to Alice. 'Did you curse Mistress Bowman?'

'What, fifteen years ago? How should I remember that, boy?'

'Are you saying that you might have cursed her?'

'If she threw me out of the inn, then I expect I said something. Wouldn't you?'

Actually, I have, when much younger, been thrown out of that inn. I too have no idea exactly what I said at the time. I wasn't in a state to remember.

'Very well,' I say to Nell, 'she may or may not have cursed you. Thank you for clarifying that. Now could you please tell us what possible relevance this has to the murder of George Barwell?'

'Because she has the power to do these things. She cursed me and it worked. I'm barren. If she cursed Barwell too, then it's no surprise he ended up dead within a couple of days. She believes she's a witch. She *is* a witch. She can harm any of us by calling up evil spirits to kill us in whatever way they choose. It's just like the Rector says.'

There's a general murmur of approval. They can see that. After the ringing endorsement Taylor has given me, they'll be expecting me to see that too. Famous Cambridge University must have taught me something. That's what it does.

'Very well. I've noted that,' I say. 'Did you see Mistress Mardike on the day George Barwell was murdered?'

'No.'

'Do you know anything about her movements that day?'

'No.'

'Is there anything else you can tell us that might help us discover who killed George Barwell?'

'No.'

'Then that will be all,' I say.

Nell pauses for a moment, then says: 'You asked Margaret Platt if she possessed silk stockings.'

'Yes,' I say.

'She said she didn't.'

'I believe so.'

'Well, she does. George Barwell bought her some. I saw them.'

This ripples across the room, like the first cold gust of wind that troubles the millpond when a storm is on its way. Even if nobody quite understands why I asked Margaret about hosiery, the possession of silk stockings does not stand in Margaret Platt's favour. Not in a village that has contented itself with good English wool since the Norman Conquest.

'Thank you, Nell,' I say. 'You've been very helpful.'

'I'd say that was brave of her,' says Taylor.

'I'm sure it wasn't easy,' I say.

I make a note of this last point, but I can see the page much less well than before. Outside, the sky has darkened and the snow is falling again. Large, insistent flakes. Several of the villagers look nervously through the windows, and not for the first time. They'll be wondering if they'll get home today, unless they go now. One or two are already standing, torn between one fear and another.

'The snow, sir . . .' says Henry Hardy, more courageous than the rest. 'Looks bad, sir. Very bad.'

'I am adjourning this hearing for today,' I announce. 'We'll meet here again at ten o'clock tomorrow, weather permitting.'

Nobody protests or decides to linger. But Taylor, almost the last to leave, pauses at the door, hat still in his hands.

'I hope that you now understand our concerns, Sir John,' he says. 'Where there's one witch in a village, they infect others. You can't store good and bad apples together. Witchcraft is a rottenness that needs cutting out with a sharp blade. Better it had been done a year ago, before that Platt girl got ideas. Maybe she can still be saved, by God's grace, but Mistress Mardike is a lost cause, you must see that now. The sooner that one's thrown out of the barrel the better. If it's not done before Christmas, then I won't be answerable for the consequences. We'll be looking to you, Sir John.'

'I shall ensure that everything is done properly and according to the Law,' I say.

'Good. That's all we're asking for. Witchcraft is illegal and we want it stamped out. According to the Law. I don't want anyone else cursed the way my son-in-law was.'

I nod, but this last remark reminds me of something that has been troubling me. 'Who told you about the curse?' I ask.

'Why do you ask that?'

'Because, when you told me, you gave me a very full account of what both sides said. Mistress Mardike informed Barwell it wasn't proper to promise the girls things so they'd let him do his dirty business with them – not with a wife of his own and with a baby on the way. That's what you said. You weren't there yourself. I doubt if George Barwell would have informed you of anything quite so much to his discredit. So, either you made it up or somebody else who was there told you exactly how your son-in-law was accused of fornication with half the village.'

Taylor frowns, then shakes his head. 'There's no reason why you shouldn't know,' he says. 'It was Nell Bowman. She told me.'

He claps his hat on his head, turns and strides out into the driving snow. A gust tugs at his cloak but he pulls it more closely round him. A dozen paces, and he is lost to sight. I close the door with some effort, fighting the wind. Suddenly everything is still. The house is finally at peace with itself.

'You did well to end the proceedings there,' says Sir Felix, when we are in front of the sitting-room fire again. 'They were ready to hang Margaret Platt for possessing silk stockings.'

'Then the weather saved her,' I say. 'I hope that everyone got safe home before the roads and paths became impassable.'

'Those living further out will have found shelter with those living close by,' says Sir Felix. 'The village looks after itself.'

'I asked Ben to ensure that Alice Mardike reached her house unmolested.'

'Then I'm sure he will, though the distance to her cottage will not please him. I'm not certain the storm will last long, though. The windows are rattling less than they were. The gale must already be slackening. If I believed in divine interventions, then I'd say we've just had one. Perhaps the Lord does not condemn silk hose or oppose witches as much as the Rector believes.'

'I don't understand Nell,' says Aminta. 'Why would she tell William Taylor what Alice Mardike said about his son-in-law?'

'People do spread gossip,' I say.

'But not Nell. Or she never did in the past. I often deride Ben for not listening to what his customers say to him, but actually that's not a disadvantage for an innkeeper – or his wife. Men say things drunk that they dearly wish they had not said once they are sober. If Ben repeated everything he heard by way of his trade, then he would have many dissatisfied clients – or, at the very least, clients who resolved to spend less money the next time they visited his establishment. Nor does Ben take sides in arguments. One man's silver is as good as another's.'

'That is very true,' says Sir Felix. 'During the late wars, Ben declared himself neither a Royalist nor a Parliamentarian. And it was a long war. Say what you like about Ben, he can hold his tongue in exchange for cash.'

'Nell isn't stupid,' Aminta continues. 'She knows as well as Ben that that's how it is done. And yet she goes straight to Taylor and reports what she's heard Alice say about George Barwell. Every last word.'

'To be fair, Barwell may not have spent much money at the inn,' I say. 'Ben said he hadn't been there lately. Which is odd because it's the only inn in the village, and Barwell must have wanted to get away from his father-in-law from time to time. His absence must have been enforced. So, maybe he had money before but not now?'

'Ben thought Amy might have forbidden him to frequent the inn,' says Aminta. 'Or he may have exhausted the money he brought with him. Taylor certainly does spend money there – and freely. But Nell can't have known how he would take the news. He was unlikely to be pleased. He might have blamed the messenger every bit as much as his son-in-law.'

'Perhaps Nell just liked Taylor better than Barwell,' I say.

'I doubt it. Barwell, for all his misbehaviour, seems to have been quite popular, with the women of the village at least. Nobody, conversely, really likes Taylor. His men fear him. Most of the villagers respect him, because he's rich. But I can't see Nell going out of her way to take his side. Anyway, as I say, Nell doesn't spread gossip. It was a strange thing for her to do, however you look at it.'

'Well, she never used to spread gossip but she was very free to tell us what Margaret Platt had done too,' I say. 'I don't understand her belief in witchcraft either. Have you ever heard her say anything like it before?'

'Not witches, nor ghosts, nor goblins,' says Sir Felix. 'A remarkably level-headed young woman. Until now. But people do change their minds. Look at all the folk who were Republicans ten years ago, when Cromwell ruled, but who are Royalists now. Being a Royalist is no more rational than being a Republican, but only a fool would claim to oppose the King now. Being a Royalist is the safe thing to do.'

I nod. I too was a Republican once. 'If it were Ben who had had the sudden change of heart on witchcraft, I have no doubt that we'd soon know the reason why. Just a question or two to him would reveal all. Ben never has learned to lie convincingly. But Nell keeps her own secrets almost as well as she once kept the secrets of others.' I look out of the window. The storm is, as Sir Felix predicted, proving to be a short one. The sun is about to emerge again through the iron-grey clouds. I can just see the chimneys of the inn on the far side of the Park. The snow on the ground is deeper than before, but not much.

'I'm going into the village,' I say.

'To talk to Nell?' asks Aminta.

'No, to talk to her honest husband,' I say.

Chapter Twelve

Ben attempts to lie to me

Snow is piled against the entrance of the inn in a soft, dazzling, white swoop, but happily the rough oak door has always opened inwards, and I need only to place my thumb on the latch and push gently. It swings open for me on its well-greased hinges. I step carefully across the snowy threshold and stamp my boots clean on the rush-covered floorboards. Ben looks up, surprised that he has a customer and such a noisy one.

'Sir John!' he says. 'I wasn't expecting to see anyone this afternoon, least of all yourself. Have you run out of ale at the Big House? Or is it just that you'd like something half decent to pour down your throat?'

'I'd rather drink your ale than any other in the county,' I say.

Ben nods. Though Royston is the furthest he's ever travelled, and thither only once, he's never doubted there's no house in England that can better his ale.

'A pint then?' he asks.

'No more, no less,' I say. 'And remember that I'm now responsible for enforcing all ordinances on weights and measures.'

Ben's hand moves from the tankard he was about to give me to one that is slightly larger. He draws a golden stream from the barrel behind his counter. I pay him a silver penny.

'Your good health, constable,' I say, raising the battered grey mug to my lips.

He waits for me to nod in appreciation of the excellence of the brew, then says: 'Constable, am I? So, it's an official visit, I take it?'

'I wanted to thank you for seeing Mistress Mardike safe home.'

'Almost died of cold.'

'You or her?'

'Me. She only had to go there. I had to come back as well. Escorting witnesses is no part of my job, Sir John. If she was a prisoner, that would be different. They're in my charge. Witnesses are expected to find their own way home, so the poor constable doesn't have to expire of frostbite. I'm not doing that again unless you charge her with a capital offence.'

'You could have stayed at her cottage for the afternoon, if the way home was so dangerous to your health.'

'Only if I wanted to be turned into a toad or a rat. I left her at the door. I wasn't going too far into a witch's house.'

'It's all fairly normal in there, apart from a dead snake in a jar. Though actually, Ben, you are starting to look a little like a toad, so maybe you should have stopped at the garden gate.'

I take a drink of Ben's excellent ale. He doesn't seem too worried that he's turning into a toad. He has something else on his mind.

'Somebody else had been there while we were all at your hearing,' says Ben. 'The first thing Mistress Mardike said, as I stood at her door, was, "Where's that come from?" There was silver somebody had left on her table, you see, Sir John. Whole pile of it. Then she looked at her bottles of medicines and nodded as if she knew who'd done it.'

'Did she say who?' I ask, looking down into my tankard.

'Why, is it illegal to buy potions from her?'

'No,' I say.

Not illegal, but perhaps not advisable at present. Unless you have to.

'Wasn't me, anyway,' says Ben. 'As constable, I wouldn't risk being seen buying anything there. Wouldn't be right for somebody representing the King's Majesty. Could lead to all sorts of trouble for the purchaser.'

'So you never buy from her, Ben?'

Ben shuffles his feet a bit, looks out of the window, then says: 'No.' I wish that the spies Arlington sent me to catch dissembled as badly as Ben does. It would have saved so much time and effort for everyone. I probably wouldn't even have the scar on my face.

'That's very wise, Ben,' I say. 'How about Nell?'

'Nell? She wouldn't go there. If anyone's told you she did, then they're lying. She never did, and that's all there is to it.'

'I believe you, Ben,' I say. 'Nobody's said anything.'

Well, the last sentence is true anyway.

Ben looks relieved. 'They wouldn't have,' he says. 'Because she didn't. So, they couldn't have seen her there, whatever they've told you. I mean, why would she?'

Indeed. That's what I'm wondering. Why would she? She must have had a reason. And Ben would know what it was.

'Does Nell really believe Alice cursed her?' I ask.

'She said so, didn't she?'

I shrug. 'It really has no relevance to the murder investigation. But I'd still like to know. Does she truly believe that you have no children because she threw Alice out of the inn?'

Ben takes a very deep breath and shakes his head. 'How are we supposed to know what women really think?' he asks me. 'You're a married man, Sir John, just like me. You've been to the University. You've studied Law. You ought to be cleverer than an innkeeper. So, you tell me how we're supposed to know what they're thinking or what they want us to do about it. Can't be done, can it?'

I nod. My tutor at Cambridge never tried to teach me what women think. The idea that women were capable of thought may not have occurred to him. He rarely met any, except the one who made his bed and washed his clothes.

'But Alice really did curse her?' I ask.

'So she says. I don't recall it myself. Can't see why Nell would say it if it didn't happen, though.'

'And she's always blamed Alice?'

'Well, as a married man, it may not surprise you to learn that she occasionally blamed me. In some ways, I'm not unhappy it's Alice Mardike she wishes to hang at the moment. Lets me off the hook for a few days.'

'Well, there's no doubt she cursed Barwell anyway. She admits that she did. But, Ben, the man was clearly strangled. There is no need to invoke witchcraft.'

'Witchcraft can take many forms. A man may sicken and die after he's been cursed or he may be set upon by Devils or he may be kicked by his own horse. Barwell's was a strange death. That's what people are thinking. Nobody here wants to think another villager would have killed somebody like that. Witchcraft's more comfortable, somehow.'

'The fact that people here don't want to believe something doesn't change the rules of the evidence.'

'If you say so, Sir John. I'm sure you know what you're doing.'

There is less deference in this last statement than you might think, reading it on the page.

'Look, Ben, Taylor had hoped for a son-in-law who would look after his only daughter and take the farm over in due course. Barwell clearly met neither requirement. Taylor had just been told by Nell that Barwell regarded his recent marriage as no impediment to his future conduct. Taylor's own reputation in the village was at stake, with a son-in-law of that calibre. Barwell's timely death, leaving Amy as a respectable and still eligible widow, must have come as a great relief. Taylor was out on the hill that day, though nobody has yet come forward to say they saw him in the wood. He's not a kind man, as I'm sure his hired hands must have told you, after a pint or two of your excellent ale. And he'd like to see Alice hanged quickly, legally or not, with no further questions asked. I just need a witness willing to testify they saw him in the wood, preferably dragging Barwell by the ear.'

Ben shakes his head. 'Sorry, Master John, but that doesn't work at all,' he says. 'You say Barwell was strangled with a silk stocking. Well, that's not Taylor's way, is it? If Barwell had been strangled by a strong pair of hands, or more likely bludgeoned to death with a heavy wooden staff, then I'd go out and arrest Taylor myself . . . subject to possessing a valid warrant from your good self, of course. But Taylor would never use a woman's stocking, even to strangle Barwell. That insolent baggage Margaret Platt, on the other hand – she might. Everyone knows Barwell had promised to marry her, though she tried to deny it at first. Nell's said that's where she got the stockings from. Margaret wanted him dead. She'd tried to get Alice Mardike to kill him. So, why shouldn't she lure him up to the hill with the promise of more of what he liked best, then strangle him with the very gift he'd given her in happier times?'

'You think that's how she did it?'

'Trust me. That's what she's like.'

'She was certainly out of her house at the right time,' I say. 'She told me so.'

'Well, there you are then.'

'You don't like her much, do you?'

'Like I say – she gives herself airs that don't rightly belong to her. You'd think she was the daughter of the Lord of the Manor, begging your pardon, Sir John. Her father's just a yeoman farmer when all's said and done, even if he does have money. Well, she can hang in her silk stockings for all I care.'

'Would she really tear off his face like that?' I ask.

'Yes. She's spiteful enough.'

'You might take one lump out of his face out of spite. Two would require a very strong stomach. And she'd have got blood over her linen apron. Her father or mother would have noticed that.'

'Not necessarily,' says Ben. 'You wouldn't necessarily see something like that.'

Ben is again less convincing than he thinks. He knows that blood stains are not that easy to hide or remove. But Margaret Platt's visits to Mistress Mardike seem to have made an unfavourable impression on him. Once Ben gets an idea into his head, it is not always a simple matter to shift it somewhere else. And this week's idea is that a witch killed Barwell. It's just that he hadn't realised until today that Margaret aspired to be one. Perhaps he is not so wrong, though, for all that. She had a sound reason, an opportunity and the murder weapon. And, to be fair, I'm not currently being asked to believe that she did it with witchcraft. She just walked up the hill and strangled him. Maybe I need look no further on a cold winter's day.

But I'd still like to know exactly why Nell went to see Alice Mardike. If I ask Ben, I'll know when he's lying but I still won't know the truth. But there's somebody else I can ask.

I drain my tankard.

'Another?' asks Ben.

'Thanks, Ben, but I have some work to do,' I say.

The sky, through the window, is now bright blue. And Mistress Mardike's cottage is not too distant for a brisk walk, in spite of Ben's warning that it may kill me.

Of course, now I come to think of it, it's very much easier on a horse. As I trudge through the village it strikes me that nobody else has chosen to take a stroll this afternoon. Most of the old wooden shutters are closed and smoke rises from every chimney. The road, as it runs between the low, half-timbered cottages, is smooth and unblemished. Everything smells cold and fresh and clean. The sky is an intense blue, such as I can rarely remember seeing. The bare-limbed trees are covered with their own white clouds. My eyes are starting to ache from the dazzling reflected light. Snow, sliding in a sudden cascade from the untidy thatched roofs, is a constant hazard. But, eventually, I wade through the last of the feathery drifts and can knock on Alice Mardike's low door.

'Thought you might call in,' she says, without looking up from tending her fire.

'Another correct prediction,' I say. 'Once may be a lucky guess but twice points to witchcraft.'

'Well, I thought you might and then I thought you might not, so I was bound to be right one way or the other. That's the way witchcraft works most of the time. Decide what's going to happen anyway and then offer to do it for cash. So, I don't need you learning me what's witchcraft, boy. I'm a bit too old to be given lessons by a young lad like you.'

'I'm thirty years old and a knight of the realm,' I say.

'Are you? Which part of that am I supposed to be impressed by, John Grey? Like I say – you're no more than a child, even if you are allowed to sit in judgment on your neighbours. So, what do you want this time, boy? Come to arrest me, have you? That's what they all want you to do.'

'Yes, they made that fairly clear. But I've merely come to thank you for the cough medicine.'

'You paid too much. The money's still on the table. You need to take back two Shillings.'

'If it works as well as usual, then it's cheap at what I gave you.'

'Is it? I'd better start charging more then. In the meantime, if you've no use for the two Shillings, they may as well be mine as the next witch's.' She makes no effort to gather up the coins, but fixes me with her gaze. 'Well, boy, if you've thanked me all you're planning to, you can clear off again before the snow starts again. I don't have enough food here to give you supper, so don't think you're staying for that.'

'I want to know about this curse you placed on Nell Bowman,' I say. 'After you cursed her, if you did curse her, did she ever mention it to you again, until today?'

'Just the once.'

'When?'

'About a week ago. Maybe a bit more. Just when the cold weather started. She came over here. When she walked across the threshold, I thought maybe she wanted something for her aches and pains, but she said no. Apparently I'd cursed her years before and now she couldn't have children and she wanted me to lift the curse. She'd pay me to do it. Well, I thought, that's the easiest money I'll ever earn.'

'And that was all?'

'No, she wanted me to tell her husband that the curse was lifted and that all would be well and they'd have a baby soon.'

'So did you?'

'Course not. I'm not that cruel, whatever folk think. How could I tell Ben Bowman they'd have a baby? It's one thing to lift a curse, it's another entirely to know what life has in store for each and every one of us. Why should I raise his hopes when I've no idea whether they can have a child? Plenty of folk can't. If they hadn't had one by now, then they'll probably never have one. Told her that if I'd ever cursed her I was truly sorry. I hadn't meant it. And I certainly hadn't meant her not to have children. For what it was worth, she could consider the curse lifted. No charge for that. But more than that I couldn't do.'

'What did Nell say?'

'She was cross. Wanted me to talk to Ben and say a baby was on its way. Said I was an evil old witch for not helping her. I couldn't argue with that, could I? So I told her to go away and stop bothering me. Said to forget about the curse being lifted too. It was back where it was, until she got a civil tongue in her head.'

'So, she believed in the curse and in your powers?'

'Seemingly. Didn't think she would, being from London and all, but she did. Maybe she's been here too long. Like me. You should get out while you can, boy.'

'Ben must believe it too, if nothing but your word would convince him the curse had been lifted.'

'Can't see it matters what he believes. He just has to do the same thing, curse or no curse, if he wants a child. I should imagine he knows what it is by now. Same thing all you men are doing all the time. It's always easy for the man. A bit too easy, if you ask me.'

'I don't understand,' I say.

'Which bit, boy? Ain't got all day to explain things to you.'

'Nell. The curse. Telling Ben.'

'Maybe you don't need to understand it,' says Alice. 'Can't see it has much to do with George Barwell's murder, and one more person calling me a witch in your dining room doesn't make it any truer than it was before. No point in digging up evidence they won't listen to. They all think I deserve to die anyway.'

'They think Margaret Platt is a witch too,' I say.

'Stupid girl. She's no witch and never will be. Her mistake was to trust George Barwell. And to strut around the village as if she owned it. Silk stockings! What did she want them for?'

'I doubt that she was planning all along to murder somebody with them. But she did want Barwell dead,' I say. 'And she did ask you to kill him.'

'She couldn't kill a toad in a jar.' Alice pauses as if remembering something, but she shakes her head.

'You'd be surprised who can kill, if they need to. It was

certainly an unpleasant surprise the first time somebody tried to kill me. You never know who has the stomach for it until they do it.'

Alice nods and looks at me, almost with respect. 'Well, you're still alive, so you seem to have outsmarted them all so far. Now, listen to what I'm going to tell you, John Grey, and listen carefully because this may be the last chance I get to say it. If you have to hang me, I won't hold it against you. Not a bit. You may not want to do it, but they may give you no choice in the matter, for all that you're a knight of the realm and thirty years old. I'm a lot older than that. I'll die sooner or later anyway. This winter, like as not, unless there's a thaw very soon. You get to a certain age and you get tired of life in a way that you never expected you would when you were twenty . . . or thirty. So, it makes little difference to me. But Margaret Platt, fool though she is, is not yet seventeen. If you're going to have to hang one or other of us, then hang me while I'm still around to be hanged, and leave her alone. If I have to confess to things I didn't do, then I pray that God will forgive me for it, because it won't be the worst thing I've done. And don't think you can just arrange things the way you'd do in London. London's a long way from here. A very long way. You got all that, boy?'

'Yes,' I say. 'I've got all that.'

'The light has almost gone,' says Aminta as I enter our own house again. 'The days are so short now – I feared you might be stranded out there without a lantern. The Rector has just called and we provided him with one to get back to his house.'

'I can find my way blind drunk from the inn to any part of the village,' I say. 'Once it was a very necessary skill. But Ben would have lent me all I needed to walk back across the Park. And my journey was not in vain. I now know that Nell visited Alice to try to get the curse lifted. And that Nell believed Ben was equally concerned and needed Alice to reassure him that the curse was removed. But more important, Ben has convinced me that Taylor would never have wielded a stocking as a murder weapon. Taylor's a proud man, conscious of his own worth and his standing in society. He would never have crept up on his son-in-law and pulled the noose tight from behind. He'd have confronted him, beaten him with his staff and felt legally entitled to do so, Barwell being a member of the family. Margaret conversely had as strong a reason as Taylor for wanting Barwell dead and was in possession of exactly what was used to kill him. A pair of them, in fact. Ben thought that her mother and father wouldn't notice the blood on her apron. I told him he was wrong, but I think they'd have lied for her anyway. They'd have probably felt that she did right to kill him.'

'I agree she could, and probably should, have strangled him, but how exactly did Margaret destroy his face?'

'Quickly, and trying not to vomit as she did it. She could have used one of his own woodworking tools, if she'd somehow managed to get her hands on them. It was his fair face that led her on to her ruin. She didn't want to leave him even that.'

'Then she's tougher than she seems,' says Aminta.

'What did the Rector want, calling so late?' I ask.

'He left the paper on the table over there. He said that he found it on Barwell's body when he was covering it in a more decent way than it was left by the shepherds. It was tucked inside his coat, in a pocket.'

'Have you looked at it?'

'You arrived not long after he left. I had to go to Charles and administer some more of Mistress Mardike's syrup, otherwise I might have done so straight away. The Rector did not instruct me not to read it, and if he had I should have only been more inclined to do so.'

I pick up the paper, unfold it, and Aminta and I scan it together.

MEET ME AT THE WOODS AT TWO O'CLOCK TODAY. I HAVE SOMETHING FOR YOU. THE SORT OF THING YOU USED TO LIKE VERY MUCH. SHE'LL NEVER KNOW. WILL SHE? MARGARET.

Chapter Thirteen

Margaret Platt tells me some of the truth

I scarcely recognise this new world. Almost all of the landmarks that I know have vanished and been replaced with smooth white domes and ridges and ripples. I have not yet dared to light my lantern. Above me is a cloudy sky, concealing the bright moon and stars. I have enough light to tell where the heavens end and the roof of the inn begins, but not much else. Soon I shall be at the main road, but for the moment I trudge on across the Park, step by tedious step.

I am making my way on foot because I have very necessarily lied to my wife and my steward. Though I need to make urgent enquiries about the letter, Aminta has forbidden me to stir from the house until it is light. She has subverted my steward sufficiently that he too has informed me that it would be inadvisable to go out in this treacherous weather. Should I behave in an honest and open manner, Aminta and Morrell will, between them, find a way to keep me at home, knight of the realm though I am. I have therefore told the household that I am at my desk, studying my Law books, and am not to be disturbed. Since I cannot call for my horse or be seen on my way to the stables, I have slipped out through a side door and made my way cautiously towards this point, where the Park ends and the high road begins, and where I may perhaps take out my tinderbox without risk that the flash will be seen by my wife or any of the servants.

And why is it so important that I take this small risk? Because I have evidence that I must not withhold, but which may kill a seventeen-year-old girl when I reveal it. A seventeen-year-old girl who has been seduced and abandoned by an older man. I have to know whether it is what it seems to be and then I have to think what I am going to do about it and how legal that is likely to be. I pull my cloak more tightly around me and press on, stumbling often but never quite falling. Almost but not quite.

Then I get some unwelcome help. The door of the inn opens, and a burst of candlelight reveals the way ahead. It also reveals Ben, who seems to be on his way to the woodpile with a large wicker basket.

'Good evening, Sir John,' he says. 'I am most flattered that you should visit me twice in one day.'

I pause. If I drink with Ben, it will prevent his questioning my journey, but it will also delay my reaching the Platts' farmhouse and, more important, endanger my timely and wholly undetected return to my own residence.

'I'm going elsewhere, Ben,' I say. 'Once I've lit this lantern.'

Ben does not ask why I am lighting the candle only now. After all, I may have perfectly good reasons for risking breaking a leg by crossing my own parkland on a dark night with my lantern unlit. He raises a more important question.

'With the snow starting to fall again?' he says. Because the light from the open door shows that a few large flakes are descending.

'I have to interrogate a witness further. I have new evidence – a note written to Barwell.'

'Saying what, Sir John?'

'I'll tell you tomorrow, when I'm sure who sent it and why.'

'As constable, surely I should see it now?'

Ben's right, of course. He ought to see it now. But there's something in his eagerness that makes me uneasy. Once Ben sees the signature, it will confirm his most cherished suspicions. And I'm not yet sure whether it's what it seems to be.

'Tomorrow's soon enough,' I say.

Ben looks at me thoughtfully. He knows I've told him all he needs to know, but, on the other hand, there aren't that many people likely to be accused of anything tomorrow. And I'm clearly going in the direction of the Platts' house, not Taylor's. Ben can add up his takings as well as any other man in the village.

'So, this note . . . it's from Margaret Platt?' he asks.

'That's what I need to find out, Ben,' I say. 'The signature may be forged.'

'Forged?' Ben looks shocked. More shocked than he seemed when we found Barwell's body. 'Then just show it to her tomorrow in front of everyone. Confront the little witch with it. Don't give her a chance to deny it now, Sir John, because that's what she'll do. It sounds as if you have the evidence you need against her without wandering through the snow.'

'Taylor would certainly agree,' I say. 'But I need to find out the truth, then have time to think how I'm going to deal with it.'

'Well, you know best, Sir John,' Ben says. 'If you want to freeze to death on a night such as this, and all for so little, then I'm sure that's the right decision.'

For once his irony is entirely justified. I am about to visit another reputed witch and will probably discover nothing of value. If I should have learned one thing from my time with Arlington it's that you should never walk into danger unless you know exactly why you are doing it. This visit may just convince the village that I habitually consort with practitioners of the black arts. Which, now I think of it, is what I do.

'Yes, Ben, I know best,' I say, though the scar on my face is clear proof that knowing best is not always as helpful as you would think it might be.

I trudge on into the swirling darkness, a circle of yellow light from the lantern now bobbing ahead of me. I do not look back, but I feel Ben's eyes on me until I turn the corner.

There is enough evidence of lighted taper through the shutters to show that the Platts are at home, though I do not know where else they might be on such a night. Though Margaret might be wise to flee the county, this is no weather for going anywhere. The wind stings my cheeks. My cloak seems scarcely to provide any protection at all. My fingers are numb inside my thick leather gloves. This is cold that can kill, if you stand still long enough.

I bang on the door with my fist. There is a silence, then the shuffle of feet, then the noise of a large bolt being pulled back, clean, oiled metal sliding over metal. The door swings open.

'Sir John!' says Jacob Platt. 'Why . . . But you must come in. You will freeze out there. And no horse – you walked here? Surely not?'

'It was more convenient in many ways,' I say.

Platt raises his eyebrows, but makes no protest. I have done enough lately to convince the village of my oddness. Choosing to walk when I could ride is not as strange as my refusal to believe in ghosts and witches.

'Do you wish to speak to me, Sir John?'

'I need to speak to Margaret again,' I say.

'Could it not wait until tomorrow? Margaret is much fatigued by today's proceedings, as you will imagine. She is asleep.'

'I've come a long way on foot on a cold night,' I say. 'If it could wait until tomorrow, I would be in a warm bed myself, under a heap of blankets.'

Platt nods. 'Of course,' he says. He knows from my previous visit that I am not to be put off easily and certainly not after a dark walk on a snowy night. 'I'll wake her. My wife will bring you some mulled ale while you wait here by the fire.'

I rub my hands and hold them as close to the flames as I dare. In the next room there is a whispered conversation, too quiet for me to make out any words, and then feet ascend the wooden stairs to the next floor. I look round the parlour. After my cold walk it looks even more inviting than it did last time I was here. Logs smoulder quietly on a deep bed of grey ash in the great fireplace. The new silver gleams on the oak dresser. The country grows comfortable, and the Platts with it. I am the King's representative here, but it is men like Platt on whom the King depends for their support and for their taxes. The King's ministers can send their candidates to stand in Parliamentary elections, but it is Platt and his fellow freeholders who decide whether they will be returned. This King, unlike the last one, will not risk dismissing Parliament and ruling alone. Things are not as they were when Sir Felix was born.

Mistress Platt fusses in with a tankard of hot spiced ale. A loose, shapeless woollen robe, reaching almost to the floor, completely covers her nightgown. Her hair is tucked neatly into a clean linen cap. She curtsies to me. She is not yet aware that the King now bows to her husband's will. 'I am sorry we have nothing better, Sir John. I imagine that at the Big House you drink only Sack and Canary.'

'Sir Felix certainly does,' I say. 'Or he would if we let him. But a steaming tankard is welcome on a cold night. I am very grateful for your kindness, Mistress Platt.'

'I hope you won't have too many questions for young Margaret,' she says anxiously.

'So do I,' I say.

'She's not a witch,' she says. 'She just imagines things. She's only a child . . .'

I nod. I am already beginning to discover that you start worrying about your children when they are born and stop when you die. Most of the people in my dining room today looked at Margaret and saw a witch. Mistress Platt looked and saw a small frightened girl.

'Of course,' I say.

She curtsies again and leaves me to my ale. I sip it. It is strongly spiced. Gone too are the days when only the rich could afford the bounty of the East.

Margaret appears after a few minutes, wrapped in a large, brightly embroidered shawl. Her hair is loose and she has not had time to comb it as she may have wished. She looks very worried.

'What is the matter, Sir John? I told you all I could at the Big House today.'

I silently hand her the letter. She reads it and frowns.

'But . . . what is this supposed to be?'

Her puzzlement seems genuine, but if everything I was told was true then George Barwell would be alive and still have a face.

'It was found on Barwell's body. The Rector brought it to me this evening.'

'And you think I wrote it?'

'It is signed by you.'

Her puzzlement is slowly turning to terror. 'Somebody has signed it with my name . . .'

'You deny writing it?'

'I've never seen it before. You have to believe me.'

'So whose work is it then?'

'Somebody who wanted to lure George to the woods.'

'He would not have found this letter improbable?'

Margaret looks down at the floor. 'No,' she says.

'Had you written similar notes to him?'

'I wrote him proper letters. I didn't write this . . . disgusting thing. Somebody else wanted to meet him and . . .' She shakes her head. Whatever the intentions of the author were, deadly or amorous, she does not care to contemplate them further.

'So, we return to the question of who might know that and want George Barwell dead.'

'His wife,' says Margaret. 'Isn't that obvious?'

'She knew of your relationship with him?'

'Of course she did. Everyone did. You know that.'

'Can she read and write?' I ask. 'Most of the younger ones in the village know their letters, but some do not.'

'She'd be able to read the notes if she found one. She'd be able to write this.'

'Is this her hand then?'

She looks at me as if trying to work out what I might be prepared to believe. She gives me an honest smile. 'Yes, I think it could be, Sir John. I do think that that might be her hand. In fact, she once wrote me a note and the writing was almost identical. Truly, that is her writing. I'll swear to that if you want me to.'

I nod. When giving evidence, it is a good idea to know when to stop. What I am sure of is that she would find it convenient if I believed that her one-time friend Amy lured her own husband to his death. There might be many reasons for that.

'Had you in fact arranged to see George Barwell the day he was killed?' I ask.

Again there is a long pause. 'Yes. I admit that, Sir John. We were to meet by the well. At noon. But he didn't come. The weather was getting worse . . .'

'Or perhaps he didn't keep his appointment with you because he received this?' I say.

'Because *his wife* sent him this,' she says with great emphasis.

'It's not impossible,' I say.

'She has silk stockings too,' says Margaret Platt with a sudden fury. 'And she goes to Alice Mardike's cottage. It's not fair. Why aren't they saying that Amy Barwell is a witch? She could be a witch every bit as much as I could.'

'What did she visit Alice Mardike for?' I ask.

'Love potions. How else do you think she snared George?'

'I don't think George Barwell needed much snaring,' I say. 'Or expensive potions. He was quite economical in that respect. Do you know who else he was attached to?'

'Eliza Grice.'

'The girl who accused you of being a witch?'

'Yes. And others. Some of the married women in the village too. Some of the older ones. I think he may have got money from them.'

I pause. My mother always had an eye for an attractive young man. And she undoubtedly had money, at least after her second husband's death. I wait to see if Margaret plans to tell me anything more, but she doesn't, even though she was very willing to name Amy Barwell as a murderer and author.

'Thank you. That was helpful,' I say.

'Don't you need to ask me anything else?'

'Not at the moment,' I say.

'You should arrest Amy Barwell,' she says. 'Jumped-up little flirt.'

I nod. That's relatively mild, under the circumstances.

'I'm grateful for your advice,' I say.

I give an involuntary grunt as I rise to my feet. I have a long journey back and it will certainly be no warmer than it was before. Though the room is warm, my leg aches a lot.

'Margaret told you the truth,' says Mistress Platt as she sees me safely out into the snow. It's falling much more heavily now. Occasionally, on reflection, you realise that your wife was right. And your steward.

'She told me some of the truth,' I say. 'Even perhaps as much of the truth as she could. The question is: who knows the rest of it? Somebody certainly does.'

Mistress Platt looks at me, puzzled. The door closes behind me, but I do not hear the bolt being slid back in place. It is well oiled, after all.

*

I retrace my steps by the light of my lantern. It is slow work with the snow and the old wound in my leg. White flakes are descending, in overwhelming numbers, covering my hat and shoulders. I can no longer see my old tracks leading to the house. It is fortunate that I know my way, drunk or sober. Fewer lights now show in the cottages. People rise and go to bed early here. They would scorn to use candle wax in the profligate way we do in London.

My feet crunch through the soft new snow and the frozen crust below. The lantern lights up a small circle round me, making strange shadows whose shapes constantly change. Half-timbered walls, iron-studded doorways and diamond-shaped leaded panes emerge from the darkness and vanish back into it again. A deep silence has fallen on the village. You feel that you would hear even a pin dropped into one of the velvety, yielding drifts.

It is with relief that I see the outline of the inn, its chimneys and gables rising black against the dark grey clouds. A warm yellow glow spills out between the gaps in the shutters, providing a beacon in this trackless waste. Just the walk through the Park now. I think I can make out a light in the Big House, shining uncertainly across the snow. Somebody has left a shutter open there. Hopefully no one has yet missed me. I stop just short of Ben's establishment and adjust my cloak, trying to wrap it round my face and ears. It really is so much colder now. Even the smallest gap in my outer clothing admits an icy chill. There is a noise somewhere behind me, but the sound is dulled by my success in muffling my ears. Snow falling from a roof, probably. No matter. This is more important. My frozen fingers finally secure the cloak in place. Then I hear the noise again, much closer this time. I'm not the only one out tonight, it would seem. I shall turn and greet them, wish them a safe journey home.

Then I fall forwards, with some force, into the soft snow. I don't understand why, but I know that my head is suddenly on fire. If I allow the darkness to close in on me, then I also know I shall freeze to death here, because what I am lying on is very cold indeed. But my lantern, the glow from the inn and the distant lights of the Big House all go out together.

Chapter Fourteen

I encounter a delay

'You might have died,' says Aminta.

'But I didn't,' I say. 'As you can see.'

The bright sunlight, enhanced by the snow, floods through the bedroom window. It hurts my eyes, but it is difficult to turn my head. Somebody has made a mess of the back of it. I have examined it with my fingers as well as I can through several layers of bandage. It's bad but it could have been much worse. Why isn't it?

'You didn't die only because I came to find you in your study,' says Aminta. 'And even then only because, after that, the servants searched the house very quickly and efficiently, allowing us to conclude that you had done something stupid. And even then only because Morrell and I decided to follow some almost-erased footprints across the Park. And even then only because you were fortunate that we saw you lying there, half covered in snow as you were, close to Ben's door. Another fifteen minutes and you'd have frozen to death. In God's name, why did you need to go to the inn at all?'

I think she is not entirely pleased with me. But then, I'm not entirely pleased with myself. Not checking behind me when the slightest sound could mean danger? It's some time since I made a mistake as stupid as that.

I try to shake my head, but it hurts. I keep it very still and say: 'I didn't go to the inn at all. I went to confront Margaret Platt with the note to Barwell. I was returning and just happened to have reached the inn when somebody came up behind me.'

'Who?'

'He didn't introduce himself. Somebody who didn't like me.'

'Somebody who wanted to kill you.'

I try to shake my head again. It's no better than before. I'll have to use words again, though the sound of my voice also hurts. 'If he'd really wanted to kill me, there would have been nothing to stop him hitting me again once I was down. If he wanted to rob me, though, then he had a very poor reward. I had only a few Shillings in my pocket. And the note to Barwell.' Aminta and I look at each other. 'Check the right-hand pocket of my coat,' I say.

My coat is draped over a chair. It doesn't take long. Aminta, correctly thinking that my memory may not be good, also tries the left-hand pocket.

'Two Shillings and ninepence,' she says. 'No papers. I don't think there's much doubt why you were waylaid. Who knew the contents of the note?'

'You,' I say. 'The Rector. The Platts.'

'Well, I have an impeccable alibi, and anyway I'd have hit

you before you went out rather than after. I'm not foolish enough to traipse around in the snow unless I have to. The Rector had only just given the note to you. I doubt he'd have wanted it back quite so soon. Was there nobody else? Did you speak to anyone on your way there or back?'

'Yes, of course,' I say, remembering. 'I spoke to Ben. But I told him only that I had a new piece of evidence. It's true he guessed it concerned Margaret Platt, but even if he had read the whole thing there and then, why should he wish to deprive me of it? Nell wants Margaret convicted along with Alice – you heard what she said at the hearing. Ignoring his obligations as constable for a moment, and the possibility of a fine or imprisonment for destroying evidence, Ben would scarcely risk Nell's anger by damaging the case against the Platt girl. No, it must have been Jacob Platt. It wouldn't have been his wife or daughter.'

'His son, Adam?'

'Still away in Colchester, so he said. Platt implied his son may have been a friend of Barwell's. But if Adam Platt's been staying on the other side of the county, he'd have had no chance of getting back into the village last night. The only Platt who could have overtaken me was Jacob. Were there any footprints where you found me, other than my own?'

'We were far more concerned with getting you home alive than examining the ground for evidence,' says Aminta. 'You seem to show very little gratitude that we did or contrition at your conduct. I'll instruct the kitchen to send up only the thinnest and most unappetising gruel for the next two days.'

'I'm not staying in bed for another two hours, let alone two days. I have a hearing to conduct at ten o'clock.'

'It is already past noon. Morrell and Ben have been round the village to let people know that the hearing is adjourned because the Magistrate is an idiot. Ben's making enquiries in case anyone else was seen out yesterday evening. I told him not to reveal exactly how stupid you were, so that your attacker might still give himself away by revealing too great a knowledge of the circumstances. He's not optimistic he'll discover anything, but then Ben never is.'

I try to sit up and fail. There seems to be only one position in which my head is in any way comfortable.

'I'm sure it was Platt,' I say, subsiding carefully onto my pillow. 'He wanted to recover the evidence against Margaret. It wouldn't take much more than that to convict her. Perhaps he did see blood on her apron that afternoon and already suspected she had killed Barwell. But the Rector saw the note and so did we. It will do him no good destroying it.'

'What did Margaret Platt say when you showed it to her?'

'She said she had never seen it before. She claimed it was Amy's writing. I suppose that's what I should have expected.'

'In which case there was no need to go out at all, was there? Somebody said that to you last night. I suppose you don't remember who that was?'

Since Aminta seems to know the answer to that last question, I decide it's safe to ignore it.

'The theft of the document by her father suggests that Margaret was lying to me. That at least is useful information.'

Aminta remains unimpressed. 'Margaret had been clearly lying all day. Your expiring in the snow would have been a high price to pay for confirmation of that.'

'She also said that she'd arranged to meet Barwell the day he was killed, but that he didn't come. And that Eliza Grice and at least one unnamed married woman were closer than they should have been to Barwell. And that Amy Barwell had visited Alice Mardike, possibly to procure a love potion. She wants me to arrest Amy Barwell.'

'Arrest his grieving widow? Shall I tell Ben that's what you'd like him to do?'

'No.'

'Then it still doesn't sound as if it was worth getting hit on the head for – or not if I'm expected to nurse you for the next week. I'll leave you to sleep, but if Ben has anything to report, I'll send him up to you. You don't seem anything like as badly hurt as you deserve.'

Ben's report is brief. Nobody admits to being out last night and nobody saw anything. The last customer left the inn shortly before he saw me on my way to the Platts' house.

'If anyone should have seen the person who did it, it should have been me,' he says. 'And you lying there, within a few yards of my door and my not knowing it. You should never have ventured out on such a night, Master John. Better to have called in for some good ale, as I proposed, and gone straight home. Or you could have asked me to come with you. Jacob Platt says that you visited him and talked to Margaret.'

'I had a note that was found on Barwell's body by the Rector. She denied all knowledge of it. Whoever hit me last night took it.'

'So Lady Grey told me. Must have been Platt who attacked you. Her Ladyship also said that Margaret had arranged to meet Barwell the day he was killed. That must stand very much against her.'

'They were to meet at the well at noon. He didn't keep the appointment. She went home when he failed to appear.

Obviously Barwell's not in a position to confirm things, but that's her alibi.'

'I don't see why we should be expected to believe any of that,' says Ben. 'Lying little madam.' This last phrase might have come direct from Nell's mouth. That isn't a surprise. 'How do we know he didn't meet her as planned?' Ben continues. 'They could have met and gone up the hill together. Then she killed him. That all fits in with when you think he died. Probably that's what happened.'

Ben is still too impressed by the possession of a pair of silk stockings for my liking.

'If she really wrote the note, then she'd have been expecting to meet him in the woods, not at the well,' I say.

'She didn't write the note, then.'

'In which case, we have to ask, who did?'

'Fine, she wrote it, if that's what you think. But they changed their minds and met at the well.'

'I'm not sure that works either,' I say.

'Margaret Platt killed Barwell,' Ben says firmly. 'Used her powers as a witch to lure him up there, one way or another, then strangled him with her stocking. Her father knows that full well, so he followed you last night and took back the best piece of evidence against her. Stands to reason. Platt was always too soft with that young daughter of his. That's why she turned out as she did, consorting with Alice Mardike and I don't know what else besides.'

'Taylor wasn't soft with Amy – far from it – and it seems to me she's turned out much the same. I don't think she's told me all she knows either.'

Ben shakes his head. 'No need to wade through the snow talking to every girl in the village. Not when the truth is staring you in the face. It's your choice, Sir John, but I say hang them both – Margaret Platt and that Alice Mardike. Principal and accessory – or the other way round if you prefer. I can make the arrest tomorrow and you can keep them locked in the cellar here at the Big House, if you're agreeable, until the snow melts, then we can send them to Braintree for trial.'

Ben's opinions have changed over the past couple of days, but the one constant, other than the importance of witchcraft, is that there's no need for the constable to do much more work.

'There's no proof Alice Mardike did anything,' I say. 'And very little evidence against Margaret Platt, other than a doubtful note. Well, I hope I'll be recovered enough in a day or two to resume the enquiry. In fact, if you see Lady Grey on your way out, tell her that I'm already feeling much better. Could she instruct the kitchen not to send me any more thin gruel?'

Ben looks at me dubiously. 'I wouldn't, sir, if I were you – resume the hearings, I mean. Taylor still has a trick or two up his sleeve, so you'll need all of your wits about you, and I'm not sure you have them yet. With the snow as it is, the killer can't get away. I'd wait until you're properly well. As for the order for your supper, Lady Grey was leaving as I arrived. She said she had business in the village. The kitchen won't take instructions from me. Or anyone but the lady of the house. You may have to eat gruel until she directs otherwise. It's apparently very nutritious, according to your wife.'

'I thought I should speak to Eliza Grice,' says Aminta, sitting on the edge of the bed, still in her fur cloak. 'Now finish up that gruel, John. Cook went to a great deal of trouble to make it that strange colour and so runny.'

'I am well enough to eat normal food,' I say.

'You only think that because you've had a blow to the head,' she says. 'If you hadn't then you'd know how good gruel was for you. Especially that gruel. I almost wish I'd asked cook to make some for me, but sadly I didn't. Never mind. I'll have to make do with the succulent roast pork that you will soon be able to smell even from up here. Perhaps I should tell you about the Grices another day, when you are feeling stronger.'

'I am feeling strong enough,' I say.

'I'm not sure you will be,' she says. 'Not when I tell you what Eliza Grice had to say.'

Chapter Fifteen

Eliza Grice reveals something I really don't want to know

'I don't think that the Grices have ever forgiven you for Dickon's death,' says Aminta. 'That may have something to do with it.'

'They must know that it was entirely his fault,' I say.

'A son and a brother? It isn't surprising that they give him some benefit of the doubt, as I might have done for you, if you'd frozen to death.'

'Would you?'

'Let me see . . . Would I? No, on reflection, probably not. Going out alone on a cold dark night was so clearly your mistake. Not telling anyone was your stupidity alone. And as for allowing somebody to hit you on the back of your head, without raising even the slightest protest . . . No, sometimes you have to accept that somebody near and dear to you is a moron. The Grices are however probably more generous and charitable. They therefore regard you as Dickon's murderer.'

'When he died, I was on the ground, shot through the

shoulder. There was nothing I could do to save him, even if I'd wanted to.'

'That is not Eliza's view.'

'Eliza was a mere child when Dickon died,' I say.

'She still is, though one with designs on other women's husbands. It's a skill they teach girls early round here. She clearly hoped, up to and including the day of Barwell's death, that he would run away with her to London or some other place where they could be married without embarrassment. I'm not sure such a place exists – even Londoners don't regard bigamy as one of the seven heavenly virtues. But there we are. That was her pious hope.'

'So could she have killed Barwell herself?'

'No. Not a bit of it. The Grices swear she was at the farm the whole day. In the absence of evidence to the contrary, that is where I think she was. She was quite forthcoming with information of all sorts, so long as it discredited her friends. She was very helpful in summarising Barwell's conquests, for example. They were fewer than they might have been. Amy, of course. Margaret. Eliza herself without doubt. And an older married woman – just one, she thought.'

'Barwell wasn't here long. That's still not bad.'

'Depending on your point of view, no, it wasn't bad at all.'

'Margaret also mentioned the married woman to me,' I say.

'Yes, but what one scatty young girl says should not be taken too seriously. What two scatty young girls say, on the other hand, may just be true. Especially if they dislike each other very much and cannot have been colluding.'

'And the woman was . . .?'

'I think she genuinely didn't know. But you were right in thinking that the woman had money. And, according to Eliza, she was very, very much older than Barwell. At least thirty. And possibly with a reputation for that sort of thing.'

'My mother,' I say.

'She wouldn't confirm it but, as I've said, she may not have known for certain. Barwell could be discreet, after a fashion.'

'So you mean . . .'

'Yes, and in one of the beds in this house – quite possibly the one that you are lying in now. But probably not those sheets, so stop wriggling like that. It's still a perfectly good place for you to recover. Of course, it may just be that that's what Eliza wants us to think. The Grices really don't like you. Not a bit. Or your mother. Mistress Grice implied she practised witchcraft.'

'My mother used to say the same thing about Mistress Grice. They both made herbal remedies. And preserved fruit. My mother thought her own were better in all respects.'

'Does Alice Mardike do very much more than that?'

'No,' I say. 'She doesn't. Not very much more. But she lives in a much smaller house without a proper fireplace. That's what makes her a witch, and my mother and Mistress Grice respected inhabitants of the village who just happen to make medicines.'

'Of course, since your mother's dead, there's little anyone can do about her making medicines or indeed preserving fruit.'

'No,' I say.

But still, I think the thing I have been told is not going to go away quietly. It will sit with me, in companionable silence, and decide what to do with me in due course.

I am allowed to walk across the Park to the inn. My hat obscures the bandage. If, like Sir Felix, I had adopted this new fashion of periwigs, then one of those might conveniently have done the same thing, but I am not yet that vain.

It has not snowed since the day before last, but nor has the snow retreated. Is it thus with the rest of the world? We have no way of telling.

'It's good to see you up and about,' says Ben. 'Though your face is paler than usual.'

'They fed me gruel,' I say. 'And you didn't stop them.'

'I'm sure that Lady Grey knows best,' says Ben solemnly.

'I don't want what's best,' I say, 'I want boiled beef. I want roast pork. I want something I can actually taste in my mouth.'

'Would a slice of ham be acceptable?' asks Ben. 'Only don't tell her Ladyship I gave it to you.'

'If you don't tell her I ate it, you have a bargain,' I say.

He cuts a thick slice off the smoked ham by the fireplace and hacks me a large hunk of white bread. He puts them on the table, on a pewter platter, along with a tankard of ale. The tankard would appear to contain a full pint. Ben might yet become a law-abiding innkeeper.

'On the house,' he says.

'Feeling guilty about overcharging me in the past?' I ask.

'Feeling guilty about not seeing you lying there. If I'd just gone to the wood stack later . . .'

I see he does not protest that he's always served me as much beer as I'd paid for. It would seem I was never quite the drunkard my mother claimed I was.

'You had no way of knowing,' I say.

'No,' says Ben. He seems relieved this conversation has gone no worse than it has.

'Nobody's reported seeing Platt out the other night?' I ask.

'No. But then, everyone would have stayed indoors if they

could. I've told nobody that you were ambushed, as Lady Grey asked. Just that you had had an accident walking home in the snow. The man who did it may still give himself away. But we both know it was Platt anyway.'

'I don't understand how he crept up on me.'

'It was dark,' says Ben, 'and that's all there is to it. Don't blame yourself, Master John.'

'But you learn to listen for things . . . He would have had to follow me closely through half the village. It's not easy to walk silently in the snow. Not all that way. Remember the sound of Taylor's footsteps up on the hill that afternoon?'

'Maybe the Devil can walk quietly,' says Ben.

'I thought his feet burned the ground where he walked?' I say. 'I think I'd have heard a hiss of steam behind me.'

'So, it was Platt, then,' says Ben. 'Just like I say. You just didn't hear him for some reason. It was cold and dark. You had your cloak wrapped round your ears.'

'True,' I say.

And yet, I know I ought to have heard him. Ben has little experience of following or being followed. It's not something innkeepers need to do. And he's made up his mind. He's not going to tell me that it might have been anyone other than Platt. Or the Devil.

'Ben,' I say, 'did you ever hear any rumours about George Barwell and my mother?'

'In what way?' Ben tries to make his query sound casual and harmless.

'I mean that she might have been enamoured of him – that she might have given him money. Barwell certainly did have money once – maybe still had it – and nobody seems to know where it came from.'

'Didn't Amy Barwell say he'd made a lot of money in Cambridge?'

'Yes. I'm just not sure how much I believe her. A Cambridge college would pay the going rate for a carpenter – neither more nor less. And he'd have to pay for his lodgings there. It wouldn't leave him much money at the end of the day.'

'Who says your mother had anything to do with George Barwell anyway?' Ben asks.

'It's only that there's a rumour in the village that one of the older married ladies . . .'

Ben frowns. 'I had heard something of the sort. But I hadn't believed it. Didn't want to believe any of them would be so foolish. And certainly not your mother, may she rest in peace.'

'Eliza Grice more or less accused her of it. Can that be right?'

'Eliza Grice did?'

'Yes.'

Ben considers this, as though wondering what answer I want. He seems happy to confirm or deny any rumour as I choose. 'Well, if that's what you've heard, Sir John. They do say your mother was very close to Sir Felix too, when your father was away at the war. And at other times.'

I look at him very hard. That is a totally different rumour and a little too close to home. Ben notices the icy silence and reassesses his position.

'Not that I believe gossip of that sort, Sir John,' he adds. 'Or any of the other gossip about her, for that matter. A woman of quite exceptional virtue, your mother. Never come across anybody with virtue exactly like hers. May she rest in peace.'

I think we may be back where we started.

'Well, if you've heard nothing yourself . . .' I say. 'I just wanted to know. It can't be of any relevance to Barwell's murder.'

'No,' says Ben quickly. 'Certainly not.'

'So there's no point in bringing it up at the hearing.'

Ben nods. I'm making myself clear at last.

'Of course, Sir John. After all, it was Margaret Platt who killed him, wasn't it? Nothing to do with your late mother.'

Is Ben trying to strike a deal with me? I condemn Margaret Platt, as his wife wishes, and he won't embarrass me by accusing my mother of adultery? If that's what he thinks, he's missed my point. I simply don't want to find my mother is interfering with my investigations from beyond the grave, in a way that would undoubtedly have pleased her. My mother rarely worried what the village thought of her when she was alive – she'll mind even less now. Barwell courting her at her age. She'd probably be quite flattered if people thought that. I just don't want to have to discuss it for half an hour at the hearing. I have a horrible feeling that my mother may yet have a part to play in this.

I drain the tankard. 'I've got work to do,' I say. 'We'll resume the hearing at ten tomorrow. Unless the snow prevents us.'

'I'll let everyone know,' says Ben. 'You going home now, then? That would be very wise.'

'Yes,' I say. 'It would. If that was what I was doing.'

'I'm pleased to see that you are up and about,' says the Rector. 'I had feared that your accident might keep you in bed for some weeks. I hope that your head is not too painful after your fall.'

'I was ambushed,' I say.

I look at Bray's face but see only consternation.

'To what end?'

'The theft of a document,' I say. 'I am sorry that I have lost the letter that you so helpfully found.'

'That is very fortunate for your friend, Margaret Platt.' The Rector gives me a sideways glance. Can he actually think I lost it deliberately? There is still this mistrust, this disappointment in almost everything I do. He had been given good reason to expect better. Doubtless he would have first heard of me from my mother. She may have spoken well of me. Sometimes it happened unintentionally.

'We both saw the letter. I can remember almost exactly what it said. I shall include it in my report to the Assizes.'

'I should hope so, Sir John. I too remember the words, just in case you have forgotten any details.'

'That's kind,' I say. 'I'm infinitely obliged to you, Dr Bray. But there's one other thing I wanted to ask you about.'

'I am at your service, Sir John, as always.'

'Barwell reputedly had money that might have come from one source or might have come from another. I'm anxious to know which. So, to repeat my question at the hearing: how much did you pay him?'

'As I told you, I cannot recall. But I have nothing to hide. It ought to be in the Parish accounts book. I can look it out for you and let you know in a day or two.'

The Rector smiles and caresses the silken scarf on the table in front of him. It is embroidered with crosses and doves and other pious symbols. He thinks I should be happy with his reply. He's about to learn that I'm not.

'Is the book not here?' I ask.

'It is somewhere here certainly. In one place or another.'

'You do not know where?'

He smiles. I know that smile. It's the one I use myself.

'As I say, I shall bring it to you,' he says smoothly. 'I would not wish you to have to tarry here on such a cold day. The Rectory is never warm. It is an ancient building, unlike the Platts' splendid new residence. Allow me to consult the ledger properly and then wait upon you at the manor house, by your own blazing log fire, in the fulness of time.'

'I'll see it now,' I say.

'It may take a few minutes. Perhaps longer. I owe it to Lady Grey not to over-tire you.'

He wags a finger at me. Occasionally I have to remember I am a knight of the realm. I think this might be one of those times.

'Now,' I say.

The Rector swallows hard and waits to see if I will say anything else that might qualify my request. I don't.

'I understand that you have to do your job, Sir John, but this is an excess of zeal. Perhaps it would assist you if I explained that the ledger is church property. I think I should consult the Bishop before allowing anyone to view it—'

'Now,' I say. 'The book. On this table. Now. I think that's as clear as I need to be. Or I'll have Ben arrest you for obstructing the King's justice.'

'Since I am a clergyman, you have no right to do that.'

'On the contrary. Pursue that line and you will find that benefit of clergy is not what it was,' I say. 'Whether this is murder or witchcraft, I have a right to do whatever I need to do to track down and arrest the perpetrators. And, if I have to imprison you on the way, I'll do it. Where are your accounts, Dr Bray?'

'I do not understand why you feel you have to do this, but

very well. I hope, for everyone's sake, that you know what you are doing.' The Rector goes over to a cupboard and takes out a thin leather-bound ledger. Not so difficult to find, then. And I haven't died of the cold while waiting, after all. My wife will be so pleased. Bray opens it and consults it.

'Just give it to me,' I say. 'I want to see the entries for myself, not have you read them out.'

'Are you not prepared to accept the word of a man of God?'

'No,' I say.

He thrusts the book at me, and stands, back straight, defying me to say what I'm about to say.

'There's no record of any payment to George Barwell,' I say.

'I said it ought to be there. Not that it was. I am somewhat behindhand with my accounts. The correct amounts will be entered very soon. I would have done it, had you given me but a few minutes. If you have to include this in your report, then all you need to say is that I paid him for the work, but that the amount had not yet been entered into the book, the payment having been made only a short time before and I having been busy with other matters, as you know well I have. Say that and nobody will question your zeal or my good intentions.'

I run my finger down the column of figures. 'These are well-kept accounts, Dr Bray. Clear – and almost up to date. I congratulate you. According to this record, there would have been ten Pounds, four Shillings and ten pence to your credit before the payment to Barwell. Let us examine your strong box together and see what it contains. That should reveal precisely what you paid, should it not?'

'There's no need to do that,' he says. 'No need at all, Sir John.'

'Why, is the chest empty?'

'No, it contains exactly ten Pounds, four Shillings and ten pence. Let me tell you the truth, Sir John . . .' Bray looks at me as if weighing up exactly which truth to tell. 'You see, I paid Barwell myself. Out of my own pocket. I told you that, in all honesty, the work did not need doing. I could scarcely charge the church – use the hard-won pennies that my parishioners put into the collection plate on Sunday. I gave him the money myself, out of my own . . . earthly treasure. Building up, perhaps, in exchange, some treasure in heaven. Presumptuous of me, perhaps, but you cannot doubt my good intentions. I hope that is sufficient explanation for you?' The Rector smiles at me again, but I do not smile back.

'How much?' I ask.

'I keep no records of my own,' he says. 'The Bible instructs us—'

'A lot?' I ask.

'Enough,' he says. 'Exactly enough. And no more. Surely you understand me now, Sir John?' He raises an eyebrow.

'No,' I say. 'I don't. So why don't you explain what you mean?'

'If you truly do not understand . . . Then there is nothing more I have to say to you, Sir John. I paid him myself. I do not remember how much; nor, in giving alms, is it right that I should remember or that I should be questioned further on an act of charity. That should be sufficient for any report that you need to write. Perhaps I was misinformed about you, Sir John, on your character and your loyalties. Perhaps I have been placed in a false position as a result.'

Well, that's what my mother was best at.

'Perhaps you have,' I say.

I adjust the hat on my head, being careful of the freshly changed bandage, and fasten my cloak.

'What do you call that silken scarf on the table there?' I ask.

'This? A maniple,' he says. 'Of course,' I say. 'That's what a maniple looks like. Thank you. We never had them at Cambridge. Not in my time there. But I can see they might be useful. It's surprising what you can learn in a short conversation.'

'And you think Barwell was blackmailing the Rector?' asks Aminta.

'Why else would he give him money, out of his own purse, for work that did not need doing?' I reply.

'It is perfectly possible that it may be Christian charity,' says Sir Felix. 'I am told that such things still happen.'

'He said he had paid Barwell *enough*,' I say. 'And he seemed to think I should understand what he meant. He expected me to be more sympathetic than I am. He expected me to accept his word, however improbable. I don't know what my mother said to him, but it has not helped.'

Increasingly my mother's shadow hangs over this. She, like Bray, seems to have been close to Barwell. She, like Bray, seems to have given him money. Is there something that she might have revealed to me, had she lived? Would it have explained why Bray clearly expects more from me than I have done?

'I doubt your mother said much to him at all,' says Sir Felix. 'Other than to pass the time of day after Matins.'

'But she would have appointed him to his post,' I say.

Sir Felix shakes his head. 'She had no right of appointment – not now. The Wests did indeed possess the advowson in the distant past. So did the Cliffords before the war. But it was one of many things that I had to relinquish. The manor was sold to the Colonel, your stepfather. But the advowson went elsewhere.'

'Who purchased it?'

'Nobody. The state confiscated it. Cromwell wanted to ensure that compliant ministers were appointed in Clavershall West, and in many other places, I think. The right to appoint rectors here passed to the Crown at the Restoration. His Majesty has shown no sign of wishing to give it up, any more than he has shown signs of wishing to reimburse those of us who ruined themselves supporting his father.'

'So, Bray was appointed directly by the King?'

'Yes. Nominally. But you know His Majesty at least as well as I do. He'll scratch his own dog under the chin if it needs doing, but dull tasks such as allocating vacant parishes to deserving clergymen would be delegated to his ministers or to his mistresses.'

'Which ones?'

'I don't know who would have dealt with this appointment. Buckingham? My distant cousin, Sir Thomas Clifford? Lady Castlemaine? Your very good friend Lord Arlington? Probably whoever had some kinsman or client in need of a well-paid position. This is not the richest parish in the country but it is not the poorest either. It would have been of interest even to the most gentlemanly of clerics.'

'Bray is the sort of man the King would approve of.'

'And many of his ministers are of the same opinion, religiously speaking. Clifford and Arlington especially. It is not surprising that a parish where the Crown has the right to appoint should end up with somebody like Bray.'

'It would seem that Bray has friends in high places, then.'

'Acquaintances in high places, certainly,' says Sir Felix. 'Whether they like him is another matter. This would also be a good place to send somebody you didn't much want to see again.'

'Does anyone know where Bray came from?' Aminta asks.

'Now I think about it, I don't think we do,' says Sir Felix. 'Most clergymen will talk a great deal about their previous parish, if only to compare their new one unfavourably with it. But I'm not sure Bray has ever told me where he was before this. I think your mother may have told me he was somebody's chaplain or secretary. She was rather vague about it. I don't think he was a parish priest anyway. One or two people have told me that, for his first few months, he conducted services in a way that suggested he had not done it for some time.'

'A teaching post at one of the universities, perhaps?' I say. 'He claims to hold the degree of Doctor of Divinity from one of them or the other.'

'He certainly never encouraged me to enquire about his past,' says Sir Felix, 'though I did once catch him understanding French a little too well. That too may or may not be significant.'

'Many high church clergy would have fled overseas during the rule of Parliament,' says Aminta. 'Just as we did. Whether he lived in Paris or Bruges or Brussels, he would have learned some French.'

'And perhaps picked up some of the ways of the local clergy,' I say. 'Silk vestments, for example. The means of murder may not have been a stocking after all. He may have actually had the weapon on the table beside him when I spoke to him.'

'So, you think that Barwell blackmailed Bray and that Bray strangled him with what . . . a silk scarf?' says Sir Felix.

'It's called a maniple,' I say.

'It's called a piece of Popish nonsense,' Sir Felix says. 'Far too much of it around these days. But Barwell was lured to the woods by a letter from Margaret Platt?'

'A letter that Bray himself gave me,' says Aminta.

'Exactly,' I say. 'A letter that condemns Margaret Platt and that Bray had just, rather conveniently, discovered. The shepherds reported finding nothing of the sort. Bray may of course have lured Barwell there in some other way entirely, writing the letter on Margaret's behalf only when he saw that it might be needed and giving it to us as soon as the ink was dry on the paper.'

'Bray is also very anxious that Alice Mardike is found guilty,' says Aminta.

'Yes,' I say, 'he is. His fervent belief in witches, like the discovery of the letter, is just a little too convenient to be true. He'd like somebody – anybody – hanged for the murder and no further questions asked – least of all questions about his payments to Barwell.'

'But Bray is a friend of Lord Arlington or some other minister?' says Sir Felix. 'He could appeal to them if Barwell was threatening him.'

'I'm not sure. Somebody Arlington genuinely wished to help would become Chaplain to the King or Archdeacon of Winchester, not the Rector of a small, if prosperous, parish in North Essex. Bray's credit with Arlington, if that's who it was, may have already run out.'

'It's a pity that your mother isn't here to recount what she knew about Dr Bray,' says Aminta. 'She'd have got him to tell her all of the things we're now speculating about. She had a way of doing that. Which sadly you don't seem to.'

I nod. A high church clergyman with an obscure past and a desire to hide himself away in the country. A good-looking young carpenter who was turning the heads of all the girls in the village. Unaccountable payments from the clergyman to the carpenter for doing work that did not need to be done. What part of that would not have interested my mother?

And yet, if Sir Felix is right, she could have played no active role in bringing Dr Bray here. After all, she did not know Arlington or any other minister. She knew Arlington's predecessor, John Thurloe, of course – at least a little. And she knew Thurloe's deputy, Samuel Morland, much better. Samuel Morland, who never did things the straightforward way if there was a crooked way available and had no principles other than his own advancement. Samuel Morland, who was still working for Arlington when I last heard of him. Yes, she knew Morland well. It's a tenuous link, but the fact there is any link at all is deeply suspicious.

'But you don't think your mother is involved in this, surely?' asks Sir Felix.

'No,' I say. 'She'd have loved it, but she's dead.'

Chapter Sixteen

I discuss religion with the only Quaker in the village

It is a bright, diamond-clear morning, with Christmas almost close enough to touch it. There has been no further fall overnight. The snow is still dazzling white but has acquired everywhere a thin, brittle crust. A network of tracks has appeared, where villagers have ventured out, to draw water from the cold but unfrozen depths of the well or buy warm, frothy milk and stiff slabs of butter from the farms. My cob makes easy work of it, adding his own horseshoe-shaped indentations to those that we are following.

I stop outside the blacksmith's. If-Christ-had-not-died-for-thee-thou-hadst-been-damned Davies, fortunately also known as Ifnot, has been up and about for at least an hour. December days possess four and twenty hours, just like their cousins in June, but everyone is aware that the minutes of daylight in which money can be made are scarce. He sees my approaching figure and his heavy hammer ceases to ring on the anvil. He shields his eyes against the low sun with his hand, then smiles and raises the hand in greeting.

'Good day to thee, friend John,' he says.

I dismount and offer up my hand to his vice-like welcome. I do not wince, as I once would have done. I think his grip is no less powerful than it was, but I have become more used to pain. A neighbourly greeting from Ifnot is better than being shot through the shoulder at close range. Almost.

'Good morning, Ifnot,' I say. 'How's business?'

'Quiet,' he says. 'Nobody is out riding, except thee, and horses that don't leave the stable don't lose shoes. Does thy cob need shoeing?'

'All four intact,' I say. 'He's as sure-footed as any creature in the village. I'm here because I'd hoped you might be able to tell me a little about the new Rector.'

'The Rector? Thou knowest that I do not frequent steeple houses.'

Ifnot walks miles every Sunday to neighbouring villages and hamlets so that he can worship with others who will address him in the correct and traditional second person singular. There aren't many Quakers in this part of Essex. He's the only one in the village.

'But you know him?' I ask. 'Even if you don't attend St Peter's . . . steeple house.'

'Of course. We've spoken.'

'And what is your view of him?'

'He lacks the inward stillness that is required if we are to know God.'

'He has chosen the wrong vocation then?'

'That is not for me to say. He is thine own minister, friend John, not mine. And he is learned, after his fashion.'

'After his fashion? What do you mean by that, Ifnot?'

'I mean that he is a Doctor of Divinity but, when I quoted to him from the Psalms, he seemed ignorant of the origin of my words.'

'He'd forgotten?'

'Perhaps. It would certainly be strange if he'd never read them at all.'

'He certainly knows St Paul,' I say. 'Though perhaps not Exodus,' I add, thinking of his error concerning the injunction against witches.

'Just so. Some parts of the Bible are familiar to him but not others.'

'That would be odd in a clergyman. After all, every service includes a Psalm.'

Of course, if Sir Felix is right then Dr Bray may not have conducted many services immediately prior to coming here.

'So I am told,' says Ifnot. 'But silence is better if thou wishest to hear God speak unto thee.'

I nod. I too have found silence useful. Sitting quietly in a dark corner of an inn, wrapped in my cloak, I have heard much that proved useful both to me and to Lord Arlington. Arlington's never asked me to spy on God, so I can't say whether Ifnot's method works for that.

'Your smithy is close to the road, Ifnot. You must see most people who pass by.'

'Some. There is also a footpath that runs behind my house. Others go by that route. The way is rough, but it is passable for one who has time to spare and who does not wish to be seen on the highway. Art thou asking me, friend John, if I saw Dr Bray on the road the day that Barwell was killed?'

'It would be helpful to know if you had.'

'Yes, I did see him. He greeted me. It was about midday. He was going that way.'

Ifnot indicates the road to the woods. 'But he wasn't skulking on the back path,' he adds.

'You didn't mention any of that before,' I say.

'Thou didst not ask before. And if he was intent on evil deeds, I doubt he would have taken such a well-observed path when a more obscure one was available to him. Thou canst not think that the Rector would countenance murder?'

I stand there. We both listen to the silence for a while. If God speaks, I do not hear him. Perhaps God thinks it's wiser to say nothing for the moment.

'Do you know anything of Dr Bray's past?' I ask.

'No, he spoke very little of that. But I think that he knows London and that he has mixed with the court there. Knights, such as thyself. Lords and ladies. Generals at land and sea.'

'Did he mention any names?' I ask.

'Lord Arlington,' says Ifnot.

'Did he seem to know him well?'

'I believe so,' says Ifnot. 'Rarely have I heard a man of God utter such foul oaths against anyone.'

'I have told everyone to be present by ten of the clock,' says Ben. There are some parts of the job of constable that he enjoys, and issuing instructions is one of them. It makes a change from taking orders from everyone else. And trade is slack at this time of the morning, so he has not lost much money by doing it. Indeed, some witnesses may wish to fortify themselves at his establishment before undertaking the short walk across the Park.

I am back in my study at the Big House and almost warm

again after my visit to the blacksmith. My snowy boots have been whisked away by Morrell for cleaning. I have been doing a lot of thinking.

'How well do you know the Rector, Ben?' I ask.

'I go to church as often as the Law requires,' Ben says defensively.

As constable, he is an office holder under the Crown and therefore, arguably, required to take communion once a year. It is one of His Majesty's more pious Acts of Parliament. It may be my duty to enforce it. I have another eleven months to find out.

'Did you know he was paying money to George Barwell?' I ask.

'I do now.'

'Have you actually noticed any of the work that he did?'

'I'll look next time I go.'

'The work, such as it was, was unnecessary. Bray paid Barwell out of his own pocket. I think Barwell was blackmailing Dr Bray.'

'About what?' asks Ben.

'Something in his past. Perhaps something to do with why he was appointed here.'

'So what are you saying then? The Rector killed Barwell?' Ben laughs, then sees that I am serious. 'That isn't possible. A Doctor of Divinity. A man of the cloth.'

'He was seen on the road to the woods at midday. Not many people were out then.'

'Have you asked him why he was there?'

'Not yet.'

'I'm sure he'll have a good reason.'

'He had a good reason for wanting Barwell dead, if he was

being blackmailed by him. And Dr Bray seems to be well acquainted with Lord Arlington.'

'So are you,' says Ben.

'That's what I mean,' I say.

'Look, Sir John, may I give you some advice?'

'If you must.'

'Everybody in the village knows it was the witches that did it. But you seem to want to accuse Taylor and Jacob Platt and now the Rector. They can't all have done it, can they? And what if one of them did? Barwell won't be missed. Not by me and not by most sensible people here. The easiest thing is that we just commit Alice Mardike to the Assizes and let the wise and learned judges there decide what to do about it. What the judges do needn't be on your conscience, or mine. Nobody should blame us for the acts of a judge and jury in Chelmsford or Braintree, should they? And nobody in the village *will* blame you, I can promise you that. But Taylor's got friends. So's Platt. And I can't imagine what will happen if you go accusing the Rector, especially if he does know Lord Arlington. Listen to the evidence this morning, then just say you'll commit Alice Mardike. You don't even have to report Margaret Platt if you don't want to. Just Mardike. Who'll object to that, eh?'

Nobody, I think. Not even Alice Mardike, if it will save Mistress Platt's young neck. I stare at the fire in silence for a while. Yes, why not just commit her for trial by the County Court and then sit back and enjoy Christmas with my family and loyal tenants? It's what any prudent Justice of the Peace would do.

'Sorry, Ben,' I say. 'It isn't as easy as that. I'll see you here at ten o'clock. Then maybe we'll begin to make some progress.'

Chapter Seventeen

I reconvene a hearing

The dining room is even more packed than before. The roads, at least within the village, are a little clearer now and word has spread that the Big House offers good entertainment on a cold day. Even the farm labourers, it would seem, have been given the day off, though not Taylor's shepherds, as far as I can see.

Everyone rises as I enter the room, preceded by Ben. I leave them standing, just for a moment, to remind them all of the gravity of the proceedings, then I bid them all sit. Just as I do so, Taylor enters. He has a young girl with him. He is frowning, she is sulking. I think they may have had words outside the house, though it is difficult to see why she thought any protest of hers would change Taylor's mind on anything. He sends her to the back of the room, while he makes for a large and comfortable seat that has been reserved for him in the front row. He is a person of importance, it would appear. Ben, standing by the door, shows no surprise that

Taylor has decided to bring a randomly chosen village girl with him. Perhaps Taylor had warned him in advance. I have to remember that Ben is the loyal servant of many masters. Though he is my constable, he is also the man who sells ale to almost everyone present. And next year he won't be constable.

'I'm sorry, Sir John,' Taylor says, removing his hat. 'I was delayed by . . . circumstances. We are all present now – all of us who need to be.'

'You have missed nothing, Mr Taylor,' I say. 'In any case, I hope that I shall not have to delay you or anyone else for very long. We have already heard a great deal of important evidence. I have only one or two people left whom I wish to question. Mr Platt, Mr Davies, the blacksmith and I may need to recall Dr Bray.'

This last causes a few puzzled looks, not least from Bray himself. He shifts uncomfortably in his seat.

'We'd also like you to hear what Jane Ruggles has to tell you,' says Taylor.

Jane Ruggles is presumably the girl that Taylor is storing at the back of the room. The Ruggles are a large family, and I am not sure whose daughter she is.

'*We?*' I say. 'Who are you including in that?'

'The village,' says Taylor.

'You speak on behalf of the whole village now, Mr Taylor? That is very thoughtful of you,' I say.

'I speak on behalf of those who wish to see justice done.'

'I would include myself in that group and I do not remember your consulting me.'

'I never doubted your support, Sir John. I have simply spoken to those I need to speak to. And what we say is that the girl must be heard.'

For a moment we look at each other. I could simply refuse to let her speak. But to what end? The point of this hearing is to show that I have taken all the depositions that I need to take. Perhaps her evidence will be something other than improbable accusations that Alice Mardike has bewitched her, but I am not optimistic. 'Very well. So long as she is brief and what she has to tell us relates strictly to the matter in hand.'

'You'll find it relates well enough,' says Taylor.

'Then I'll hear her now, Mr Taylor,' I say. 'Come and stand over here, Jane.'

Jane Ruggles is pushed, with some force, to the front of the room. She stands there resentfully, snub-nosed and freckled. She looks like any of the younger village girls, wearing what was probably once her elder sister's dress, a dull red beneath the layer of rural grime. As with most of the girls and women here this morning, the lower third of her skirt is unavoidably sodden from dragging it through the melting snow. Winter is somehow kinder to men. There is a clean white scarf covering her untidy hair – an attempt perhaps to make her a little more presentable and believable. Her right index finger is cleaning out her nose prior to speaking.

'What do you have to tell us, Jane?' I ask.

'I don't know,' she says, flicking something onto my carpet.

'Tell her about the toad,' says Taylor.

The voice is one of command, but Taylor is not her mother or father. She doesn't even turn to look at him.

'What about the toad?' she demands, examining the tip of her cleaning finger. She seems happy with the results of her labours but wipes it on her skirt just to make sure.

'Tell the Magistrate what you saw Alice Mardike do with it,' says Taylor. He speaks softly but not in a way that can safely be ignored. Even Jane must be able to see that. 'The orders she gave to it. Then what it did. You remember that, don't you, girl?'

'This is Jane's evidence,' I say to Taylor, 'not yours. If she has anything to say, I'd like it from her, please.'

Jane decides she wishes to get this over with and to resume her place out of sight at the back of the room. 'I saw Alice Mardike,' she says, 'with an old toad.'

'And what did she do with it?' I ask

'She had it in a jar. Then she opened the jar and let it out into her garden. She spoke to it. Then it hopped off down the lane.'

'Sending her familiar into the village to do her evil work,' says Taylor. 'Only witches can command animals in that way. Consult your books, Sir John. What she did was contrary to the King's Law.'

'I would remind you again, Mr Taylor, that it is Jane giving evidence,' I say. 'And I'll consult my books when I need to. Do you have anything else to say, Jane?'

'No, sir.'

'Then you may return to your place,' I say. I look at Taylor. 'Do you wish to waste my time in any other way, Mr Taylor? We have all day, after all.'

'You've just heard evidence that Mardike is a witch,' he says. 'Keeping a familiar is—'

'Contrary to the King's Law. Yes, I think we've agreed that is the case. And I can apparently find it set out in my books, should I retain any doubts on the matter. Very well. Alice Mardike, you heard Jane: did you release a toad into your garden?'

'Yes,' she says.

'Why?'

'Didn't need it any more.'

'Did you speak to it?'

'Yes. I told it to piss off before I put it in the pot along with the nettles. Best advice that toad ever had.'

'Was it your familiar? Did it possess any magic powers? Has it ever said anything to you of any significance?'

'No, it was a toad.'

'Then I think we have cleared that matter up,' I say.

'Are you letting her get away with that?' Taylor demands.

'Yes, I believe I am,' I say. 'Now perhaps we can turn to more important matters.'

'I can't see who else you have left to take evidence from,' he says.

'You,' I say. 'Perhaps you would be kind enough to stand, Mr Taylor. I have one or two questions.'

'I assume I am no more under oath than the others?' Taylor says. Now it comes to it, he is not one bit happier giving evidence than Jane Ruggles was.

'You assume correctly. But I still expect the truth from you, as from everyone.'

I pause and observe Taylor. It's one of the things I can do. It's my hearing and nobody can make me proceed faster than I wish. There's a bead of sweat on Taylor's forehead. He's worried about something. Of course, I've no idea why, but he doesn't know that. Let's allow him to worry if he wants to. I smile. He doesn't smile back.

'Now, Mr Taylor, when did George Barwell arrive in the village?'

'When? I'm not sure. About a year ago – last winter.'

'And where did he come from?'

'He was a Suffolk man. He'd been in Cambridge lately. Don't you know that already?'

'I do indeed. But thank you anyway. Had he ever lived in London?'

'Yes, he had once.'

'What work did he do there?'

'He had a commission from one of the foreign ambassadors. A big job. Several weeks.'

I note this on the paper in front of me.

'Anywhere else?'

'He was in Derbyshire for a while working on one of the great houses there. As a carpenter he travelled all over the country.'

My quill hovers above the paper. I do not record this. It is all very interesting, but not leading anywhere much.

'What was his religion?' I ask.

'The normal one. Same as you or me.'

'Did he attend church?'

'No more than he had to.'

I pause again, then write: 'Devout Anglican'. There must be something in Barwell's past to link him to the Rector. What is it?

'Was he a good son-in-law?' I ask.

'I've no sons, Sir John. My wife died before we could have any more children. I'd hoped Amy would marry a man capable of taking over from me. When Barwell first arrived here, he knew nothing about farming. I've taught Amy all I could – she understands the workings of the farm and how to load and fire a gun. She's stronger than she looks. I'd have taught Barwell the same, sooner or later. Amy deserved that at least.'

Yes, I think that's true. Taylor would have imposed his

will on Barwell. Barwell would have been made what Taylor wished him to be – a competent sheep farmer, capable of doing his accounts, chastising the hired men and acting as church warden. In the fullness of time he would have become a more circumspect, if not entirely faithful, husband. There would have been no point in killing him. Not yet. After all, Taylor was married for some time before his wife fell down the stairs. He's a patient man.

'Did he leave your daughter well provided for?'

'I have enough money, God be praised, that there was no need to worry about that.'

'But did he?'

Taylor now pauses. This is his own business and there is no reason why the village should know about it. 'He had about two hundred Pounds in gold,' he says.

There is a collective gasp within the room. Silver is the usual currency within the village and it would take over ten years for most of them to earn two hundred Pounds. Even for a rector in a highly desirable parish it would represent more than a twelve-month's income. Barwell could afford to drink at the inn, whatever Ben thinks.

'That's a lot of money for a carpenter to have in his purse,' I say. 'Cambridge colleges must pay well.'

'I've no idea. Maybe the job for the Ambassador was profitable.'

'Which ambassador was it?'

'How should I know that? I don't mix with ambassadors.'

There are nods around the room. They don't usually mix with ambassadors either.

'Did your son-in-law say how much he had been paid for his work at the church?'

'He never spoke of it,' Taylor says. 'Look, Sir John, I don't know where his money came from. But he left Amy well enough provided for. That's all that matters.'

'Thank you, Mr Taylor,' I say. 'I'd like to call Jacob Platt next.'

'Just a couple of questions for you, Mr Platt,' I say. 'I called on you the other day and showed you a letter, purporting to come from your daughter. Can you remember what it said?'

Platt swallows hard. He'd rather not say. 'It asked George Barwell to meet her at the woods.'

This produces the biggest response of the day – greater than for George Barwell's gold, greater even than the village's collective denial that they knew any ambassadors. One or two of the women experiment with calling Margaret a strumpet and a hussy, but surely this goes beyond even that? At last we have proof of one of the witches' guilt.

I demand silence and am pleased to find that I get it. 'And do you believe that the letter actually came from her, Mr Platt? Was it her hand?'

Platt shakes his head. 'No,' he says. 'I should know my own daughter's writing, and I do not believe that it was.'

There is a sigh of disappointment within the room. Just for a moment they had thought there might be a hanging before dinnertime.

'Do you know where the letter is now?' I ask.

He shows genuine puzzlement. 'You took it away with you,' he says.

I think there is little point in asking him whether he struck me over the head to recover it. Ben has clearly followed, in making enquiries, my order not to mention the theft of the letter. That's a pleasant surprise. Platt genuinely believes I still have it, though somebody in the room knows better.

'Thank you,' I say. 'I should like to hear Mr Davies now.'

'I cannot swear an oath, friend John,' he says. 'Thou knowest that.'

'I demand it no more of you than the others,' I say. 'And we can, I think, finally abandon our discussion of witches. On the day of the killing, where were you, Mr Davies?'

'In my smithy, as always except on the Lord's Day.'

'And your place at the anvil commands a good view of the road to Saffron Walden?'

'Yes.'

'And hence of the road to the woods on the hill?'

'Yes.'

'Were there many travellers that day?'

'No, the weather was bad. I saw only one person pass the smithy that morning.'

'And who was that?' I ask.

'The Rector,' he says. 'Dr Bray.'

There is a gasp from almost everyone. This is the best yet. Why didn't my predecessors as Lord of the Manor arrange Christmas entertainments of this sort? Some people are having to explain it to others amid the din, but most have turned to look at the Rector. He is not happy. And I am about to recall him to give evidence.

Dr Bray's mouth is set defiantly, but his eyes show fear. Everyone knows exactly why I am asking a few more questions. 'There is a perfectly simple explanation—' he begins.

I hold up my hand. He'll answer the questions in the order

I ask them. 'I just want you to confirm one or two things you told me yesterday,' I say.

'If you must.'

'That's right, Dr Bray. I must. You said that you paid Barwell from your own pocket for his work on the church.'

'I said that I did it out of charity.'

'It seems that he was richer than most people here. You've heard evidence he had two hundred Pounds when he died.'

'I had no way of knowing that. I believed him to be poor.'

As did we all. I'd placed too much reliance on Ben's evidence that Barwell could no longer afford ale. Perhaps he had other reasons for avoiding the village constable.

'Have you yet recalled how much you paid him?' I ask. 'Could it have been as much as two hundred Pounds?'

'Of course not.'

'So, how much?'

'But when thou doest alms, let not thy left hand know what thy right hand doeth,' says Bray. 'St Matthew, Chapter six, verse three.'

'Was it alms? Or did Barwell oblige you to pay him?'

'I have no idea what you mean,' says Bray. He tries to say more, but I think his mouth is dry.

'Was he blackmailing you?' I ask.

'I must protest,' says Taylor, from his seat. 'Dr Bray stands accused of nothing. You can't possibly believe that a clergyman murdered my son-in-law. Why then should he be made to answer that question? It is wrong that you, as Lord of the Manor, should be so disrespectful to the Rector of your own Parish. This is not the way things should be done. Not here in Essex.'

'This is my hearing and my witness,' I say. 'I'll decide what questions are and are not appropriate. And I want an answer from you, Dr Bray.'

'I have given it already,' says Bray. 'I decline to respond to any questions relating to my own charity.'

'Very well. I shall have to draw my own conclusions, as will the County Court. Let us turn to the question you wished to answer earlier. You heard Mr Davies give evidence that he saw you on your way to the woods on the day that George Barwell was killed. Is that true?'

'Yes,' he says.

'Did you go there to meet Barwell?'

'Yes . . . no.' Bray may or may not have killed Barwell, but he would certainly like to kill me. 'You are right that I wished to talk to him that day. I was in the village, visiting the sick. I saw him pass by. As soon as I could, I followed on the same road, but the snow was getting worse and I turned back, well before the woods. I was wearing only ordinary shoes – not boots – the going was difficult and my stockings were getting wet. I felt there might be a better occasion to speak to him.'

'It must have been an important matter for you to go so far as you say you did.'

'I went only a short way beyond the smithy.'

'It's a pity that nobody saw you coming back,' I say.

'I—' he says.

There is a cough somewhere in the crowd. Bray pauses as if distracted. He looks behind him.

'You were about to say that somebody *did* see you?' I ask.

'No,' he says. 'I don't think they did, but—'

'Well,' says Ben, from his position by the door. 'I for one

believe the Rector. He went out on the road and returned almost at once. If nobody saw him return, what does that signify? Mr Davies must have to leave the anvil from time to time to work the bellows or fetch charcoal. And in the snow, anyone might pass by silently enough.'

'Thank you, Ben,' I say. 'I agree that anyone might have gone through the village unseen and unheard that day. But again, I am taking evidence from Dr Bray and only Dr Bray. I'd be grateful if you would allow me to do that.'

'It's what I think though,' says Ben.

'I don't need your advice, Ben.'

'It's what everybody thinks.'

'If I need you to give evidence, then I'll ask for it,' I say. 'And if I need to know what everyone thinks, then I'll ask them.'

'You know best, Sir John,' he says.

Well, I've heard Ben say that before. I turn back to Bray. What was I going to ask him next?

'Dr Bray,' I say, 'you'll recall finding the letter, purporting to come from Margaret Platt, in one of Barwell's pockets?'

'Yes, I gave it to you. Then you lost it, Sir John. Under circumstances that you seem unwilling to reveal in their entirety.'

Well, I can't deny that. I scan the room to see if anyone seems to understand what Bray means. Ben does the same. But the puzzlement on people's faces suggests that my attacker is either absent or more than usually skilled at deception.

'Mr Platt says that it was not her writing,' I say.

'If she didn't write it, who did?' Bray asks. 'You are not suggesting that it was my hand?'

'Since it is lost, we'll never be able to tell,' I say.

Taylor is on his feet. 'This is preposterous, Sir John. Are you saying that the Rector killed Barwell, then forged the letter, gave it to you and finally attacked you to steal it back again?'

They all look at the Rector, a slight figure in a black suit and white linen bands, smiling benignly. But I've been shot at by less likely killers.

'I hadn't yet suggested that,' I say, 'but it has clearly occurred to you, Mr Taylor.'

'You can't do this, Sir John. You've as good as accused me and Dr Bray of murder. You've reprimanded your constable without just cause, when he was merely trying to tell you what everyone here was thinking. You may represent the King, but you do that because it is the custom here and it is one we respect. It is also custom for the Lord of the Manor to respect the authority of the Rector and the constable in their own domains. We've given you the evidence that Alice Mardike is a witch. She brews potions. She keeps familiars and gives them orders. She cursed Nell Bowman. She cursed my son-in-law. She *says* she is a witch. And when we threw her in the water, she swam. You saw her. How much more evidence are you going to ignore?'

It's a good question. But before I can reply there's a voice from amongst the mass of people in front of me.

'Of course he'll ignore it. His mother was a witch!'

Chapter Eighteen

I adjourn a hearing

I turn and look at Mistress Grice. She is standing, pointing at me, her face red with fury.

'His mother was a witch,' she repeats. 'That's why he's in league with them.'

'Mardike's wearing one of his mother's best cloaks,' says somebody else. 'She had it made twenty years ago. I remember it well. Now Mardike's got it.'

After that, there is complete silence in the room. Nobody yet is supporting Mistress Grice. But then nobody is supporting me either. It's rather like the other night. But this time they're all in my dining room and the pistols have been stored away.

'She only made potions,' says Harry Hardy. 'That's not witchcraft. Gave them away free, too. Most of you are the better for having taken them.'

'I never did,' says Jacob Platt.

'Nor me,' says somebody else.

Henry's helpful intervention does not seem to have

worked in my favour. Everyone seems anxious to distance themselves from my mother in what was until recently her own dining room.

'She was no witch.'

Everyone turns to Alice Mardike.

'She was no witch,' Alice Mardike repeats. 'And if I'm supposed to be a witch then I ought to know one. Her cures were every bit as good as mine, but that wasn't witchcraft. That was ancient country lore, that was. And what else is she supposed to have done apart from cure your aches and pains? Any of you ever see her flying on a broomstick? Any of you see her talking to a toad?'

'She had a cat,' somebody says. He seems to realise this is not particularly damning. He looks round to see if anyone has anything better.

'Two cats,' says somebody else. 'And a dog.'

Well, that's slightly more convincing.

'Listen,' says Alice. 'I am wearing her cloak and very grateful I am for it too. None of you ever offered me something warm to wear. But every one of you, more or less, benefited from his mother's kindness and generosity. She didn't always have money to spare, but when she did she gave it freely enough, especially after she married the Colonel. And she cared for all of you, as Sir John does now, if you'd only let him do his job. I may be an old witch, but at least I don't show the ingratitude that you all do, it would seem. You should be ashamed of yourselves.'

I think they are, on reflection, deeply ashamed and they show it by shouting insults at Alice. Every variant of 'witch' and 'whore' is exploited in colourful detail.

I bang the table and there is silence again, but it is the sullen, temporary silence of a reprimanded child.

'I have said that I shall ensure that justice is done, but it will be done strictly according to the Law,' I say. 'If anyone wishes to accuse my mother of witchcraft it is a separate matter to be heard by another magistrate at another time. I gave Mistress Mardike the cloak, because frankly she needed it after you'd made her other clothes soaking wet. So, don't blame me or her for that. That is your doing. And I can still have everyone who was at the millpond charged with assault if I wish.'

Ben has been sniffing the air to see which way this will go. He decides it is safe to stand by me. 'You've all bought medicines from Alice Mardike,' he says. 'You know you have. And you're still buying. When I took her back the other day there was half a crown on the table for medicine that somebody had taken while she was out. And they'd overpaid her.'

'But we were all here,' says Harry Hardy. 'None of us could have left money then. Or rather we were almost all here. Just one or two people from outside the village were not here . . . and Mr Taylor's shepherds . . . and some of Sir John's servants.'

Suddenly everyone is looking very thoughtful and Ben turns to me open-mouthed. We both know what he's done, and his fixed gaze is now clarifying matters for those who are slow on the uptake.

'Is your constable giving evidence that you purchased potions from Mistress Mardike?' Taylor demands.

'No—' says Alice.

'You may all wish to lie about buying from Mistress Mardike,' I say, 'but I have no intention of following your lead. Yes, I have bought cough syrup from her. I make no apologies to anyone for doing so.'

'You gave her money?' says Taylor. 'While you were investigating the murder? And you overpaid her? The very thing you have criticised the Rector for doing over the church repairs? If so, you are unfit to conduct this enquiry. You should stand down immediately and let somebody else take over.'

'Thank you for your opinion,' I say, 'but I am appointed by the King and only the King can oblige me to stand down. I have no idea who might take over. You have me as your Magistrate a while longer.'

'Let's see what other people think of that,' says Taylor.

'Well, what I think is this,' says Aminta, from her seat behind me. 'You should all listen to my husband. You have no authority in the matter – none of you. And especially you, Mr Taylor, since you are as likely to have killed George Barwell as anyone. These snows will not last for ever. Sooner or later this village will be part of the wider world again. Then you will have to answer for your actions.'

'And if we choose not to fall into line and do as you say?' asks Taylor.

'Then you'll be safe enough, Mr Taylor, since you own the freehold to your farm. Of course, many of those whom you claim to speak for are copyholders, without your security of tenure. They can be evicted from their homes with much greater ease.'

The crowd, which had been enjoying the exchange up to this point, suddenly starts to look concerned.

'You're not saying you'd turn everyone out of their houses if they don't do as you say?'

'As you've pointed out to us, loyalty cuts both ways.'

My admiration for Aminta increases by the day. I'd honestly forgotten just how effective crude threats of arbitrary retribution can be. The Cliffords have generations of this type of action behind them. If Aminta didn't go through with it, it wouldn't be because she didn't know how.

Everyone is looking backwards and forwards between Taylor and Aminta. They're trying to work out how much Taylor will be able to help them when the evictions start.

Harry Hardy, as so often, sums up the views of the village. And, like my father-in-law, he clearly knows not to charge a well-defended enemy line. 'What do you want us to do, Sir John?' he says to me. 'We'll abide by your ruling.'

Taylor turns on him. 'Fool!' he says. 'You're all fools if you listen to Harry Hardy. What's the use to you of your copyholds if you're struck dead by a witch's curse? You can't let her live – not now. She'll get each of you one by one and that son of a witch isn't going to save you. You've seen how he ignores all of the evidence that runs against her. How he belittles the Rector. He's a lawyer when all's said and done, and nothing he says can be trusted.'

This last point is even more telling than my being the son of a witch and a whore. It seems to have turned the debate.

'Hang the witch,' somebody calls out. 'Hang both of them.'

'There will be no hanging,' I say.

'Burn them, then.'

'There will be no burning,' I say.

'Try to stand in our way,' says Taylor, 'and you'll hang alongside her.'

Nobody wants to be the first to volunteer to put a rope round my neck. But it may only be a matter of time until they find a way of doing it.

But Alice Mardike is on her feet. 'This is wrong,' she says. 'I won't let this happen. I confess now to being a witch. I confess to having a toad as a familiar. I confess to cursing George Barwell. I confess to cursing Nell Bowman. I confess to providing you all with medicines. I confess to finding what you've all lost over the years. But Margaret Platt played no part in any of it. She's no more a witch than any of you are. You can see that. Nor was Sir John's mother, and you know that well enough too. So, just hang me, if that's what you want to do, and let that be an end to it.'

Taylor turns to me triumphant. 'You heard her, Sir John,' he says. 'Convicted out of her own mouth. Very well, we just hang her. The Platt girl goes free if that's what you want.'

'No,' I say.

'No?' says Taylor.

'No,' I say. 'Think about it. The one thing that she hasn't admitted to is killing Barwell. Because she didn't. Nobody has been able to come or go from the village since the murder. That means that the murderer is still here amongst us. Some of you may know who it is. Some of you may have seen something and not yet realised its significance. In either case, you're even less safe than the rest of us. It isn't the Devil you need to fear at the moment. It's somebody in this very room, who didn't hesitate to strangle George Barwell and then hack his face off. Do you think they won't kill again if they have to?'

'We understand what you are saying, Sir John,' says Harry Hardy, 'but Taylor's right too. We're afraid of the witch, and that's the truth. If we do as you say, you may still never catch this person you say killed Barwell, but we'll all have Alice Mardike amongst us.'

There is a general murmur of approval.

'Sir John will find the killer. He just needs more time,' says Aminta.

'How long?' asks Taylor. 'A day? Two days?'

'A week,' says Aminta.

'And have a murdering witch with us over the holy time of Christmas? That's not right. You can't expect us to do that.'

'Very well. Until Christmas Eve,' says Aminta.

'Christmas Eve,' says Taylor. 'We'll have the hanging then. I look forward to it.'

Ben declines to escort Alice safe home. But I think a deal has been struck. Nobody will lay a hand on her before Christmas Eve – and certainly not our copyholders.

'Well done, both of you,' says Sir Felix. 'I think that went rather well. The hearing has held them off for a few days, but the thaw didn't come when we needed it. A truce until Christmas Eve was as good as we could have hoped for under the circumstances. The weather may still change. Or something else may turn up. Or we'll find some trick for spiriting her away. Or, who knows, you may even catch the culprit.'

'This weather looks set in for a while yet,' says Aminta. 'The snow melts a little during the day, but then freezes hard again at night. Even if it got very much warmer, it would take days for the drifts to melt away and for the roads to be clear again. Flooded roads may be worse than the snow.'

'Then you have enormous faith in my ability to find the killer,' I say to Aminta. 'I hope it is not misplaced. Christmas is almost upon us.'

'It's what Arlington has paid you for all these years, my dear husband,' she says. 'He's not stupid – just devious, self-serving and unprincipled. He knows what he's doing. And he always said you were his cleverest agent. I've bought you two whole days. My only advice is don't get stabbed or shot this time. You're running out of places without scars.'

'I'll bear that in mind,' I say.

Chapter Nineteen

I interrogate my mother and disagree with an innkeeper

I have dined on roast pork. If I am to tramp the lanes again, I simply cannot do it on thin gruel. But before I venture out, I am doing something I should have done before. My mother has left an untidy mass of letters and other papers which I had hoped to go through at my leisure after the funeral, and perhaps would have started had a man not had his face removed on a low hill, just inside the woods.

So, I am sitting in her bedroom, surrounded by her carefully folded dresses, her shoes, her cloaks, her petticoats and a faint residual scent of rosewater. The walls are lined with tapestries, showing men and women of Queen Elizabeth's time hunting chestnut-coloured stags in a faded blue forest. There are heavy, rose-pink silk curtains at the windows; between their sweeping folds I catch a fine view of the sunny, snowy Park. On the table in front of me is a pile of letters, account books, receipts, bills, all heaped together as she left them. Had it ever occurred to her that she might die one day, she might have allowed Morrell to put some of them in some sort of order.

The oldest of these documents go back many years. A few are in code and doubtless date from the days when she corresponded with Samuel Morland – the days when they were both in risky and treasonable contact with the threadbare, exiled pretender Charles Stuart (now addressed as His Gracious Majesty King Charles II). These are not without interest to me, but decoding them will take time and they can, I think, wait. There are letters from me, at University and in London. These last appear tedious and self-absorbed, and I put them to one side, to be used for kindling the fire tomorrow. There are letters from aunts and uncles that have long outlived the sender. There is a copy of her will, which I have still to read properly. The general outline is clear – the Big House, its contents, the surrounding land and a certain amount of money come to me, Aminta and our heirs. Sir Felix has been left a life interest in the small house – the so-called New House – that he has lately rented from my mother. He appears to have moved in with us here, however, so what becomes of that kind gesture remains to be seen. There is a long list of lesser bequests, which she must have enjoyed adding to and deleting over the years. I still have to work out which codicils cancel out which, and what I am left with at the end. Some choice items, such as her pearl brooch, may have been left to more than one person, and perhaps not by accident. It is a task I have deferred as long as I can and that Sir Felix has offered to help with, knowing most of the legatees and the likelihood that my mother will have changed her mind about them. I am interested to note that she has left her oldest and least fashionable dress to Mistress Grice 'in memory of our long and most sincere friendship'. Some of the better dresses have, I know, already gone to more deserving cases in the village and there will soon be a few poor widows drawing water from the well decked out in last year's finery and old Brussels lace. I quickly search, in great trepidation, for a bequest to George Barwell, but either the rumours are false or my mother felt that he had already been adequately recompensed. I put it all to one side. Sir Felix will enjoy it more than I.

Then, without knowing exactly what I am looking for, I find it. Tucked inside an account book is a new-looking letter, folded and folded again. I recognise the writing immediately. I had suspected something of the sort might exist. Because it had to.

Lord Arlington begins by greeting my mother in the most cordial terms. He continues:

I have a small favour to ask of you. One of my agents is obliged to seek somewhere safer to live. He has worked for me for some years and has lately been playing a dangerous double game with the Dutch, they believing that he was spying on me when he was in fact spying on them. Somebody has alerted the Dutch to the possibility that he is my man rather than theirs. Understandably, he wishes to leave London before they are certain this is the case. Indeed, he desires to find some safer form of employment for the foreseeable future. As you know, the advowson of your own Parish belongs to the Crown, and the King is minded to appoint our man to the living, he having studied theology at Oxford in his youth and being reasonably well acquainted with both Bible and Prayer Book. However, the risks of making a mistake are considerable. Should he be found out, and should a report be made to the Dutch of his hiding place, then they would certainly wish to make short work of him, as I would if he had treated me as scurvily as I instructed him to treat his Dutch masters.

My request is therefore this: would you be willing to interview him and report back to me whether he would sit happily in this post or no? Could he pass in your Parish for a man of the cloth? Would anyone betray him if they did guess his past? The gentleman concerned is a High Church Anglican, and as such commends himself mightily to His Majesty. I would ask your son to do this for me, but as you know his Puritan leanings might make it difficult for him to form an impartial view, whereas you, dear Lady, are (according to Mr Morland) sound in your beliefs – or sufficiently flexible to accommodate those of my friend. If you are willing, I shall send him to you and he will introduce himself as Dr Bray, the name and title by which he would prefer to be known from now on. Should you be unable to do this, I should be grateful if you would tell nobody of my request, not even your son. Once Bray is installed in Clavershall West, if that is what you recommend, then I leave it to your discretion what Mr Grey may be told and when.

Your most humble servant, Arlington

Very well, Dr Bray, or whatever your real name and title may be. I think we finally have you.

'So,' says Aminta, 'Bray comes to Clavershall West and your mother gives him a clean bill of health. He is as good a clergyman as the village needs.'

'I assume so,' I say.

'Bray is installed as Rector,' Aminta continues. 'He is understandably rusty to begin with, because he has for some time had relatively little to do with the Bible or Prayer Book, but your mother is able to coach him on how his predecessor did things and how to ingratiate himself with the village – a sermon or two against witches, for example. Sometimes Bray is still caught out, as both Ifnot and my father noticed, by a piece of doctrine or a passage in the Bible that most Church of England clergymen would know but that he has either not yet come across or has forgotten. In time however these slips get rarer and rarer. Bray settles into the life of a country parson. It is less exciting than spying, but he thinks he is safe.'

'Then Barwell discovers his real identity,' I say. 'We know that Barwell worked for one of the ambassadors – maybe more than one. If he worked for the Dutch Ambassador, then perhaps Barwell saw him there, under a completely different name. That alone might be enough to arouse his suspicions. Or perhaps he overheard a conversation about Bray?'

'Did Barwell really speak Dutch?' asks Sir Felix. 'I doubt the Ambassador would have obligingly spoken English so that things would be clear for him. Of course, I may be wrong. I was a soldier myself, not a diplomat. We conversed mainly by means of foul oaths.'

'I agree it's unlikely he spoke Dutch,' I say. 'But we finally have the connection between Bray and Barwell – or a very likely one. And a definite one between Bray and Arlington. However Barwell found out, my guess is that he was blackmailing Bray that he would reveal his true identity – to the Bishop or to the Dutch. Either way, Bray would lose a comfortable living for life. If the Dutch found out, Bray faced a painful death at their hands – unless he could flee them again. He had every reason to bribe or to kill Barwell. As one of Arlington's agents, he would have seen no reason why he shouldn't try each in turn.'

'Why remove his face? How does that help?' asks Aminta.

'I don't know, but until half an hour ago we had no idea what might connect the Rector and Barwell. Now we do. Perhaps if we ask a few more questions, we'll understand that part of it too.'

'How do you propose to find that out?'

'I'll ask him,' I say. 'But I'll speak to Ben first. There may be trouble if I arrest the Rector. I need to ensure that we are prepared.'

The air is fresh and the sun is shining, not yet enough to melt the snow noticeably, but enough to suggest that this cold will not last for ever. I have in fact three visits to make. The first is to Alice Mardike.

'Good afternoon, Mistress Mardike,' I say, ducking through her low doorway. 'I trust you are well.'

'You're a fool, John Grey,' she says to me, without getting up. 'How are you going to get Taylor to confess to murder before Christmas?'

'I don't think it was Taylor, and hopefully I have the proof already,' I say, with a cheerfulness that I do not feel. 'Two days may be enough. If not, I'll need to ask my wife what we do next.'

She squints at me across the smoky room. She too has confidence in Aminta, but not that much.

'You should have let them hang me,' she says. 'That's how I'm going to die sooner or later. That's what happens to witches.'

'You won't hang,' I say.

'Listen,' she says. 'There are worse things than hanging. Do you know what will happen if you don't get a confession from somebody?'

'They'll try to hang you but we'll stop them,' I say.

'No, before that. First they'll take me and strip me naked to check for the Devil's marks on me. Anything will do – a wart, a mole, a boil. They can all be Devil's marks if you look hard enough and have enough belief. I saw them do it to my mother. She almost died of shame. They stuck pins in her, because witches are supposed to have spots where they can't feel pain. The only way she could stop them doing it was by biting her tongue so she wouldn't scream. That meant they thought they'd found a dead spot and didn't need to stick the pin into her again. Because they don't stop until they find one. Then they walked her up and down for hours to get her to confess to anything she hadn't already confessed to. Afterwards they sent her to the County Gaol and starved her until it was time to hang her. There was a trial before that of course, but there was only one possible outcome. She'd given them more than enough proof. A lot of people die of gaol fever while they're waiting for trial, but my mum wasn't that lucky. I wasn't that lucky either, because I had to watch it all, from beginning to end, and the hanging wasn't the worst part of it. Not by a long way. If I'm to die, I want to die quickly, not have it dragged out over the next six months, looking each day for a reprieve that never comes.'

'They can't stick pins in you,' I say. 'Torture is illegal.'

'Doesn't mean they won't do it.'

'I already have some new evidence,' I say.

'Then keep it to yourself. They'll hang you too, boy,' she says. 'If they think you're trying to defend witchcraft. They'll hang you or they'll creep up on you one night and stick a knife into your back.'

'Don't give up hope, Alice.'

'Hope?' she says.

I nod. It's probably not something she's had a lot of use for over the past sixty years.

'William Taylor wasn't best pleased,' says Ben. 'He wanted his hanging there and then.'

'It's my enquiry,' I say. 'I can't have other people telling me how to run it – I certainly can't have people who may have committed the murder telling me how to run it. Especially Taylor.'

'You still suspect him of killing Barwell?'

'I certainly believe he killed his wife. And the more I see of Taylor, the less I like him. Nothing would give me greater pleasure than to commit him to the next assize, but I think the killer's more likely to be Bray. Look at this.'

I show Ben the letter from Arlington.

'Well, I always thought there was something odd about the way the Rector ran his services,' says Ben.

'How many have you been to?' I ask.

'One or two,' says Ben evasively. 'But it can't be the Rector. I mean, a clergyman . . .'

'He's one of Arlington's agents with a Degree in Divinity,' I say. 'Those are the standards by which we need to judge him. Barwell had probably discovered his true identity after encountering him in London, and was threatening to reveal it to the Dutch.'

'But if Barwell was blackmailing him, why not call on Arlington? He could send somebody to deal with Barwell.'

'He could certainly send another of his agents to persuade Barwell of his folly, but Bray could do the same on his own account and more efficiently. Anyway, Ifnot said that Bray hated Arlington – or words to that effect. There may have been a falling out that prevented an appeal for help.'

'Well then . . . Perhaps you're right,' says Ben. 'But why remove his face like that, all the same?'

I agree. That still puzzles me, just as it puzzled Aminta. As an agent you learn to do as little as you need to do, then get out fast. You don't risk being caught carrying out some time-consuming and completely unneeded act of revenge. Bray might have done it if he needed the body to be unidentifiable, but that was never going to be possible. If Barwell disappeared and, the same day, a body was found on the hill, nobody was going to be fooled into thinking it was anyone else, face or no face.

'Well, he certainly went up to the woods,' I say.

'Ifnot saw him go past,' says Ben, resuming his polishing. 'But he turned back. Nobody saw him and he saw nobody. He said so. As I said, I think we have to trust the Rector.'

Of course. That's it. The question I was going to ask Dr Bray.

'No, that's not right,' I say. 'He said nobody *saw him* – then he paused. I was going to ask him whether he saw anyone else, but you interrupted me.'

Ben's cloth comes to a sudden standstill, then continues again at a much-increased rate.

'Did I?' he says.

'Yes.'

'I don't remember it like that at all,' says Ben. 'He just said he hadn't seen anyone, and, him being a man of the cloth, I think we should believe him, don't you? You shouldn't doubt the word of a man of God.'

'He wasn't working for God,' I say. 'He was working for Arlington. Different masters entirely.'

'Well then, even if he had said he'd seen somebody, he'd probably have been lying,' says Ben triumphantly.

Ben has a point, but maybe not as good a one as he thinks.

'Ben, do you know who Dr Bray saw?' I ask.

'Why do you ask that?'

'Because you've been polishing the same spot on the same tankard for five minutes,' I say.

Ben stops polishing, in the hope I'll believe what he says next.

'Why should I know anyway?' he asks.

'I've no idea. Unless you were out near the woods yourself. Then you might.'

Ben smiles. 'I was here all day until I was called to inspect the body,' he says. 'Ask anyone.'

'I may ask,' I say. 'Everyone in the village is a suspect until I am certain who killed George Barwell.'

Ben leans across his counter. 'Look, Master John,' he says confidentially. 'We all know it was the witches who did it. Or if they didn't, then they've done something else equally bad. Because that's what witches do. If you convened a jury here – any twelve men you want to pick – they'd find Alice Mardike and Margaret Platt guilty in five minutes. They'd all be agreed on it. So, why do you think you know better than the rest of us? You've scarcely lived here for the past ten years. You think you know Alice Mardike, but you don't really – not like we do. All witches are evil, deep down, even the ones who seem decent when you talk to them, as you apparently do. Fine, let's say that it wasn't her this time. George Barwell's no loss, is he? Lots of people here would have had good cause to kill him. A father whose daughter he's seduced. Or a husband whose wife's been bedded by him. Or a girl he's deceived. Or a man he's blackmailing, for that matter. Whatever it was, good riddance to Barwell, I say. If anyone's going to swing for it, then better Mardike than anyone else in the village. An honest man saved, like as not, and an evil witch put out of the way. Now, I can't do that for the village, because I was born to be an innkeeper, as you see. But you can do it for us. Like Lady Grey said, most of the people here pay their dues to you as copyholders, every Quarter Day. And, if you ask yourself honestly, what have you ever done to deserve that? God bless you, Master John, they don't resent that you were born richer than they were and can dress in fine clothes and drink Canary while they dig the frozen soil and drink small beer. They accept that that's how things are and always will be. They just want you to do right by them in return.'

'I'm going to talk to the Rector,' I say.

'Do you need me to come with you?' asks Ben.

'You still have pots to wash,' I say.

The Rector is standing in the churchyard, looking out over the snow-covered fields. He stares north, towards Cambridge. Perhaps that is where he plans to run. Further from London and the Dutch Ambassador.

'The snow is starting to melt,' I say. 'The roads may soon be clear.'

'I hope not,' he says. 'It's probably safer as things are. You really think I killed Barwell, don't you?'

'I have a letter from Lord Arlington,' I say, 'consulting my mother over your appointment here.'

He nods. 'She was supposed to destroy it,' he says.

'While she kept it, she had something on Lord Arlington. Proof at least that he owed her a favour. It would have been too valuable to use to light the fire.'

'Yes, of course,' says Bray. 'I'd have kept it too and for the same reasons. Arlington rarely commits his promises to paper. You'd better come into the Rectory. It will be easier to talk there, away from prying eyes and ears.'

'Thank you,' I say.

It occurs to me that I am unarmed. Bray could have anything stored behind his theological texts or wrapped in his popish vestments. Well, I shall be as ready for him as I can be. He may be the more experienced agent – and quite capable of silently tracking me through the snow in order to ambush me outside the inn – but I am twenty years younger at least. And I think that he may still retain some notions of fair play that I lack.

'Brandy?' he asks, as he motions me to a seat by the fire.

'Is that what you're drinking?' I ask.

'Both drinks will come from the same bottle,' he says. 'You can choose which glass you drink from.'

'Poison can be slipped in as you pass the glass to me,' I say.

'Please excuse me, Sir John, if I have not made myself clear. It goes without saying that I don't expect you to choose until the glasses are on the table in plain sight,' he says.

He places two wine glasses before me and pours. I select the one on the right and raise it. 'To your good health, Rector,' I say. I wait until he puts his own to his lips, because it is not unknown for both glasses to have poison in them, then I drink. It seems to be just brandy. If it isn't I'll know very soon.

'You're right,' he says, settling back into his chair. 'Barwell was blackmailing me. He was doing work at the house of the

Dutch Ambassador on a number of occasions when I was there. So he later told me. I never noticed him at the time. He was just one of a number of English workmen. I always spoke good Dutch to the Ambassador. It all seemed perfectly safe. Later, as you know, I had to tell Arlington that our Dutch friends no longer trusted me as they should. Things were becoming quite unpleasant. I advised his lordship that I wanted to quit. He could provide me with a pension somewhere safe, unless he wanted me to go for a comfortable retirement in Amsterdam. I knew a lot that the Dutch would pay well for. He prevaricated, as you know he always does. My life was worth quite a lot less to him than I imagined. Eventually he offered to find me a parish far enough from London that I wouldn't meet any Dutchman and with a large enough income that I would not starve. I had actually been a curate many years ago before I took to espionage. The idea that I should vanish from London and return to that way of making a living was not unattractive. It is pleasant enough, if your parishioners let you alone.

'There happened to be one or two vacancies. For reasons I did not then understand, Arlington suggested North Essex. As you now know, he contacted your mother to ensure that it all happened as smoothly as it could. Morland had recommended her as somebody who could act with discretion, as indeed she did. She gave me a lot of useful advice – for example, that I would be the more readily accepted here if I conformed to the prejudices of the village in matters such as witchcraft. I have to say that my sermons on the subject were well received. Of course, I had no idea that one of my parishioners might soon be accused of it, or I would have left myself more room for manoeuvre. Still, I have a lot to thank your mother for. I miss her very much.'

'Why not me?' I ask. 'Arlington could have taken me in to his confidence. I was working for him then.'

'It's as it says in the letter; he trusted your loyalty to the King, but not your religion. Anyway, your mother was here and you were in London. But both Arlington and Morland led me to believe that I could nevertheless turn to you if things got difficult.'

'Unfortunately nobody told me that,' I say. 'My mother died before we could discuss it.'

'It took me a while to work out that that was the case,' he says. 'Your questioning of me seemed unkind under the circumstances. I bear Alice Mardike no ill will but I could scarcely be expected to contradict what I had told everyone in church only a few weeks before. Your attempts to make me do so were awkward.'

'So you don't believe in witchcraft?' I ask.

'You've been an agent yourself. It's not enough to claim to be somebody you aren't. If you're not going to get caught, you have to believe in your own fiction. Dr Bray believes in witchcraft. That's all that mattered. Anyway, that's beside the point. What I wanted to tell you about was Barwell. He didn't often come to church, but when he did he looked at me oddly. It was after the service on Palm Sunday that he said to me, as he left the church: "We've met before, Rector. In London. At the Dutch Ambassador's house. You were dressed rather differently in those days." Then he smiled and went on his way.'

'So he threatened to tell the Dutch where you were?'

Bray shakes his head. 'No. He had no idea that they were even after me. He just knew that the new Rector had been some sort of Dutch agent, and that the Parish had been cruelly misled as to my origins – perhaps that I wasn't a priest at all. His immediate threat was to report it to the Bishop. It wouldn't have done him much good since the King had appointed me, but the fuss might have alerted certain people to where I was ... and other things. And I couldn't be sure exactly how much he knew that was not to my credit. There's quite a lot over the years. So, I bought him off.'

'Two hundred Pounds?'

'Of course not. Ten, then another ten.'

'And that was enough?'

'Who knows? I have no doubt he imagined he could come back for further payments. But then he was killed, so I can afford the excellent brandy that we are drinking. Would you like some more?'

I allow Bray to refill my glass. 'How much did he know?'

'I never found out. After he discovered who I was, he may have made further enquiries at the Embassy. He might have established that I was a double agent.'

'Then twenty Pounds was cheap.'

'I thought so.'

'The Dutch would have paid him far more to locate you.'

'They certainly have more money for their operations than Arlington does.'

'But why not get Arlington to dispose of him? That would have cost you nothing.'

Bray looks at me. Then suddenly I understand. 'You were really working for the Dutch all along, not Arlington,' I say. 'That's why you couldn't call Arlington in. Because he might talk to Barwell and finally discover what your game had been. And that's why there was no point in Barwell betraying you to the Dutch. They had no interest at all in killing you. You were always their man.'

'You seem surprised.'

'Only that Arlington didn't find you out. He's no fool.'

Bray nods. 'For a while, I thought that you had found me out. Hence your hostility to me. That worried me a great deal. But needlessly, it would seem. It must just be your Puritan character that made you so sour and unbending.'

'And you're not concerned I'll go to Arlington now?' I say.

'You'll never prove it,' says Bray. 'I'll deny saying any of this. I doubt if the Dutch will be very forthcoming. And the only witness is dead.'

'So, that's why you killed him,' I say.

'Kill him? When his price was twenty Pounds a year? I wasn't going to risk going to the gallows for so little. There's no benefit of the clergy for murder, as you know – even if the Judge accepted my slightly dubious status as a clerk in holy orders. Anyway, I was learning a lot about Barwell's little tricks. After twenty years of working as an agent for various masters, I have become quite adept at finding things out. Two can play at blackmail, and by the time he died I knew a great deal about George Barwell's past. All of no value now, of course.'

'Did Barwell know what you'd discovered?'

'Oddly enough, I was about to tell him, the day he died. I was at a parishioner's house when I saw him hurry past, going in the direction of the woods. I made some excuse and ran out of the door in a most unclerical manner. I thought I would catch Barwell and tell him why he'd be giving me a generous New Year's gift. But the snow had become heavier and, exactly as I told you, I gave up my chase. After all, it was not urgent. Blackmail requires no salt to keep it fresh in winter. Like treasure stored up in heaven, neither rust nor moth can get at it. I came back by the same road I'd gone out on. I didn't see Davies the smith as I passed his house. As Ben said, he was probably fetching more charcoal. I made my way back to the Rectory. The village streets were deserted. I stoked up my fire and poured myself some of this brandy. I knew nothing about Barwell's death until Ben brought me his body. I was not pleased. Not now I was in a position to turn the screws on the dirty little thief, praise be to God for his infinite mercy and compassion.'

'Was my mother's name ever mentioned in connection with George Barwell?' I ask.

'Not that I recall,' says Bray. 'Had you expected it to be?'

'No,' I say. 'Not at all. He did have a lot of money when he died.'

'Not from me,' says Bray. 'He may have been blackmailing others. As I say, he was quite good at it and there was no lack of opportunity.'

'If he had money all along, why did he stop going to the inn?' I say.

'I've no idea,' says the Rector. 'Perhaps his wife prevented him? As a married man you would know whether that was possible. Or maybe he found religion? It does that to some people.'

He pours me some more brandy and we sit for a while and look at the fire. The flames dance merrily and a thick stream of grey smoke rises up the capacious chimney.

'There was only one other question I had to ask you, Dr Bray,' I say.

'Please ask, Sir John,' he says. 'It would be a great pleasure to assist you.'

'When I questioned you, I thought you were about to tell me that somebody did see you while you were out. Perhaps as you returned.'

'Yes. I said nobody saw *me*, but, as you have so astutely deducted, I did see *somebody*. They had come along the track behind the smithy – it's very rough, so I assume they did not wish to be seen. I saw them where the track rejoins the Saffron Walden road, going up the hill as fast as they could. I wasn't going to mention it. There seemed little incentive since you were so unsympathetic and I was no friend of George Barwell's. Why should I betray his killer for your benefit? But we are getting on so well now and you are about to swear that you will say nothing of any of this to Lord Arlington ...'

'I too have retired from his service,' I say. 'There may be no point in troubling him with such a minor matter ... especially if you help me with my current difficulty.'

'I hoped you would see it that way.'

'So, who was it?' I ask.

'Nell Bowman,' says Bray. 'Another brandy, my dear fellow? You look as if you need it.'

The sun has vanished. Dark clouds are gathering again. A vicious wind lashes across the surface of the fallen snow and whips a cold spray up into my face. It also powders the grimy walls of the houses with clumps of white. From my vantage point on the back of my horse, I can see the roof of the Big House. Five minutes' ride will get me there, but I have one more call to make.

I have known Nell for many years. She has served me with much good ale. She has overlooked many of my youthful follies. But she has murdered George Barwell; and I am now the Magistrate and must do something about it. Ben's argument that Barwell is no loss is sound morally, but not in Law. His argument that it would be better that Alice Mardike hangs for the greater good of the village is all the more understandable now that I know – as he must have known all along – that his wife was out and about at the time of the murder. His many prevarications and interruptions no longer seem as clumsy as I had believed. He has in fact played a poor hand very well. And I think I now know who the married woman was who was so enamoured of Barwell. It was not my mother. I can't blame Nell for straying after so many years of being married to Ben. I can understand why she might kill him to prevent the village knowing. Or out of revenge. But murder is murder.

Nell came so close to getting away with it. I don't think however that I can expect much help from my constable in making this arrest.

I press my thumb on the latch and the inn door swings open as before. Ben takes care of what is his.

Nell is at the counter. The parlour is otherwise empty. 'Where's Ben?' I demand. They may as well both hear together what I have to say.

'Gone to see William Taylor,' she says. 'Do you need him? He's done more than enough work as constable lately and we needed to get in more supplies from Taylor's farm. The weather seems to be turning again . . .' Her voice tails off. She is looking at my face. 'What's the matter, Sir John? You look very serious.'

'I've been talking to the Rector,' I say. 'He saw you going up to the woods just before the murder occurred. I have come to arrest you for the killing of George Barwell. You were there at the right time. You are in possession of something very much like the murder weapon. And I think I know exactly why you did it. You may hang for this, Nell.'

For almost a minute Nell can say nothing at all. Then she laughs. 'Well, they may find me guilty but they won't be able to hang me,' she says. 'Not now I'm with child.'

Chapter Twenty

I find that the village can still surprise me

'You're right,' says Nell. 'I had good reason to kill Barwell. I should never have listened to him. I should never have laughed at his jokes. I should never have let him into my bed when Ben was at the market. Or when Ben went to one of the farms to buy meat. Or when Ben was occupied downstairs and Barwell had crept in through the back door. None of the times was it right or even sensible. But you haven't been married to Ben for as long as I have. You haven't spent days without count working at a village inn. You don't want to scream until you weep at the tedium of life in a small Essex village, everything the same, season after season after season – the same faces in the parlour, the same stories, the same jokes, the same orders for ale, ham and bread, the same weather, the same mud, the same husband ...'

'I've lived here too,' I say.

'But you're a *man*. You've never tried dragging your skirts through the snow in the winter and the wet leaves in the autumn and the mud in the spring and the mud in the summer. You've never looked at the other women with haggard faces and a dozen screaming children in tow and thought: Yes, I'd like that too, that's as good as it gets. You can put your breeches on and mount your horse and just ride and ride until you are somewhere else. Then, when you get there, you can decide what it is you'd like to do with the rest of your life, and your father and your husband can't tell you you can't do it. That's the difference between us, John. That's why you aren't raving mad and I am.'

'It's why I went to London,' I say.

'I conversely went the wrong way. I came from London to here. I had a job – yes, a job – in the theatre. I didn't write plays like Lady Grey, and when I was there it wasn't legal for women to appear on stage, though I did several times. I helped my father manage the theatre. I did his accounts. I sold tickets. I managed the costumes and the swords and the armour. And I was really good at it. Better than the man who did it before me or the man who came after me. I was the best in London. Then I came to visit my aunt in Essex for a month. I met Ben. It was May and everything here was so fresh and so clean and almost dry in places. There was blossom and green leaves and lambs. It was like paradise after hot, dusty London. Even now, I'm almost sane, sometimes, during May. By the first of June that year I was married. If only I'd visited in November, I'd have seen it as it really was. If I'd stayed two months I'd have seen Ben as he really was. But it was May and I had permission from my father to be away for one month. And as a woman, your father's word is Law, until you get a husband. Then it's your husband's word. Can you imagine Ben's word being Law?'

'I have some idea of what that legal system would be like,' I say.

'You'll have heard all sorts of stories about George Barwell,' Nell continues. 'That he was a nasty, sneaking seducer of young girls and of women who were old enough to know better. That he was completely unprincipled. That he was a liar and a rogue with a false tongue.'

'You're saying it's all untrue?'

'No, that's exactly what he was. He was wonderful really. He was also the best-looking man in the village. Don't misunderstand me, John – most of the girls fell into a swoon every time you walked by, and that scar on your cheek might have been designed to make you look dashing. But it's not worth hanging around the well all day hoping to be seduced by a Puritan lawyer. It doesn't happen that often. But Barwell would flatter you the moment he saw you and keep flattering you until you thought: Well, why not, eh? He'd bring you presents, pick flowers from the fields, laugh at things you said . . . When you've been married to Ben for fifteen years and the last time he listened to you properly was November 1657 . . . but maybe I've said that once or twice already. You'll see the difference between Barwell and Ben quite easily. Nobody has ever looked at Ben and thought, There goes a danger to women's virtue. You wouldn't want to marry Barwell, but you would want to go to bed with him if he asked very politely.'

'The baby is George Barwell's, then?'

'That seems likely, doesn't it? Ben managed nothing in fifteen years. Then once or twice – all right, maybe a dozen times – with Barwell and I'm pregnant.'

'After you killed George Barwell, I can see why you'd want Alice Mardike blamed for it. I don't understand why you claimed she made you barren, when you clearly weren't.'

'For exactly the reasons I've given. For fifteen years, Ben and I had been trying to have a child. Then Barwell comes along and, lo and behold, we have one. You don't think Ben won't suspect something? Men are slow on the uptake sometimes, but not that slow.'

'So, if Alice Mardike had cursed you and then lifted the curse ...'

'Precisely. That would explain why we'd had no luck for fifteen years, but were now blessed with a beautiful son or daughter.'

'But one who unaccountably resembled George Barwell. That would suggest a curse only partially lifted.'

'All babies look the same. It would have been years before Ben suspected anything.'

'And that's why Alice had to tell Ben herself. So that the story didn't just come from you? It was fully corroborated by the very person who had cursed you. Would he have believed that?'

'Who can tell what he might have believed? The old witch wouldn't do it,' says Nell. 'I begged her and she said no. I offered to pay and she said no. I threatened her and she said no. Then, after Barwell died, I thought, well if she hangs and I seem to fall pregnant almost straight away, that's pretty convincing too. There are plenty of stories of curses being lifted once the witch is dead – or even just arrested. Any fool might believe that one was the result of the other.'

'And did Ben believe it?'

'He doesn't know yet. I can't conceive officially until she lifts the curse or dies or you at least arrest her properly.'

'Won't he suspect if the baby is born after just six or seven months?'

'He's a man. I'll just tell him that sometimes it's like that.'

I nod. The women will know of course, but they may not let on.

'Well, I can understand why you killed Barwell,' I say. 'And I can understand why you hacked away at his face. The face that had so cruelly seduced you—'

'That isn't what happened,' says Nell. 'I didn't do either of those things.'

'But I've said, you were seen. There is a witness.'

'Whose story is this?'

'Yours.'

'In which case, can I finish telling it, please?'

'Yes,' I say.

'Good. Thank you very much indeed. So, by the time I realised I was pregnant, Barwell had already gone back to that silly little Platt girl. He felt, and rightly, that having two mistresses at the same time would lay him open to accusations of fickleness. He stopped paying me compliments. He stopped bringing me presents. So, I told him that I was with child, but sadly he didn't see that was a problem for anyone. I was married, after all. Nobody would comment on a married woman having a child. It was normal. He wouldn't even see me after I told him. He didn't visit the inn any more – something that Ben noticed but was unable to account for. I told him that Barwell could no longer afford it. But I knew the reason perfectly well and I knew that, deep down, Barwell really loved me better than Margaret or his silly little wife. At first I thought that Amy would come to see her mistake and throw him out – I did my best to hurry things along by telling her father about Barwell's behaviour. Then it occurred to me that I just needed to get George Barwell alone and remind him who he liked best. And, having reminded him the best way I could, I was going to suggest that, as soon as the snow cleared, we both ran away to London or Colchester or anywhere with more life in it than Clavershall West. A letter from me wasn't going to tempt him out, but a letter from Margaret would. So, I wrote one. I knew the sort of thing she'd say.'

'You proposed a tryst in a snowstorm?'

'The weather was still relatively mild when I wrote it and left it under a stone by the wall – our usual place for exchanging correspondence of an incriminating nature. And, again, I have to remind you that we are dealing with a man. He would have dropped his breeches in a blizzard. I was confident he would be there, even after the weather turned and the snow started to fall.'

'What did he say when you arrived?'

'Not a lot, because he was dead and his face had been hacked off.'

'So ...'

'I didn't kill him, John. I was late – I think I've mentioned the problem of snow and skirts? Try it if you don't believe me. Oh, and petticoats, they get soaking wet too. I arrived long after the time I'd written – after the shepherds who found the body. I hid in the bushes and watched them standing there, talking, then they both went off in different directions, and I was able to creep up and see what had happened. It's fortunate that I have a strong stomach. Somebody else, a little more nimble than I, had got there first. Somebody who knew Barwell would be there. Somebody who had reason to kill him. Somebody who had perhaps seen my letter.'

'So they must have either found it where you left it or somehow seen it here before you took it to the hiding place ...'

The inn door swings open behind me. 'Well, the two of you must be having an interesting conversation,' says Ben. 'What's it all about, then?'

Chapter Twenty-One

Ben attempts to lie

'I went to see the Rector,' I say. 'He told me that he saw Nell heading towards the woods on the day that Barwell died. Nell says she did go there but that Barwell was already dead when she arrived.'

Ben swallows hard. 'And do you believe her?' he asks.

'What I think of it myself probably matters very little. In as much as I can be confident that anyone will tell the judges the same thing that they have told me in private, Dr Bray will give evidence that he saw Nell on the Saffron Walden road at about the time that Barwell was killed. The jury will have to consider what else she might have been doing there on a snowy afternoon in December when she presumably had other duties to attend to here at the inn.'

'Couldn't Bray have killed him and then seen Nell on his way back?'

'Yes, but the question of what Nell was doing there, heading up the hill as fast as she could, doesn't go away. The jury would still find that interesting. So, it would then be his word against hers. Bray's a clergyman, albeit one who has also worked for Arlington, properly appointed by the King after being interviewed for his suitability by the lady of the manor. A jury might be inclined to listen to him. For what it's worth, I do actually believe Bray when he says it would not have been worth the risk for him to kill Barwell.'

'Then who was it, if it wasn't him or Nell?' Ben demands.

'Where were you, Ben?'

'I was where we are now,' he says. 'I've told you that. Nell was out. Somebody had to be here running the inn. Ask any of the customers who were here that afternoon.'

I look at Ben. He could be lying, but it would be so easy to test this alibi that there would be no point in trying to deceive me. In which case . . .

'Then you will have to agree that things do not look well for your wife,' I say.

'But why should Nell want to kill him? Have you considered that?'

Neither Nell nor I say anything.

Ben suddenly sits down in one of the chairs that he so thoughtfully provides for customers. He puts his head in his hands. 'I knew this would happen,' he says.

'What?' I say.

Ben turns to Nell. 'Do you think I didn't know about you and Barwell?' he demands. 'Do you think I didn't notice you together in the evenings? When the village girls started telling tales about him and an older woman, I knew it had to be you.'

His voice tails off into silence. He hasn't asked Nell how she could do this to him. He's worked it out for himself. I respect him for that.

'I'm sorry, Ben . . .' says Nell.

'And I know about the letter,' he says, turning to Nell.

'How?' she asks.

'I saw you writing something, then tuck the paper away in a cupboard, as if hiding it from me. When you were out of the room, I went to the cupboard and found it behind the pile of candles. It was to Barwell, but you'd signed it "Margaret". I couldn't understand why, but it didn't bode well, whatever your reason was. The afternoon Barwell was killed, you went out, even though snow was threatening. Then one of the shepherds came down and told me that Barwell had been murdered, at exactly the time and in exactly the place that the note specified. And finally, just before I set out up the hill, you came back. Your skirt was soaking wet and you looked terrified.'

'So, once you saw the body, you were quick to agree that it must be witchcraft,' I say to Ben. 'You didn't want me to look any further.'

'It wasn't just me. It was what everyone thought. Taylor. Tom. Dick. The Rector. Why should I say any different?'

'You'd have seen Alice Mardike hang, even though she was innocent?'

'Yes, if it was her or Nell,' says Ben.

Nell nods approvingly. After fifteen years, Ben's finally got something right.

'Where's the letter now?' I ask.

'I burned it,' he says. 'I hoped it must have been lost or that Barwell destroyed it before he set out. Then you called by and told me that you had new evidence connecting Margaret to the killing. When I first saw the letter – before it was sent – it was obvious to me that it was Nell's hand. Sooner or later somebody else would recognise it, too. Maybe not you or Jacob Platt, but somebody in the village. I had to get the letter back.'

'So, it was no coincidence that I was ambushed close to the inn?'

'I waited until I saw the light of your lantern. I hid round the corner. I tried not to hit you too hard, Master John. And I only hit you once. I thought I'd see you get up within a few minutes, or call for help. I was just going to come back and get you when Lady Grey appeared. I wouldn't have let you freeze to death.'

'Really?'

'You weren't lying there for more than two or three minutes.'

'Aminta says I was half covered in snow.'

'A quarter covered at the most. I'm very sorry, Sir John.'

'I had to eat gruel for two days.'

'I did give you some ham.'

'My wife called me an idiot.'

Ben says nothing. There's no point in lying when he doesn't need to.

'I should have you arrest yourself for assault,' I say.

'I'll do whatever you say,' he says.

I rub the back of my head thoughtfully. It's not as bad as it was.

'I do believe Nell,' I say. 'She described accurately what happened after the murder, with Dick and Tom finding the body, then both going off in different directions. That means she probably did stay there as she described and I don't think she would done that if she'd killed Barwell. Of course, we still have the small difficulty that she had a reason to kill him and went there to meet him, having sent him a letter in somebody else's name.'

'What if I admitted to it?' says Ben. 'I could say that I saw the letter and went there ahead of Nell, confronted him and strangled him in a jealous rage.'

'And then hacked his flesh away?'

'Yes.'

'With what?'

'One of his tools.'

'How did you get it?'

'He brought it with him. To defend himself. But we fought and I took it off him.'

'Why was there no sign of a struggle?'

'I overcame him very quickly.'

'You actually reckon you'd be able to do that?'

'Possibly.'

Ben seems exhausted just by describing this hypothetical encounter. He'd have had a considerable weight advantage of course, but I think he'd have lacked the necessary agility. He might have just crept up behind Barwell of course, then hit him on the head. We both know he can do that.

'So, where is this sharp implement now?' I ask.

'I carried it away with me.'

'What did you do with it then?'

'How should I know? I just took it. Or maybe I threw it in the bushes. Is it important?'

I pause. Ben has raised a good point.

'Yes, I think so,' I say. 'We've spent a lot of time on the murder weapon – was it a silk stocking or a silk maniple? Who in the village possessed such things? But we've forgotten the blade that was used to disfigure him. Because, after all, he was already dead when that happened. So it wasn't that significant.'

'We didn't forget that at all,' says Ben indignantly. 'We agreed that it must be one of Barwell's own woodworking tools. They'd be sharp enough and he could have had one with him, just like I said.'

'But why should he have one with him? If he'd wanted to defend himself, then a knife or cudgel would have been better. And anyway, why would he take one to a meeting, as he thought, with Margaret Platt? What danger did she pose?'

'So you don't think it was one of those tools?'

'No, I do think it was exactly that. What I don't understand is how the killer got their hands on it. Then what they did with it after the murder. Those are the questions we should have been asking. First light tomorrow I'll need you here with your boots on, Ben. We're going back up the hill.'

'You don't think I should just confess to the murder?'

'Only if you want to be convicted for contempt of court,' I say. 'You never could lie. I don't advise doing it in front of a County Court judge.'

'Well, at least we've now all told each other everything we know,' he says.

I look at Nell. There may be other things she'll have to tell Ben at some stage. Before the baby's actually born.

'Oh, and have your thickest cloak on too, Ben,' I say. 'It'll be cold up there in the early morning.'

It is good to get back to the Big House. Once the sun is down, the wind is more bitter and the ice more treacherous. Aminta is in the drawing room, giving instructions to one of the servants. She dismisses him and turns to me.

'You were almost late for supper,' she says. 'I hope you've discovered something useful.'

'Bray's a double agent working for the Dutch, but Arlington doesn't know yet – unless I decide to tell him. Barwell was blackmailing him, but was relatively cheap. Bray didn't kill Barwell but saw Nell heading for the woods. Nell's pregnant with Barwell's child, but Ben, like Arlington, still has much to learn. Ben did understand what was going on just well enough to decide to hit me over the head, steal the letter Nell had written in Margaret's name and leave me to die in the snow.'

Aminta nods. 'Not bad,' she says. 'Not bad at all. In fact, it's almost as good as what I've found out.'

Chapter Twenty-Two

In which a more serious attempt is made on my life

'Your problem,' says Aminta, passing me the dish of boiled beef, 'is that you're not very good at interviewing young women.'

'I did well enough with Nell,' I say.

'Once Bray had passed you all the ammunition you needed. Anyway, I meant the younger village girls.'

'I could tell Margaret Platt was lying,' I say, spooning some more of the beef onto my plate. The gravy is thick and brown and glistens in the candlelight.

'Everyone knows when Margaret Platt is lying,' says Aminta. 'But did you get the truth out of her?'

'How should I know?'

'Precisely. So that's why I went to talk to Amy Barwell. And could you kindly leave some of that beef for the rest of us? I realise you're hungry after a busy day, but so am I.'

'So am I,' says Sir Felix. We look at him. 'No, I really have had a very busy day,' he says. 'But let's listen to Aminta first.'

'Yes,' says Aminta. 'Let's listen to me. So, I rode over to Taylor's house, knowing that he would be out in the fields and that Amy should be home. I knocked on the door and said that I hadn't paid my respects properly after her husband's death.'

'Did that take her in?' I ask.

'Of course not. She's a woman. She knew I was after something. So, she smiled and I smiled and we sat by the fire and drank tea and talked about the difficulties that husbands, living and dead, constantly presented. That took some time to cover adequately, as you will imagine. Then, just as I was about to leave, I turned the subject to her mother. She agreed that her mother had suffered more than she had, poor woman. Her father could be demanding and forceful. I took the opportunity to enquire if the black eye that Amy currently had could be attributed in any way to her father. She conceded they had had a slight disagreement that morning. I sympathised and started to dig a little deeper on her mother, who you will remember died after a fall down a flight of stairs.'

'Amy Robsart died the same way,' says Sir Felix. 'Married to Lord Robert Dudley back in my grandfather's time. Queen Elizabeth objected to the marriage on the grounds that she wanted Dudley for herself. A little later Amy Robsart was found dead at the bottom of a flight of stairs.'

'And people believed it was an accident?' I ask.

'Not that I know of,' says Sir Felix. 'The rumours followed Dudley for the rest of his life. But nobody could ever prove it wasn't accidental. The injuries from a fall like that are not dissimilar to those you'd have if you were hit over the head. And people do fall down stairs, though more frequently, it would seem, when they have violent husbands.'

'In this case, there was a witness,' says Aminta. 'Amy saw her parents arguing at the top of the stairs. Then her mother fell and just lay there at the bottom. She didn't understand what had happened, but her father walked slowly down the stairs and knelt by his wife. Then he looked up and saw Amy. He just put his finger to his lips.'

'And Amy said nothing to anyone at the time?'

'She was five or six then. All she knew was that her mother was gone and she had to keep quiet about it.'

'And later?'

'What could she do? Her father was all she had. She just had to stay and make the best of it. You wouldn't be able to get a conviction now any more than they could then, but I don't doubt it was murder.'

I remember Nell's words about a man being able to put on a pair of breeches and ride off wherever they wanted to go. I could see that Amy's choices were even more limited than Nell's.

'So Taylor has already committed one murder in the village,' I say.

'Yes, but there's more. That wasn't the first time he'd tried to kill his wife. Amy remembers hearing her parents arguing before. That time, she came running into the room to discover her father with his hands round her mother's throat. He backed away when he saw Amy, but still . . .'

'It wouldn't be the first time he'd tried to strangle somebody,' I say.

'Exactly. We were very wrong when we decided that the only way he'd deal with Barwell would be face to face, with fists or cudgels. If he's angry enough, he'll try whatever he can.'

'So, after being brought up by a violent father, she finds herself married to Barwell.'

'Yes. Taylor might have understood, even approved, if Barwell had beaten Amy. It would have shown that Barwell was more of a man than he seemed. Taylor was clearly less tolerant of Barwell's blatant infidelities. The Bible sanctions a great deal that men wish to do, but not that. After Nell told him what Alice Mardike had said at the well, Taylor challenged Barwell. There was a nasty confrontation between them. And Barwell stood up for himself. That was quite brave of him when you think he was quite small and Taylor rather large. But it made matters worse. It ended with Taylor threatening to kill Barwell. Amy overheard that too.'

'The two of you obviously got on well.'

'She doesn't have many friends in the village. She was very happy to talk about it.'

'If Taylor did murder Barwell, he must realise that Amy may inform on him sooner or later.'

'That's what worries me. Is she safe with him? He must know she could hang him. Would a man who kills his wife also kill his daughter?'

'But would Amy give evidence against her father?' I ask. 'She shows no sign of doing so. She just demands we hang a witch.'

'She still doesn't want to believe it,' says Aminta. 'She doesn't want to believe it any more than she wanted to believe he killed her mother. Hence, as you say, the accusations against Alice Mardike.'

Quite right. Amy has chosen not to believe it. Like Bray, if she's going to live a lie, then she'll live it properly.

'So now we have an actual threat against Barwell from somebody who has killed before. A violent man, who would not shy away from a little blood and who deeply resented his good-looking son-in-law's activities. And Taylor would have had access to Barwell's tools,' I say. 'I'm going back with Ben in the morning to see if the blade used on Barwell is still in the woods. The snow will have melted a little up there. Getting around is much easier than the evening when I went to see Platt.'

'Well, this time, make sure you don't get hit over the head by anybody,' says Aminta. 'I'm not coming all the way up to the woods to find you.'

'You also said you had been busy today, Sir Felix,' I say.

'Me?' he says. 'Oh, that was nothing compared with what you and Aminta have discovered. Just one or two minor queries concerning your mother's will. It's slightly odd, but it isn't urgent.'

'Tomorrow then,' I say with a yawn.

After all, we have established that the older woman who befriended Barwell was Nell. None of this can have anything to do with my mother.

The sky is still pink in the east as we set out. It has been a clear, cold night. The snow is crisp, and there are sheets of ice where it melted in yesterday's sun. I am mounted on my cob, Ben on his gelding. We pass Ifnot's smithy. On this last Sunday before Christmas, his forge rests cold and idle, but he is standing at his front door and waves at us. He does not ask us where we are going so early on a Sabbath morning, along a road that is blocked with snow after the first half mile.

We ride in the sun to begin with, then the lane narrows and the trees crowd in from either side. The surface becomes more icy and both mounts stumble. Everything is silent. The world awaits the results of our work.

We dismount close to where the body was found. Much snow has fallen since, but I am able to identify the spot amongst the trees, where it was always less deep and has now begun to melt.

'Strange to think of George Barwell lying there,' says Ben. 'No trace of him at all now.'

'If I were the killer,' I say, 'I'd have left the blade somewhere here. You wouldn't want to be seen carrying it through the village or take it home. But Barwell's gouge or chisel left lying by the body ... that would give away nothing at all.'

'Unless we're wrong and the killer used his own knife,' says Ben. 'You wouldn't leave that close by.'

'No,' I say. 'You wouldn't. You take that side of the clearing, Ben. I'll take this. And we'll see whether there's anything to find.'

For over an hour we both hunt diligently, kicking the small drifts of snow that have gathered under the trees, searching amongst the dead leaves on our hands and knees.

The sun is high in the sky, and the church bell has long since finished ringing for the morning service, by the time I am ready to admit defeat. I rise to my feet.

'Ben?' I say, because I have heard a twig snap just off to the right.

Then I see a flash and a gunshot reverberates through the wood. It's difficult to know by how little a shot has missed you. It usually feels much closer than it was. But that one did feel very close. I crouch and peer into the trees. I catch sight of a coat and pair of breeches moving quickly, then my would-be assailant is gone, heading down towards the village or perhaps Taylor's farm. Then there is another noise behind me. Dick, Taylor's shepherd, appears from the bushes.

'Somebody just tried to shoot me,' I say to him. 'Did you see anyone?'

Dick shakes his head. 'Heard a shot,' he says. 'Haven't seen anyone until I saw you, not since I left Tom on the other side of the woods.'

'What are you doing up here? I thought all of the sheep were down by the farm?'

'We came up here looking for some ewes that are still missing. A waste of time. If they were ever here, they'll have frozen to death by now. And it's Sunday, when some folk are given a day of rest. We'd have told Mr Taylor there was no point, but he sent the instruction by way of Mistress Barwell and there's no arguing with that one. She always gets what she wants, one way or another. So, we came. Tom's somewhere over there.' He points vaguely. It's easy to lose your way in here.

'Are either of you armed?'

Dick laughs. 'Us? No, bless you, sir,' he says. 'Mr Taylor wouldn't let us have one of his muskets or his pistol. Wouldn't trust us. And we certainly don't own any ourselves.'

'Well, I'd better not keep you talking,' I say. 'Not in this weather.'

'It's getting warmer, sir,' says Dick. 'But, as Mr Taylor often reminds us, we're paid to look after his sheep, not chatter amongst ourselves. So, I'll look, even if there's nothing to find.'

I watch Dick go on his way. It is surprising how quickly I lose sight of him amongst the trees and undergrowth. Then Ben comes puffing up the hill. His face should be red after that effort, but it is somewhere between white and grey.

'Thank goodness you're alive, Sir John,' he says. 'I heard a shot.'

'I think somebody tried to kill me,' I say. 'Did you see anyone heading down the hill, towards the village maybe?'

Ben nods. 'I only really saw him from behind,' he says, 'but he was holding a pistol in each hand as he ran.'

'So you didn't recognise him then?'

'Oh, yes, I'd have known him anywhere,' says Ben. 'It was George Barwell.'

Chapter Twenty-Three

The home life of the Taylors

'Barwell's dead,' I say. 'And I've never heard of a ghost with a loaded pistol.'

'Maybe he's not as dead as we thought,' says Ben.

'You have to be mistaken,' I say.

'I know Barwell,' he says.

'Taylor says the body in the church is Barwell. So does Amy. And the Rector, for what it's worth. He can't be up here with a gun.'

'Well, somebody very much like him was.'

'Precisely. Very much like him. Somebody shot at me, but it was not Barwell.'

'I was there and I know what I saw,' says Ben. He can be stubborn, though to be fair Aminta says that I can be too. There is a pause. 'It wasn't me,' Ben says. 'I'm not making it up because it was me who shot at you.'

'I didn't say it was,' I say.

'I don't even have a gun with me,' says Ben.

'I believe you,' I say. 'Did you find anything in the woods?'

'Nothing all morning,' he says. 'I assume that it was the same with you?'

I nod. 'I'll ride over to Taylor's farm,' I say. 'I can at least check if all of the tools are in the box or any are missing.'

'Do you need me, Sir John? If there's somebody trying to shoot you, maybe it's best if I stay with you this time.' Ben must be feeling guilty about the blow to my head. Normally, he'd have been pressing to be allowed to go home long before this.

'No, you go back to the inn,' I say. 'Nell will need your help. Whoever tried to kill me was last seen by both of us running away as fast as he could. I don't think he'll be on the path to the farm, even if he suspects I might go that way.'

'It wasn't me who tried to shoot you,' says Ben again.

'Whoever it was shoots as badly as you,' I say.

But I'm not telling the truth. The shot only just missed me. That shows some skill in these circumstances. And remarkable skill for a man who has been dead six days.

For a short distance Ben and I ride together in silence. I watch the trees and hedgerows carefully, but we see nobody. Then I strike off towards the farm and Ben continues down into the village.

Taylor is standing in his yard when I arrive. The day threatens to be a warm one. The yard is already a mixture of mud and dirty snow and brown puddles. The rich smell of livestock, which had almost vanished with the cold weather, has returned.

'I hope you are making good progress, Sir John,' he says.

He does not invite me to dismount, but I do so anyway, my feet slipping as they touch the ground. He puts out no hand to steady me, but I do not need it. There is a jolt of pain through my wounded leg, but I manage to stay upright.

'Good enough,' I say. 'Have you been out today, by the woods?'

'No. There was no need. I've been here. Why do you ask?'

We look at each other. He'd have had to move quickly to get back here on foot, but he could still have fired at me in the woods and run back down. He had time. But surely Ben would never confuse him and Barwell? He's very much bigger.

'I heard a shot up there,' I say.

'Somebody hunting my rabbits,' he says. 'If I catch them, I'll be reporting them to you.'

'As is your right.'

He shrugs. 'So, you've been up to the woods yourself?'

'Yes.'

'Find anything?'

'No.'

'I could have told you that you wouldn't. Don't waste too much time, Sir John. We need an answer from you by Christmas Eve. That's tomorrow, in case you'd forgotten.'

'You'll get it,' I say. 'One way or the other. I need to see George Barwell's box of tools.'

'Step this way,' he says.

We enter the house and he opens the door to a small storeroom just inside. It is cold, with just wooden bars across the window, no glass. On the floor is a small chest, made of polished elm. It looks neat and organised. I kneel down by it and try to raise the lid. It does not move. I hear Taylor behind me give a short laugh.

'It's locked,' I say.

'I never said that it wasn't,' he says. 'You just wanted to see the box.'

I stand again. 'The key, if you please, Mr Taylor.'

'I don't have it,' he says. 'There was only ever one key and Barwell kept it with him at all times. Nobody was allowed to open that precious box except him.'

'It's true.' I turn and see Amy standing by the door in what must be her Sunday best – a mustard-coloured dress, the skirt draped back to reveal the cream petticoat beneath. It's not something you'd wear in the farmyard. 'He always kept the key himself. I'm sure he had it with him the day he died.'

Yes, of course. When I first visited the Rectory, Dr Bray told me that he had Barwell's cash and a small door key stored away.

'Then I know where the key is,' I say. 'It was found on his body.'

'In which case, do get it, by all means,' says Taylor. 'But the blade used to disfigure him can scarcely be back in the box, can it? Not if the key's been in Barwell's pocket since he died.'

Ben must be long since back at the inn. Nell will be preparing his dinner, wondering when she can tell Ben about the baby. My cob is still wading through snow that is becoming softer and softer by the minute. When this freezes again tonight, the whole village will become one vast sheet of muddy ice.

I bang on the Rector's door. A maid opens it and leads me to his sitting room. Bray looks up from his writing.

'You were not at church this morning, Sir John,' he says.

'I shall certainly rectify the omission on Christmas Day,' I say.

'Well, you now interrupt the preparation of my Christmas sermon,' he says. 'I hope this is important.'

'I need something else from you,' I say.

'Anything within reason,' he says. 'We are allies now, are we not?'

'I have no allies,' I say. 'It is simply that there are some people who seek justice for its own sake and some who try to evade it or circumvent it or bend it to their advantage. I find it easier to work with one of those groups than the other.'

'So, you would betray me to Arlington after all?'

'Only if Arlington ever joins the group seeking justice for its own sake,' I say. 'Barwell had a key in his pocket when he was found. Do you still have it?'

'Of course. And the money. I offered the coins to Mistress Barwell, but she said to use it for the benefit of the church. A generous gift indeed, though not as generous as the bribes I paid her husband by some nineteen Pounds, seventeen Shillings and sixpence. I clear forgot the key.'

'So did I. But now I have recalled it to mind, it would be helpful to have it for an hour or two.'

'I shall not ask why. As Magistrate you are entitled to it, as you were to the letter.'

'I promise not to lose it,' I say.

'I'll fetch it from the vestry,' he says. 'I hope, by the way, that we are able to send for the coroner soon. With this warm weather, the earthly remains of George Barwell may not last very much longer.'

'Well, that looks like the key,' says Taylor. 'The box is still where it was.'

I kneel again and try the key in the lock. It turns smoothly and the lid springs open.

Inside, the tools are arranged carefully, so as not to blunt any edges. There is a place for each of the knives and gouges and chisels and planes and saws. I cannot see any gaps where a tool might be missing.

'Have you seen inside this box before?' I ask.

'Once,' says Taylor. 'Very shortly after he arrived. Later he guarded those tools as if they were the Crown Jewels. But, on the one occasion I was allowed to view the contents, it looked much as it does now.'

'Well, it all seems to be complete. There are no spaces for other tools.'

'I agree,' he says. 'Certainly there is no space for the sort of tool that might have been used on his face.'

'Then the instrument used to disfigure Barwell . . .'

'Was clearly something else entirely,' he says. 'As I told you, the box has been locked since Barwell left the house alive and the only key has been either in his pocket or with the Rector. It could not have been returned to its place by anyone other than Barwell.'

'I was so certain . . .'

'That's right, you were so certain. As you so often are, Sir John. But you were also wrong. Perhaps you should be searching Mistress Mardike's house rather than mine?'

I look again at each of the tools in turn. They are clean. I think I can detect the smallest trace of blood on the handle of one of the chisels, but I am not sure. And anyway, with instruments this sharp, Barwell must have cut himself from time to time.

'You'll have other sharp knives here?'

'Of course. But nothing that would have produced the injuries we both saw. You can search the farm if you wish, I've nothing to hide. It was a blade like one of those in the box, but these were all safely locked away. Of course, a witch could do that.'

I stand slowly. 'What would you say if I told you that Ben saw George Barwell up on the hill today?'

I look at Taylor's face. He clearly believes in witches rather more than he believes in ghosts.

'Impossible,' he says. 'If Ben said it, then it was a poor jest on his part.'

For once he and I are in complete agreement. George Barwell is dead and that's all there is to it. I'm not going to stop and search the farm for him.

'I'm taking the chest as evidence,' I say. 'It will be returned to you when my investigations are complete. Could you please get one of your men to strap it to my saddle?'

'You can keep it for all I care,' says Taylor. 'I've no plans to have a carpenter in the family again. They're nothing but trouble. Until tomorrow morning, Sir John. That's all you have.'

'There remain three and thirty hours before Christmas Eve reaches its end,' I say.

'Hangings take place first thing in the morning,' he says. 'You wouldn't want to see the witch hang on Christmas Day, would you? It wouldn't be right. At dawn tomorrow, we'll come for her. And we'll expect you to honour the agreement we have.'

'Are you sure you wish to do this?' asks Dr Bray.

The smell of decaying flesh is becoming apparent.

'I've had to deal with much worse,' I say. I pull back the sheet and look again at what was once George Barwell. I have three chisels and two gouges on the table next to the body. I place each of them against his face, one after the other.

'The flesh will have shrunk a little,' says Bray.

'I agree that an exact match can't now be expected,' I say,

'but this chisel is a remarkably good fit. And if you hacked into his face thus, see how it would strike the bone just there, where it is shaved away.'

'Seven or eight blows would do it,' says Bray. He looks closely at the tool. 'Is that blood there on the handle?'

'I thought I could see some that had soaked into the wood. If so, the steel blade has been well cleaned.'

'But it was locked in the chest?'

'Yes.'

'And Taylor says that is the only key?'

'Yes. So does Amy. But I can't think I'll ever find a closer match to the wounds than that blade there.'

'Interestingly, Barwell also told me, on one of his visits, that he kept his chest locked and the sole key was always with him. In which case, begging your pardon Sir John, it would have taken witchcraft for this blade to have been available to somebody up on the hill. I can promise you that the key never left the vestry from the moment that Mr Barwell arrived here. Excellent fit though it is, somewhere there must be another blade that is equally good.'

'I know,' I say. 'That's what Taylor says. I'm beginning to think so too.'

And what I'm also thinking is this: until tomorrow morning. That's all I've got. Just a few hours. Unless I let them hang Alice Mardike on Christmas Day. That is possible too.

Chapter Twenty-Four

The coming of the shepherds

'I am not sure that Barwell is correct in stating that hang-ings must take place at first light,' says Sir Felix. 'It is a convention rather than a matter of Statute. We could argue that we have until sunset tomorrow at least.'

'And in which court of Law do you propose to make that submission, my dear father?' says Aminta. 'We would do better to concentrate our efforts in finding the killer.'

'We have gone backwards,' I say. 'I thought I at least knew how Barwell had been disfigured. But the tool was locked away in the chest.'

'Unless somebody is lying,' says Aminta. 'Could there be two keys?'

'Barwell thought not,' I say. 'And it was his key. He should have known.'

I produce the key I have.

'The box is beautifully put together,' says Sir Felix. 'Look at those mitres. Barwell presumably did that himself. The lock is a cheap country-made one. That could almost be a door key.' He takes it from me and turns it over in his hand. 'Easy enough to copy, if you could get your hands on it and take it to somebody skilled in ironwork.'

'Taylor might have been able to do that,' I say. 'Though I am not sure how he'd get the key for long enough. Not if Barwell guarded it as well as everyone says. And, even then, we still don't have enough evidence against him. We need witnesses who saw Taylor at the woods that afternoon.'

'Taylor knows you suspect him.'

'I told him in court that he was a suspect. Perhaps I should have been more circumspect. He may be the man who shot at me in the woods this afternoon.'

'Somebody shot at you!' says Aminta. I can tell she already blames me rather than my assailant.

'He missed,' I say. 'Ben saw him better than I did. He thinks it was Barwell. But he only saw him from behind.'

'You wouldn't mistake Taylor for Barwell,' says Aminta.

'That's what I thought – but the undergrowth is thick and it's not easy to see. On reflection it's not impossible it was him.'

Our conversation is interrupted by Morrell.

'There are two persons to see you, Sir John.'

'Well, bring them in,' I say.

'You may prefer to interview them in the entrance hall,' he says. 'It is two of Mr Taylor's men. Two shepherds.' He looks pointedly at our carpets, freshly brushed by the maids.

'Bring them in,' says Aminta. 'It is almost Christmas. We should turn nobody away from our fire. Bring them in here.'

'Certainly,' says Sir Felix. 'In my time as Lord of the Manor, we welcomed everyone at this time of the year. The entrance hall is cold and unfriendly.'

Morrell clearly does not share their views. Christmas is a time when the tenants are to be indulged, up to a point, but to have Taylor's shepherds in the drawing room is unnecessary. He nevertheless departs, to usher in our visitors.

'They were out on the hill when the shot was fired,' I say. 'Perhaps they saw somebody later on.'

Dick and Tom shuffle in, looking round themselves with great curiosity. This will be one of the few occasions they have been in a room, other than at church, where you could not reach up and touch the ceiling. They have not attended the hearings in the dining room; and I have not sought to call them, since they have previously sworn that, when they found the body, there was not a living soul around. There seemed little point in getting them to repeat this simple fact, and thus incur Taylor's accusations of idleness. They now stand in front of us, their hats in their hands, even though their master is not watching them and they know I probably won't beat them for disrespectful use of headgear. They seem ill at ease, however.

'Can we offer you some refreshment?' asks Aminta.

'Thank you, my Lady, but no,' says Dick. 'When we visit with the carol singers, then that is always welcome. But this time we've come on business as it were.'

'Is it about the shot fired today?' I ask.

'No, Sir John. It's something else. We wanted to say something to you about the killing,' says Tom. 'And seeing you up there today . . . we talked afterwards and hoped you wouldn't be offended if we came.'

'I thought you had said all you could,' I say.

'Well, in a way that's true,' says Dick. 'We have already said it to you – or we tried to. And we don't want to annoy you again, as we did when the body was found.'

'Just tell me whatever it was you saw,' I say. 'You won't annoy me, and I'll protect you if it's likely to annoy anyone else.'

I look at Aminta. Are we about to hear that Taylor was witnessed in the act of murder? That would be a Christmas gift from the shepherds. But it would seem not. I am greatly disappointed when Dick says: 'You will recall what I said about Mr Barwell's ghost, sir?'

'That you were afraid of seeing it. Yes, I told you there was nothing to fear. You would see neither his ghost nor the Devil.'

'I said we didn't want to see it *again*, sir.'

'I don't understand,' I say.

'We'd already seen it once, sir. We'd seen his ghost as clear as day, hadn't we, Dick?'

'I know you are trying to be helpful,' I say, 'but there are no such things. You didn't see Barwell's ghost.'

'Sorry, sir,' says Dick. 'If we're being foolish then I hope you'll pardon us.'

'Ghosts are precisely that,' I say. 'Foolishness.'

'Wait,' Aminta says to me. 'Let them finish. I'm beginning to think Mr Barwell has been unusually active since his death. I'd like to hear more.'

'Thank you, my Lady,' says Dick.

'Very well,' I say. 'Tell me about the ghosts.'

I wonder what further idiocies I shall now hear, but Aminta is right. I have a feeling that I should have listened more carefully before.

'As you know, we were up on the hill, looking for sheep,' says Dick. 'When it snows, they shelter anywhere they can, but their choice of sheltering place is not always good, if you understand me. They go to places that seem to be out of the wind but where the snow will actually be deepest by morning.

They go into the woods and get lost. There's nothing as stupid as a sheep, sir. Or not much. Anyway, we decided to see whether any were taking shelter there. We'd gone a hundred yards or so, when I said to Tom: "Look, Tom, there's George Barwell." He was coming straight towards us. But when I turned back, he'd gone. Just vanished. Another fifty yards and we found him again – but this time he was dead on the ground and had no face on him at all. He couldn't have been killed in that short time, sir. When he came walking towards us, he'd already been dead at least ten minutes, I'd say. Maybe more.'

'You're sure it was him?'

'Well, we saw him through the trees, but I don't see who else it could be.'

'Could it have been his father-in-law?'

'No, sir. It could not. Mr Taylor is a large man, as you know. This man was young and agile, sir. Slim and quite short exactly like Mr Barwell, and . . . I don't know, sir, it just looked like him. I never doubted for a moment who I'd seen.'

'Did you know him well?' asks Aminta.

'Yes, my Lady. He was a bit too good for the likes of us. Mr Taylor – he'll pass the time of day with you, ask after your family – but not Mr Barwell. That's why, when he vanished, I didn't think much of it – he just didn't want to speak to us. Then we found him stone cold dead a minute later and knew it was just his ghost we'd seen.'

'Standoffish in death as well as life,' says Tom. 'Not that I wanted a ghost to stay with us and talk to us.'

'And not that we would speak ill of the dead, either,' says Dick cautiously. Ghosts are tricky things and can turn up anywhere. Sometimes it's enough just to mention their names. No point in upsetting ghosts any more than it is upsetting witches.

'Course not,' says Tom. 'He was a good man, Mr Barwell. In his way. May he rest in peace and not trouble the living.'

'Amen,' says Dick.

'What sort of clothes was he wearing?' asks Aminta.

'Himself or his ghost?' asks Dick.

'His ghost.'

'Much the same as he did in life, my Lady. I think maybe that's why we knew it was him – even in the woods. Hat. Cloak. Boots. They were his.'

'Thank you,' says Aminta. 'I understand completely.'

'Thank you,' I say. I hand the men two Shillings each. They exchange glances. If they'd known they'd get two days' pay for ten minutes' work, they'd have come sooner.

'Well, that was a fine ghost story by the fire,' I say.

'Yes,' says Sir Felix. 'But it's clear to me that whoever they saw was real and probably Barwell's killer. It's no surprise he vanished the moment they caught sight of him.'

'Or perhaps they did see Barwell,' I say.

'You believe it was his ghost?' asks Sir Felix.

'No, I mean, what if they saw Barwell himself, alive? They were remarkably certain it was him. And Ben was also convinced he saw Barwell today. In which case the person without a face in the church can't be Barwell. The thing that's puzzled me all the way through was why disfigure him when there could be no doubt who had been killed? But if Barwell himself is the killer, then it might have suited him that the identity of his victim was unknown.'

'But if any young man from the village had vanished, we'd have heard by now,' says Sir Felix.

'True,' I say. 'But perhaps he's not from here. We know how

Barwell conducted himself in this village. In all likelihood he behaved no better in any of the other places he's lived and worked. It wouldn't only be here that there were people who wanted him dead. His past may have caught up with him. So, let's assume that whoever it was followed him up the hill that afternoon. But Barwell killed him in self-defence, then, having made his victim unidentifiable, fled back to the farm – which isn't far from the woods. At this very moment he could be hiding there until the roads are clear to make his escape to London or Cambridge. Amy and her father both identified the body as Barwell's. In due course the coroner, who's never seen Barwell at all, will bring in a verdict that Barwell was unlawfully killed and the dead man will be free to start a new life elsewhere, with or without Amy. Taylor might have favoured him starting again without her and be willing to aid and abet him, including by ensuring that a witch was blamed for the murder rather than some other innocent villager. I should have stayed and searched Taylor's barns while I could. I've stupidly warned Taylor I know that's a possibility. Barwell could be anywhere by now.'

'I like the story,' says Sir Felix. 'That Barwell's past should catch up with him on a cold hillside is very effective. And Taylor's desire to see Alice Mardike hanged is excessive, and might be explained if he was trying to save a member of his family. But let's not forget that the shepherds identified the dead Barwell by his clothing. Are we saying that Barwell had time to dress his victim in some of his own clothes? Or that the victim happened, by coincidence, to be wearing something almost identical?'

'The shepherds could be lying,' I say. 'They work for Taylor. They could have been instructed very firmly to tell Ben that they thought it was Barwell.'

'Very true. But having met them, I'm not sure they would do that,' says Sir Felix. 'And they came to you today in a way in which they would not if they were in some way implicated. They fear Taylor, but they're honest and want to see justice, even at the risk of having you mock them again for believing in ghosts. In any case, the idea that the body wasn't Barwell's requires too many unlikely things to happen. For example, nobody seems to have noticed this stranger from Suffolk in the village. It's a small village and doesn't get many strangers. There are back ways where you can avoid too much attention, but a stranger wouldn't know where they were. As I say, I like the story, but I'd prefer something simpler – something that takes into account everything we know, rather than finds an improbable way round it. And I don't see what that something is.'

'I agree,' says Aminta. 'The shepherds saw a real person – somebody who lives in the village and could simply go home after the killing without attracting attention. Our problem, when you think about it, is that he resembles none of the suspects we have. Too small for Taylor – and they'd certainly know their master if they saw him. Too young for Bray. Too agile I think for old Jacob Platt. Too thin for Ben. And a man, so you would want to rule out Margaret Platt or Nell or Amy or any of the village girls.'

'There must be young men in the village who resembled Barwell,' I say.

'Not in the eyes of the young women,' says Aminta.

'What about Margaret's brother?' asks Sir Felix. 'He would be the right age, surely? And, like Jacob Platt and Margaret, not tall.'

'He's in Colchester according to the Platts,' I say.

'I suppose he might have returned without our knowing,' says Sir Felix, thoughtfully. 'Once he learned how Barwell had treated his sister, he might have decided that the reprobate should be punished. As a matter of family honour. Once he'd killed Barwell, the family could have hidden him. After all, nobody has searched the Platts' house or their barns for that matter.'

'But nobody's caught sight of him, before or after the killing,' says Aminta. 'His name has been mentioned in nobody's evidence. As a solution to this problem that seems somehow . . . unsatisfactory.'

'Well, fair play to him if he did, but I don't think young Platt's the killer either,' says Sir Felix. 'The Platts are on the far side of the village from the woods and Taylor's farm. I don't think he'd have got safely home without running into somebody he knew. You never can when you walk through the village. Anyway, how does he succeed in dressing like Barwell?'

'I agree,' I say. 'We've spent a great deal of time on this and we're no further forward than we were when I was examining Barwell's body. We're not going to find the killer in time – even if we can hold them off until tomorrow evening. We need to decide now what to do when Taylor's men come for Mistress Mardike.'

But Aminta is looking thoughtful.

'No, you're wrong,' she says. 'It's obvious what's happened, though perhaps I'm in a slightly better position to understand it than you are. When you look at everything we know – including strange little details like the permanently locked tool chest – there could only be one person who killed Barwell. And, I think, only one person who could have shot at you, though interestingly I believe they intended you no harm. There is an additional piece of information that I need to check before I can be absolutely sure. And to do that, I have to talk to Ifnot. He's the key to it all. And I'll take your cob, John. The snow's still much too deep to wade through in these skirts.'

'So are you going to tell us who killed Barwell?' says Sir Felix.

'I already have,' says Aminta. 'If you'd just listened to what I've said. But let me talk to Ifnot before you make an arrest. As John says, we don't have many hours left if we are to save Alice from the hangman. This time we can't afford to get it wrong.'

Chapter Twenty-Five

The journey of the wise woman

Aminta has returned. She is sitting in front of the fire, warming her hands.

'So, are we to know now who killed Barwell?' Sir Felix asks.

'I called at the inn on my way home,' says Aminta. 'I have asked Ben, in his role as constable, to arrest the killer. A little presumptuous of me, perhaps, since I am merely the wife of the Magistrate, but Ben concurred with my reasoning. He and the guilty party will be here shortly. Then, John, you can go and inform Alice Mardike that there will be no hanging on Christmas Eve.'

'So what did you need to find out from Ifnot?' I ask.

'There clearly had to be a second key,' says Aminta. 'Ifnot makes anything in iron. So that's where you'd get one copied. Of course, he would have had no idea what the key was or that it was in any way significant. It looked like a small door key. He would never have connected it with the box of carpenter's tools. It was just one of many orders for items like that – hooks, door latches, door keys – that he gets every month.'

'So, who ordered a duplicate key?' I ask.

Morrell enters. 'Mr Bowman is in the hallway, Sir John. He has Mistress Barwell with him. May he bring her in?'

'Yes,' says Aminta. 'Thank you, Morrell. Please show them in. That was fast work on Ben's part, wasn't it, John? He's a very effective constable when properly directed. And now you'll learn exactly how Amy did it.'

Amy Barwell is frightened but defiant. If Ben has explained anything to her, then it is with his usual diversions and vagueness. She is aware she is in trouble but perhaps not how much trouble. Aminta is about to let her know.

Aminta holds up the key. 'Do you recognise this, Amy?' she asks.

'It's the key to George's chest,' she says cautiously.

'And the other one is presumably in your room at home?'

'There's only one. I told Sir John.'

'I've spoken to Ifnot, Amy. He remembers copying this for you a month or so ago.'

'It was some other key . . .' she begins.

'Well, Ifnot was very certain about it. But I can ask Ben to return to the farm and make a search if you wish us to. He can bring any key he finds here and we can try it in the chest.'

'I'd every right to a copy of the key,' Amy says.

Had I been her lawyer, I would have told her this was a bad move. Don't change your story. Above all, don't change it in mid-sentence. It makes juries uneasy.

'Yes, of course you do,' says Aminta. 'Your very own copy. For your own use. What wife wouldn't want that? We always thought there might be a second key out there. But we knew your husband guarded the original carefully. So who would be able to get their hands on it easily? Who, if I may put it so indelicately, had access to his breeches? Well, a number of women perhaps, but nobody so regularly and dependably as George Barwell's own wife. Even without Ifnot's help, that seemed obvious.'

'Well, there you are then,' she says. 'That was no crime.'

'No,' says Aminta. 'It wasn't. A wife has the right to know what's going on. Especially if she suspects that her husband is hiding something in his work chest. Letters, for example. That's where he kept them, wasn't it? I mean, his tools were precious, but they hardly needed locking away with the care that he did. I never quite understood that until I thought about the letters and the need to hide them somewhere. Where could he always access them and you not do so? In his toolbox. How did you discover what was going on? By getting a second key cut. You wouldn't have wanted to have to borrow it constantly, with the risk of discovery every time. So, there had to be a second key.'

'Yes,' she says in a flat voice. 'That's where he kept the letters.'

'From other women.'

'Yes. From other women.'

'Which I assume you've since burned?'

'Yes.'

'Except for the very last one that you found. The one that was signed by Margaret, inviting him to a tryst in the woods. You didn't burn that, did you? Because he still had it with him when you killed him and you didn't search his pockets because you didn't have time. Not after you had taken a chisel to his face. That really was the final act of revenge. A man might have simply killed him, but to destroy his face using a tool taken from the box in which he kept the letters from his mistresses – there was the delicate feminine touch that is so often missing from murders.'

'You can't prove any of that,' she says.

She really does need a good lawyer. Far better to say in terms that something is untrue, rather than that it might well be true but cannot be proven. Especially if your accuser may have that very proof. I am interested to see if my wife has exactly that.

'You waited until he left your father's house,' says Aminta, 'then, knowing exactly where he was going, you followed him up the hill. You were aware you would have to work fast because Margaret, as you thought, would be there soon. But George was keen to get started and so was a little early. You knew you had time. You came up behind him, whispering that he should not turn round, then you slipped a silk stocking over his eyes then slid it down round his mouth, then onto his throat, pressing yourself against his back.'

'How do you know that?'

'It's how I would have done it.'

Amy nods.

'Of course,' says Aminta, 'he would have realised eventually that it was the wrong woman running her underclothing across his skin, but by that time you were already pulling the noose tight. George was not a large man – very much the same size as you. I suspect, after years of working on the farm, you were stronger than he was. And you had the advantage of surprise. Perhaps at first he thought it was a game.'

'The type of game he played with that Platt girl,' Amy says bitterly. 'I saw the letter. She promised him the sort of thing he liked doing.'

'Which, again I hope I'm not being indelicate, as his wife you would have known almost as well as Margaret.'

'Men,' she says.

'They lack imagination or variety,' says Aminta. 'Their predictability is their downfall in so many cases.'

Amy Barwell narrows her eyes. 'But in this case, if I may make so bold, my Lady, *you* are showing too much imagination. All of that could have happened, I grant you, but you have no witnesses. When the shepherds found George, there was, as they have told Sir John and Mr Bowman, not a living soul to be seen. The killer was no longer there. It could therefore have been anyone. Anyone in the village.'

'But you *were* seen,' says Aminta. 'Though Tom and Dick thought, and still think, it was a ghost. They saw somebody who was about the same height as George Barwell and – a vital clue – dressed exactly like George Barwell. Here my husband was of great assistance to you, because he dismissed their fears of a ghost without asking exactly why they were afraid. So it was only today that we knew what they'd seen. And you kept Dick and Tom away from the hearing into George's death. That was nicely done.'

'They had duties tending the sheep. My father didn't want them idling away their mornings in your dining room.'

'I'm sure he didn't. I thought it odd that they weren't there, even if my husband had, in his great wisdom, decided that two superstitious shepherds had nothing of interest to tell him. Most of the village found time to be there for at least some of the hearing. Somebody had clearly given two key witnesses other things to do. Somebody whom they could not disobey under any circumstances. That's either you or your father, in case I haven't made myself clear.'

'Perfectly clear,' says Amy.

'You see, the one thing that troubled me every time we considered that a woman might have been the killer is this: how did she trudge up the hill in skirts and petticoats? One woman did try it, to be fair, but it took a long time. If I were doing it, and I wanted to use the back ways, I'd have borrowed my husband's boots, breeches and cloak. Men's clothing is far more practical. Dick and Tom are certain they saw somebody in your husband's clothes. Let us again pause and ask ourselves who had access to those? Hmm ... who do you think that might have been?'

Amy says nothing. I wonder if she knows that the woman Aminta referred to was Nell? She doesn't ask, anyway.

'So that's what you did, wasn't it?' Aminta continues. 'You dressed in George's clothes. Useful to get there quickly. Even more useful when you are running away and need to dive into the bushes because you've just seen two of your father's men. You hoped they hadn't spotted you. But you kept them away from the hearing to make sure. You also used your duplicate key to return the chisel to the box, having washed the blood off the blade, but left a slight stain in the handle. You locked the box, confident that anyone investigating would conclude that the chisel had never left it, let alone left the house. I suppose you might have bribed Ifnot to say you'd never asked him to make the key – but he's one of the few truly honest men in the village. Him and my husband.'

I see Sir Felix is considering interjecting something at this point, then he wisely decides not to after all.

'And are you saying that Amy shot at me in the woods today?' I ask.

Aminta shakes her head. 'She wasn't shooting at you. At

first Amy thought that she had not been seen by Tom or Dick. But they must have told the story about George Barwell's ghost once too often and word got back to Amy. She heard you say to everyone that the killer was still amongst us and that some people in the village must know who it was, though they might not realise it yet. She'd hoped that Alice Mardike would be hanged quickly and people would stop looking for any other suspect. But, as the Magistrate delayed longer and longer, she knew that Dick and Tom would eventually tell their story to somebody who would understand what had happened – as indeed they did. So, she told the pair of them that her father wanted them to check the woods one last time for lost sheep, even though it was a Sunday morning. She dressed again in her husband's old clothes. She took a pair of pistols and went up the hill and lay in wait for them. Taylor told us that she knew how to handle a gun. Two targets and just two balls, unless she got a chance to reload. It was desperate stuff, but she was about to be exposed as a killer. She saw somebody exactly where Dick and Tom ought to be – and fired. She'd have known she'd missed, but there would be other chances if she got back undetected. Ben saw her running back to the farm – the second sighting of a ghostly George Barwell.'

'Taylor was at the farm when I arrived,' I say. 'Amy appeared later.'

'Having had time to change back into a dress,' says Aminta. 'You'd think she'd just attended the morning service. If you didn't know otherwise.'

'Say what you like, you don't have anything like enough to convict me,' says Amy.

'Actually, we do,' I say. 'Since your shot missed, we still have two witnesses of good character. You were in possession of the weapon used on your husband's face. We will soon locate exactly the clothing that Tom and Dick saw. You had a very good reason for wanting your husband dead. You have admitted to us that you had read the letters from his various paramours and were in no doubt of his activities. And you have shown an irrational determination to hang Alice Mardike as a witch, though that last point may not sway the Judge very much one way or the other.'

'My father has influence in this county,' she says.

'Which will not be enough to save you,' I say. 'Things have changed. They are not as they were. Do you have anything else to say?'

She scowls at me and shakes her head.

'I do,' says Aminta.

'Are you acting for the defence as well as for the prosecution?' I ask.

'Yes,' she says.

'You'd better go ahead, then,' I say. 'But the prosecution has made such a good case that I fear you are wasting your time.'

'It's like this,' says Aminta. 'Amy's mother was murdered by her father when she was six years old. Since then she's suffered ill-treatment from him every day—'

'Almost,' says Amy.

'Almost every day since then. Even now you can see where he struck her on the face.'

'I broke a jug,' says Amy.

'Ill treatment,' Aminta continues, 'that she is made to feel guilty for. Then she finds herself married to a man who, I grant you, isn't up to beating her, but betrays her with every girl—'

'Almost,' says Amy.

'With every girl in the village,' says Aminta. 'Her life has been constant beating and humiliation at the hands of men.'

'She killed one,' I say.

'But just the one,' says Aminta. 'I am amazed at her moderation.'

'If I do not have Amy arrested,' I say, 'then Alice Mardike will surely hang tomorrow. Because we either have to catch the real murderer or the village will take the matter out of our hands. It will be one or the other. And Amy is the real murderer. Why should I not hand her over to the Assizes for trial?'

'What if Amy persuaded her father to cease his accusations against Alice?'

'Yes, he would do that,' says Amy. 'I know he would.'

'The problem,' I say, 'is that we still have a dead body, slowly rotting in the vestry. The coroner will ask how it came to be there and who is responsible for it having no face. I cannot say that nobody killed George Barwell. He is too obviously dead.'

'It could have been footpads from Suffolk, Sir John,' says Ben. 'They're desperate men.'

I shake my head. It is Ben's solution to most intractable problems. And a good Essex judge might sympathise. But not even Suffolk footpads could have made their way through this snow and back across the frozen Stour to the safety of their own county.

'Ben will see you safe home, Amy,' I say. 'We'll reconvene the hearing tomorrow morning. I shall give my judgment then. Please do not try to shoot any more witnesses. And, even though the snow is melting, please don't try to leave the village. We will be able to track you down.'

'Leave? Where would I go?' she says. 'And what would I do when I got there?'

Chapter Twenty-Six

I bring tidings of great joy

'Well,' I say, when Amy has departed. 'We can at least reassure Mistress Mardike that she need not fear the noose. She has waited too long for this news. I commend your advocacy, Aminta, but whether we can also save Amy Barwell is another matter entirely. She has murdered one man and attempted to kill two more, even if one will not be missed and the others were safely on the far side of the wood when the shot was fired.'

'But she does not deserve to hang.'

'Judges, most of whom are married, take a dim view of wives murdering their husbands. They are reluctant to look for extenuating circumstances. I fear there is no likely outcome other than acquittal or death in such a case. Since she did kill George Barwell, I am not sure how any jury could acquit her. More to the point, even if I accepted your argument that the killing of George Barwell was justifiable, morally if not in Law, I don't see how both she and Alice Mardike can be saved. Alice is innocent because Amy is guilty. Unless there is something I have missed. I do at least have until tomorrow to think what might be done about Amy, but Mistress Mardike should know the good tidings at once. She was in despair when I last saw her.'

I get the servants to saddle two horses, and Aminta and I ride across the Park. The day has been dull, but the sun breaks through as we reach the inn. An orange shaft of light cleaves the dark clouds and sheds its radiance over us. It is a cold, glistening world, full of hope.

'We shall have a fine sunset,' I say. 'And Charles's cough has almost vanished, with the help of Mistress Mardike's remedy. I don't know how it will be done, but truly I think it may yet work out well for everyone. Something will happen that makes it unnecessary to condemn Amy. I know it.'

'You've heard of hubris, I suppose?'

'It is the toy of Pagan gods,' I say, 'who are not to be feared.'

'True. But let's hope they didn't hear you say that,' says Aminta.

We reach Alice Mardike's cottage. The garden is still clogged with yesterday's smooth white snow. It doesn't look as if she has stirred abroad today. No smoke rises from her chimney.

'Her fire is out,' says Aminta.

'I thought I'd sent plenty of wood,' I say. 'I'll get Morrell to arrange for another load to be delivered.'

But it is with a sense of foreboding that I push open the low door and peer into the gloom. Alice Mardike is lying, slumped on the floor. I see no sign of breathing. I kneel down and touch her hand. It is very cold. I think she has been dead since this morning. Then, close by, I see an empty bottle. Its label reads: 'Belladonna'.

On the wall she has written in chalk: 'BETTER THIS THAN TO DIE OF SHAME'.

Chapter Twenty-Seven

A Solomon come to judgment

My dining room is crowded again. Every seat is taken and even more people are crammed into any space in which a man or woman can stand. There is an air of expectation.

'As many of you already know,' I begin, 'Mistress Alice Mardike was found dead in her cottage yesterday evening. She had mistaken the label on one of her bottles of medicine and unfortunately poisoned herself with deadly nightshade. Her body has been taken to the church where it will in due course, the Rector assures me, be given Christian burial, as I have urged him to do. Though he had some reservations, which I entirely understand, we eventually agreed between ourselves that this was the best course of action for all concerned.'

I look at Dr Bray, who nods, having nothing now to fear from Lord Arlington, for thus I have promised.

Amy Barwell sits beside her father, grey-faced. She knows that I will turn next to her case and that the evidence is utterly damning.

'We now come to my conclusions regarding the death of George Barwell,' I say. 'I have considered most carefully all of the evidence that we have heard. Though a number of people in the village could, arguably, have been up on the hill at the time of Mr Barwell's death, and some were undoubtedly on the road to the woods, we have no witnesses to say that they were in fact there at the time of the murder. As you know, without two witnesses to the crime, any charges would be unsound. I have considered the evidence of the Rector, a man of great experience and of exceptional sanctity . . .' I pause and look Dr Bray in the eye. He smiles benignly. 'He has informed us – as indeed he has told you in his sermons – that the Bible states that witches do exist and that they are capable of harming even Kings. Nobody has sought to produce evidence to the contrary. These facts are therefore uncontested. The Law in any case takes the same view.'

There is a great deal of nodding in the room. This is a pleasant surprise for them.

'I have also questioned Dick and Tom, Mr Taylor's shepherds. They state quite clearly that they saw George Barwell's ghost, immediately after his death. If a ghost appeared in this way – a thing so rare as to be quite unprecedented in my experience – it would surely point to a most horrible and unnatural killing.'

'Very true,' interjects Harry Hardy. 'The ghost of a murdered man is worth ten living witnesses.'

'Thank you, Harry,' I say. 'I value, as always, your good sense and experience. The injuries inflicted on George Barwell after his death were appalling – to an extent, I can safely say, that I have never come across in my entire legal practice. Many of you have suggested that they are therefore the work of the Devil. That is a field in which I have little experience, but again nobody here has offered any testimony to the contrary. This evidence might therefore also be said to be uncontested. It is agreed that George Barwell had been cursed by Alice Mardike a day or two before he died. But, and I cannot stress this too strongly, it is impossible to say if it was that particular curse that killed him. Though I would not wish to speak ill of the dead . . .'

There is a murmur of agreement. Nobody wants that. Later, maybe, but not now.

'Though I would not wish to speak ill of Mr Barwell,' I continue, 'there were rumours of immoral behaviour on his part. Indeed, there have been accusations made in this room. But they are unsubstantiated by any detailed evidence or a confession. Under the circumstances I would choose not to believe these stories, not amongst such good and sensible folk as yourselves, though I fear that such conduct may have taken place elsewhere.'

'Suffolk,' says Harry Hardy.

There is another murmur of approval. Say what you like about Suffolk, but they certainly know how to enjoy themselves there.

'Precisely,' I say. 'Suffolk. Witches, as you know, are said to be able to do their work from many miles away. That is why witchcraft presents such problems for magistrates. In this case, there is no evidence to connect George Barwell's death directly with Alice Mardike's curse. Indeed, the curse, as described to me, was that he should die of the plague, which he clearly did not. I therefore cannot say that Alice Mardike was to blame, simply because she lived here and had cursed him the day before, and so I shall not say that in my report. It is even less clear to me that Mistress Margaret Platt could have played any part at all in the sad events that have unfolded. There was evidence – but purely hearsay evidence – that she wished to be a witch. I have heard no testimony to the effect that she ever practised as one or harmed any of you. Nobody has claimed to have suffered in any way as a result of one of her curses. I would go further and say I have been presented with nothing that would suggest that she would ever have made a competent witch, even given the necessary instruction. I would remind you that she comes from a good family that has lived in the village for as long as anyone can recall, just as most of you have done. It is true that she was seen going to Mistress Mardike's cottage, but I doubt that you would wish me to extend this investigation to cover everyone who has ever consulted her. I am sure in fact that you would agree that it is right that I say nothing about Margaret Platt or anyone else in this room who may have visited Alice Mardike for perfectly good reasons.

'In conclusion, therefore, I shall report to the coroner that George Barwell died, according to the evidence presented to me here by many trustworthy and responsible witnesses, as a result of witchcraft, and shortly after being cursed by Alice Mardike, though not, I believe, as a result of that particular curse. He will, of necessity, be buried later today, it not being seemly that he should be left to decay completely over the Christmas period. There will be no opportunity for further examination of his body by anyone, but with your help I shall have produced a very comprehensive report for the coroner. I doubt that he will disagree with any part of it. Thank you all for your evidence and for your patience. And I wish every one of you a Happy Christmas.'

There is silence then a hubbub. Harry Hardy advances on me and shakes my hand. 'A masterly judgment, Sir John,' he says. 'I'm sorry that we doubted you. I told them that you would see them right in the end. And you did. I'm proud of you, Sir John. You are the finest Lord of the Manor this village has ever been honoured to have.'

Giles Kerridge slaps me on the back. 'I'd always said my old father was killed by witchcraft,' he says, 'but nobody would believe me at the time. Those Cliffords, begging your good Lady's pardon, were always too soft on witches. Dad will rest easier in his grave now we have a Magistrate who takes such a firm hand with them. Thank you, Sir John.'

Jacob Platt catches my eye and gives me a grateful nod, before hurrying Margaret away. He doesn't quite trust her not to convict herself all over again. There are plenty of other crimes in my copy of *The Compleat Justice* that she could still admit to. Agnus Dei, for example.

Taylor has been holding back, but he now also approaches me, with Amy in tow. 'I apologise for my conduct, Sir John,' he says. 'I thought that you were ignoring custom and precedent, but I now humbly acknowledge how wrong I was. I don't have your learning, Sir John. I'm not a University man, just a simple grazier. I couldn't see what you were trying to do, but you knew where you were going all along, God bless you, sir. God bless you for your wisdom . . . and compassion. I . . . and Amy . . . are deeply in your debt. As soon as the spring comes I shall send you some good mutton – as much as you wish – no charge. And a fine lambswool coat for Master Charles. He is well, I hope?'

'Very well, God be praised,' I say. 'He has made a complete recovery.'

There is only one comment on my conduct to which I might take great exception.

'Splendid,' says Dr Bray. 'Lord Arlington himself could not have handled it better.'

'Well done, John,' says Sir Felix, quietly over my shoulder. 'Nicely judged. Your mother would have been proud of you. Perhaps her ghost can see you now.'

I look round the room. 'It wouldn't surprise me in the slightest,' I say. 'Not in this place.'

Chapter Twenty-Eight

A great gift

The sun continues to shine. Soon all of the roads will be open again. In fact one traveller has already got through the drifts to the east of the village. Another day or two and the road to London may be clear.

This morning, Christmas morning, I walked arm in arm with Aminta across the Park, followed by Sir Felix (with his grandson), then all of the servants in approximate though constantly disputed order of rank. We heard the Rector preach a Christmas sermon, which drew heavily on the idea that if we wished for forgiveness ourselves, then we needed to forgive others. He implied it was best to get the deal in writing if you could, but a formal handshake would often suffice. Many of the congregation muttered a fervent 'amen' at the end of it.

Later the mummers and the carol singers visited the Big House as they had done, openly or in secret depending on the views of the authorities at the time, for hundreds of years. For half an hour they filled the place with laughter and music.

The mummers' play was the grande finale. St George, after a long battle and a number of speeches, killed a Turkish knight. The knight's make-up did not disguise the fact that he had been born and lived all his life in Essex. Still it was a relief to all when St George, having been revived once from the dead by the doctor, thrust his wooden sword under the Turkish knight's arm, causing him to expire in a flurry of rhyming couplets. In return we offered them mulled wine and spiced pies and apples and a certain amount of corruptible treasure on earth, which St George's dragon, his fearsome green head now tucked under his arm, took care of for the group.

'It's good to see the old customs being maintained,' said Harry Hardy. 'It's good to see you and Lady Grey so happy. Long may it last, sir.' If God had responded straight away to every request to bless me, then He would have been kept very busy until noon at least.

Since then we have all eaten well. Now Aminta and Sir Felix and I sit in front of the fire again. Judging by the noise from downstairs, the servants are also enjoying themselves. Soon I shall go down and wish them a final merry Christmas and leave half a dozen bottles of Canary behind. Because that is the custom here too.

'The Platts will be enjoying Christmas,' I say. 'Their son was able to get through the snow this morning. He'd been stranded at Saffron Walden on his way home. So will the Taylors be very content – and all the better for being without George Barwell. And Ben told me this morning, as a great secret, that he and Nell were expecting a child. He is delighted.'

'I'll stop by and drop it into our conversation that some babies are born early,' says Aminta. 'It may help.'

'That would be very kind,' I say.

'But I am very sorry that Alice Mardike hasn't lived to see this,' says Sir Felix, looking into the fire. 'Her death is a great sadness.'

'For me too,' I say. 'But I know she would not view it thus. Because of her, the Platts are all together. Because of her, Amy Barwell is not now under arrest for murder. Because of her, Nell has been able to tell Ben of her pregnancy. Few people showed Alice much love or kindness when she was alive, but it would have pleased her more than I can say that she had been able to do so much for them. For her village. She was willing to die just to save Margaret Platt. There are at least three families in the village who will bless her name as long as they live – or they most certainly ought to. It's at least as good a monument as the tree my mother planted.'

Sir Felix takes a sip of wine. 'I worry about Amy Barwell, though,' he says. 'Her father beats her. He'll continue to beat her. He's that sort of man. Nothing you can do about it, of course. It's his right.'

'On the contrary,' I say. 'I took her to one side this morning after church and gave her some free legal advice. George Barwell dying may have been inconvenient for her in one way, but not in another. As a widow she is a free woman, subject to no man's authority. She can marry, buy property or simply leave the village, and nobody can stop her. George Barwell's ill-gotten gains, wherever they came from, are all hers. She's not rich, but she has some independence if she wishes to use it.'

'If she chooses to stay, I could rent her the New House,' says Sir Felix thoughtfully. 'After all, I don't require it myself – not if I'm going to live here with the two of you.'

'We need to talk about that,' says Aminta. She places the cork firmly back in the bottle.

'Amy's richer than you think anyway,' he continues. 'You remember that I wanted to ask you about your mother's will.'

'Yes,' I say. 'I still haven't read it properly.'

'Well, I have. Your mother left Amy one hundred Pounds.'

'Really? I have no objection, but why?'

'She says it is with her apologies.'

'Did she say apologies for what?'

'No.'

'Sometimes,' says Aminta, 'when concluding a story, it is better not to know everything.'

The heavy velvet curtains are drawn and the candles have long been lit, when there is a banging at the front door. I rise, but Morrell gets there before me. He appears at the entrance to the drawing room, a little the worse for wear and at a slight angle to the wall, but with his dignity intact.

'A person to see you,' he says very carefully. 'Named Atkins. The road to London is now open, it would seem.'

'Will!' I say, as my clerk comes through the door. 'You are most welcome – and on Christmas Day too! You must have some wine with us in front of the fire. Then I'll go down to the kitchen and see if the servants have left any of the goose or the beef. If not, there is plenty of ham.'

'I'll fetch it,' says Aminta. 'You have only the vaguest idea where the kitchen is, dear husband, and anyway Will must have urgent business to come all this way. You need to hear what he has to say.'

'Thank you, Sir John,' says Will. 'Thank you, Lady Grey. That's kind of you both. It's certainly been a long journey through the snow.'

'I have no doubt of it. So, delighted though I am to see you, why are you here?' I ask. 'Is there anything wrong at Lincoln's Inn?'

'No sir, your new partner is running the office very well. Your clients are very pleased with him. He is very efficient at drafting wills. He is very plausible in offering legal advice. We continue to make money in a most satisfactory way. I hope that we shall see you back in London before too long.'

'I'm not sure, Will,' I say. 'I have my duties here now. It may be a while before I visit London again.'

'Of course, Sir John. And when you do I shall ensure that you find everything in order, just as you would wish it.'

'So what is it, Will?' asks Aminta. 'You haven't come here just to tell Sir John that.'

Will reaches inside his coat and takes out a letter, sealed with red wax. I recognise the writing even before Will says: 'It's from Lord Arlington, sir.'

He places it on the table and pushes it cautiously in my direction with the tips of his fingers.

'I don't work for Lord Arlington any more,' I say. 'He knows that.'

'He says you'll want to do this one,' says Will. 'And this time there is no danger of any sort.'

'He said that last time.'

'He says this time it's true.'

'John,' says Aminta, 'I forbid you even to break the seal. Just throw the nasty thing on the fire.'

'I'm certainly not going to spoil Christmas by opening it today,' I say. I pour Will some wine and, seeing that his glass has suddenly emptied, I do the same for Sir Felix.

I look at the letter lying on the table. I resolve not to open it. Not today. Not tomorrow. This is where I belong. Here amongst my family and my tenants. Here where my family has always lived. I'm not going back to London.

Probably.

I quickly tuck the letter in my pocket and raise my glass.

'Merry Christmas, Will,' I say. 'Merry Christmas everyone.'

Postscript

December 1668

It was a fine, cold morning, just a couple of days before Christmas, and the churchyard was covered with the very lightest dusting of snow. Beyond the tower, thin black branches crisscrossed the blue sky.

Harry Hardy wedged his pruning knife, very cautiously, under his leather belt and stood back to admire his work. Where there had been a tangle of old, dry brambles, there was now a neat pile of well-cut stems, awaiting burning. Sometimes, when he worked in the churchyard, he wondered who would clear the weeds when he took up permanent residence there. It probably wouldn't be long now. Almost everyone he'd known as a boy was already accounted for, except those who'd gone off to war and never come back.

And she was here too. The Rector hadn't liked the idea of burying a witch in God's Acre, but Sir John had insisted, so they said, and paid for the fine brick tomb, topped with Purbeck marble, that lay hard by the churchyard wall. It just recorded that Alice Mardike was buried on that spot and that she'd died on the 23rd of December 1668. Nobody knew exactly when she'd been born, so there was none of this *anno aetatis suae* nonsense, as there was on some of the gravestones.

He'd been promised a Shilling for the work, which would come in handy, but what he really wanted now was a smoke. He wasn't sure whether the new Rector (as he was still called and would be called for the next twenty years) tolerated smoking in the churchyard or not. So he took out his short clay pipe with prudent caution and looked around before fetching his tinder box from his other pocket. Then he quickly stuffed them both back again. Marching through the gate came the Rector, surplice billowing out behind him like a brilliant white cloud.

'Good morning, Mr Hardy,' he said. 'I see you've made a goodly start on clearing the brambles.'

Harry Hardy, who rather thought he'd finished, touched his hat.

'I suppose you've seen none of the village women here?' asked the Rector.

'No, sir. Maybe a bit cold for them, though it's a fine day for working. Were you expecting somebody?'

The Rector paused, then said: 'Last year one or two of the women – women who wished to bear children but were unable – came into the churchyard to touch the tomb of Mistress Mardike. One told me that it was a certain cure for barrenness. I've no idea where she got that idea from, but there you are. I do hope none of them come here this year to continue the foolishness.'

'It seems a harmless notion, sir.'

'But we would scarcely wish it to become a habit, would we?'

'No, sir.'

'To touch the tomb of a saint, perhaps . . .'

'Yes, sir.'

'But Alice Mardike was a witch.'

'She never claimed any different, sir.'

'Well, she's elsewhere now,' said the Rector, 'and no longer troubles us.'

They both turned to look at the tomb.

'The inscription will fade with time, sir,' said Harry Hardy. 'They all do.'

'It's Purbeck stone,' said the Rector. He clearly wished it wasn't. 'Well, I'll leave you to finish your work. You can call at the Rectory later for your Shilling, when you feel you've done enough to deserve it.' He turned on his heel and strode off towards the church.

'Happy Christmas, Rector,' said Harry Hardy, though perhaps too softly for the departing clergyman to hear.

He'd do another half hour, he decided, and no more. Not for a Shilling. But first he was having that smoke. The Rector wouldn't be out again for ten minutes at least.

He wandered over to Alice Mardike's tomb and sat down on the sun-dried surface, as he'd done more times than he could remember. It was, he'd found, a comfortable place to be. Comfortable in every way. He took out his pipe and the old battered tinder box, struck up a flame and breathed in some cool smoke.

Then a thought occurred to him. Was it right to smoke on the grave of a woman who was, it seemed, halfway to becoming a saint? He too had heard of this business of touching the tomb on the anniversary of her death. Last year it had not been entirely unsuccessful. Two babies had been born in the autumn. And apparently somebody was coming from a neighbouring village this time. Perhaps the Rector was right: before they knew where they were, half the county might be wearing out God's grass. Saint Alice, eh? And here he was sitting on her tomb as if it was the arse end of an old elm tree. He took the pipe out of his mouth for a moment and looked at it accusingly.

Then a woman's voice behind him said: 'You go right ahead, Harry boy. Can't make no difference to me, can it now?'

Harry spun round. But there was nobody there. Nobody at all. Just the old mossy wall and a blackbird singing.

Notes and Acknowlededgments

I was angry when I wrote this book, though I can no longer remember what I was angry about. Brexit? The systematic and progressive suppression of freedom of speech? Cyberbullying? The unreasonable criticism of Arsène Wenger's management of Arsenal? Perhaps all of those. Irrational, unfocused anger is helpful when you have to spend hours at the keyboard.

It is of course difficult not to be angry, though, when writing about society's past treatment of witches. Tom Gardiner in his book *Broomsticks over Essex* wrote (in 1981) that any account of seventeenth-century witchcraft demonstrates 'a latent nastiness which is disturbing. It also reveals certain ways in which human beings do not change: belligerent group behaviour, group animosities, irrational dislikes and hatreds, persecution manias, are all still with us.' Almost forty years later, those words read as true as they did then, long before the invention of social media. The targets of our witch-hunts have changed, but witch-hunting is still a popular sport.

It was however possible to do a great deal of harm without access to the internet. The seventeenth century was a decidedly bad time to be a witch. The Middle Ages had actually been relatively relaxed. Punishment was largely in the hands of the church, which imposed penances or a brief, if unpleasant, stay in the pillory. It was the late sixteenth and early seventeenth centuries that represented a peak of anti-witch hysteria. It is no coincidence that Shakespeare's *Macbeth* dates from exactly this time. Punishments were progressively toughened. From 1604 hanging was the standard punishment for acts of sorcery, even if the victims did not themselves die.

Then there was a lull during the reign of Charles I, until the breakdown of law and order associated with the civil war allowed a fresh wave of persecutions. Matthew Hopkins, the Witchfinder General, cut a swathe through the eastern counties in 1645.

Hopkins behaved much as I have described in this book. He would arrive in a locality and offer his services. He would make a charge for an initial survey of a district and for each witch tried and sentenced – reputedly £5 each. Once he had identified them, he kept his victims awake and without food until they admitted to the charges. Sometimes he ran them up and down the room between his two assistants. The victim, usually naked, ended up exhausted and with blistered feet. If her domestic pets came to find her, that was proof they were her 'familiars' who went out into the world to do her bidding. The supposed witch could also be flung into water, left hand tied to right foot and right hand to left foot. The general idea was that floating showed you were in league with the Devil. But, as C. L'Estrange Ewen has pointed out in *Witch-hunting and Witch Trials*, 'notwithstanding that very absurd evidence was often considered sufficient, it cannot be agreed that the failure to sink per se was a hanging matter, rather the testing seems to have been a popular pastime'. Another test, carried out by female assistants, was to check the body of the witch for the signs of the Devil – marks that might be interpreted as an extra nipple, for example. Warts and boils were useful in that respect.

After Hopkins, the persecution of witches – at least in England – falls away. Cromwell did not encourage witch-hunting. A belief in witches did not die that easily, however, especially outside London. Even amongst the upper classes there were still some who retained a fear of witchcraft, including some senior judges. In 1664 Sir Matthew Hale – a great lawyer but 'as gullible as the simplest peasant' in this respect – condemned Amy Duny and Rose Cullender to death in Bury St Edmunds. A child had become ill and was taken to a Cunning Man, who advised the mother to wrap the child in a blanket that had previously been in the chimney and to burn any object that fell out of it. A toad fell out and was thrown into the fire, where it exploded. Amy Duny was later seen with burns on the arms and body. It was clear to everyone that she must have assumed the shape of a toad and bewitched the child. When this became generally known, other children came forward with accusations. When Duny touched the children they began to scream, had fits and vomited pins. This was taken as proof, but some suspected trickery. One of the children was blindfolded then touched by somebody else entirely. The girl still screamed. It seemed that the trick had been revealed for what it was, but Hale still regarded the children's evidence as credible and condemned both Duny and her supposed accomplice Rose Cullender to death.

This one example can serve to show how flimsy and full of malice the evidence usually was and how willing people were to believe it. But sometimes women died because of cowardice rather than gullibility. Justices who did not believe in witchcraft personally did occasionally give way to avoid a riot and hanged women they knew to be innocent. One example was in Bideford in 1682 at the trial of Temperance Lloyd, Susannah Edwards and Mary Trembles. Sir Francis North argued that it was better for an unjust Law to be administered by the courts than for it to be left to the mob.

The tide was, however, already turning. In 1694 Margaret Elnore of Ipswich was charged with inflicting illness on a woman who had refused to let her a house. She was searched and the Devil's marks were found on her. Evidence was presented that her grandmother and aunt had been hanged as witches and had bequeathed her nine imps. Though this would once have been more than enough to convict, Lord Chief Justice Sir John Holt decided it was insufficient. She was acquitted.

After 1684 there were no official executions in England for witchcraft. Lynchings continued, but the authorities cracked down with increasing severity. As early as 1665 members of a mob were hanged at Wakefield for taking the Law into their own hands and murdering a suspected witch. John Grey's warnings to the villagers of Clavershall West were based on good legal precedent. But it took a relatively brave official to be prepared to go against the evident will of the people, however foolish it was.

What made the persecution of witches so easy, at least for a while, was the willingness to set aside the normal rules for prosecution; the desire to believe the victims at all cost, however weak the evidence; the danger of speaking out against the accusers and the willingness of the authorities to go along with the prejudices of the mob. Once the juggernaut had been set rolling, the only safe thing to do was to travel in the same direction until, as all these things do, it lost momentum and ground to a halt.

But the fact that all things will pass should make us no less angry at the time – then or now.

I consulted a number of works on seventeenth-century witch-craft in the course of writing this book. They include:

Broomsticks over Essex and East Anglia by Tom Gardiner, Ian Henry Publications, 1981

The Trials of the Lancashire Witches: A Study of Seventeenth-Century Witchcraft by Edgar Peel and Pat Southern, David & Charles, 1969

Witchcraft in Stuart and Tudor England: A Regional and Comparative Study by Alan Macfarlane, Routledge and Kegan Paul, 1970

A Trial of Witches: A Seventeenth-Century Witchcraft Prosecution by Gilbert Geiss and Ivan Bunn, Routledge, 1997

Witch-hunting and Witch Trials by C. L'Estrange Ewen, Routledge, 2015

The Dark World of Witches by Eric Maple, A. S. Barnes & Co, 1964

The European Witch-Craze of the 16th and 17th Centuries by Hugh Trevor-Roper, HarperCollins, 1969

Two interesting primary sources, referred to in the text, that give advice to magistrates on how to deal with witches (and other matters) are:

The Compleat Justice, Justices of the Peace, 1667 edition

The Country Justice by Michael Dalton, 1618

As ever, I owe many debts of gratitude. First to my publisher, Constable/Little, Brown, and in particular to Krystyna Green, Amanda Keats, Ellie Russell, Thalia Proctor and Charlotte Cole, for their continuing faith in me, for the meticulousness of their editing and for feeding me from time to time. Second, to my excellent agent, David Headley, and to the whole team at DHH. Next, to my family (including the newest arrival, Ella, who calls me 'Grumps') for their love and support. I couldn't do it without them. And finally to the readers of my books and particularly to those who write in and say they have enjoyed them – when you've spent the day getting very angry in seventeenth-century Essex, you've no idea how nice it is to hear from somebody that it was all worthwhile. To all of the above, and to the many other people who have helped and encouraged me over the past year, my most sincere thanks.

CRIME AND THRILLER FAN?

CHECK OUT THECRIMEVAULT.COM

The online home of exceptional crime fiction

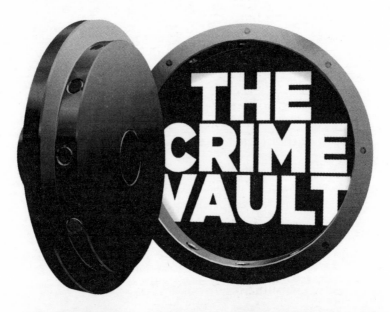

KEEP YOURSELF IN SUSPENSE

Sign up to our newsletter for regular recommendations, competitions and exclusives at www.thecrimevault.com/connect

Follow us on twitter for all the latest news @TheCrimeVault